Behind Them the Engines of the Fighter Whined in Pursuit.

A tree exploded in fire, then it was gone. The fighter sheared off to make another dive. Lar knew it would not be satisfied until it had destroyed them all, and flushed its quarry.

"Now! Run!" he yelled, and they shot into the open.

Coryelle could hear the fighter's engine as it executed a turn and followed them. Explosions punctuated her footsteps as the jezails struck the earth behind her. As she and Lar reached the bottom of the hill, the blasts ceased. The ship's engines throttled down, and there was a moment of terrible silence, a silence more dreadful than any sound.

"Quick fire! No hope. Run!" Lar shouted and pushed her away from him.

Coryelle stumbled on, but she looked back to see the flames roar toward him, spitting and hissing as they came. Quick fire would follow its prey inexorably. She saw the flames rear up as they closed on Lar. They cackled wildly, throwing off showers of white sparks.

In spite of her promise to save herself, Coryelle stopped in her tracks. He meant to die so that she might live.

She started to turn as the flames lunged for him...

Also by M. S. Murdock

VENDETTA

Published by
POPULAR LIBRARY

DYNTERYX

BY
M.S. MURDOCK

POPULAR LIBRARY

An Imprint of Warner Books, Inc.

A Warner Communications Company

POPULAR LIBRARY EDITION

Copyright © 1988 by Melinda S. Murdock
All rights reserved.

Popular Library®, the fanciful P design, and Questar® are registered
trademarks of Warner Books, Inc.

Cover illustration by Tim Hildebrandt

Popular Library books are published by
Warner Books, Inc.
666 Fifth Avenue
New York, N.Y. 10103

 A Warner Communications Company

Printed in the United States of America

First Printing: July, 1988

10 9 8 7 6 5 4 3 2 1

For Dorothy

Prologue

The dynteryx's head shot up in the cool morning air, his ears pricked in alarm, wisps of moss dripping from his mouth. He snorted, blowing air out in great gusts. His eyes rolled as he swung his head around, trying to catch the scent of danger.

He pushed his silver nose higher, but there was nothing in the wind. He whirled and surveyed his mares and foals, placidly nibbling at the greensward. He struck a trot, dappled gun-metal sides rolling with his movement, long crested neck arched with pride. He nipped the dimpled rump of a straying mare and sent her back to the herd with a squeal. When he had made a complete circuit of his band, he skidded to a halt and snorted again.

He could detect no predator, no disaster, yet his nerves tingled with danger. He could feel it all around. It rippled over his skin in waves. Frustrated, he reared, whistling. He shook his head and his snowy mane billowed around it. His white wings spread and beat the air as he uttered peal after peal of defiance. His mares stopped eating and watched their lord and master in wonder. He gave a final bellow and settled to earth, but he did not return to his breakfast. He remained alert, his ears up for the first sign of danger he knew was there, waiting in the shadows beyond his senses.

CHAPTER I

The planet Lazur was a small world orbiting a minor sun on the outskirts of the colonies of Dynt. The vast, deep seas that covered three-quarters of the planet made it a sapphire jewel in the sun's bracelet. It was so remote it housed a single settlement of less than seven score—the adventurous, the solitary, and the sought. The last category was responsible for its space dock.

Shiny and new, the slips rose majestically into the planet's lower atmosphere. When not in use they were drawn into an inconspicuous central core. The entire station could be broken down in moments. Fully extended and filled with ships, it took on the appearance of a many-layered silver blossom. In the blaze of sunset the blossom flamed gold against a darkening purple sky. There was no break in the glowing petals. The fleet was in.

The tavern-keeper, Thomas Small, set a plate of stew in front of a burly spacer. As a young man he had decided never to look beyond obvious externals. Subtle games of intrigue played around him, and he was oblivious to them. Treachery garroted its victims, and he ignored it. This made for a pleasant life devoid of complications. It also made his tavern a comfortable gathering place for all manner of men, a stopover where they would meet no questions and no curious eyes.

The tavern was full and that made Thomas happy. The gold dyntares clinking in his pockets made him happier yet. These refugees from devastated Chor were rich. How they came to be so did not interest him. The prospect of a steady flow of gold into his coffers brought an easy smile to his face.

Torrmere tavern was a rambling stone structure built on a

bluff overlooking the ocean. The climate was temperate and the long green hill ran down to the sea in a wealth of brilliant salt flowers and waving grass. Two hundred yards from the riffling edge of the water vegetation gave way to fine white sand. It had a faintly opalescent sheen. The bright blue water lapped at it, throwing up graceful shells from its depths and wearing them into sand with each surge. A continuous stiff wind from the sea swept up the hill and swirled around the tavern's fluted stone walls. They acted as a buffer to the cluster of houses and shops that completed the trading outpost.

Yellow lamplight gleamed from Torrmere's windows. A quick melody plucked from a harp was a pleasing counterpoint to the low rumble of conversation and occasional burst of laughter. The refugees were remnants of Eban Foxxe's resistance movement. Less than one hundred men and women remained after the awful confrontation with Corbin's fleet. A fraction elected to stay with the resistance. Marc Dynteryx did not blame them. To cheat death once might pass for bravery, but to taunt it daily was the act of a fool or a madman. The cause he championed was madness and he was a fool to attempt it. There was little hope of reward. He dismissed the occasional windfalls of cash and contraband from captured Gardeposts and ships. Breaking Ran Corbin's back was a thankless, impossible job, especially with the battered squadron he commanded. Sending it against Corbin's military resources was even more ludicrous than before Chor, yet he knew it must be done. He clung to Foxxe's cause as the one frail hope of an enslaved nation.

Eleven months had passed since Eban Foxxe faced Corbin's fleet to a standstill. He ransomed Chor with his life, setting himself in Corbin's path as a blood sacrifice. Chor had lost a fearsome number, but it survived, and Corbin's fleet was wounded past quick recovery. This gave Marc time to extricate his troops and regroup. They had fled to an emergency base, counted their losses, and moved again. Their progress to Lazur was a series of relocations that took them farther and farther from Dynt. Marc hoped Lazur's remoteness would give them a chance to continue Foxxe's fight. He could see no other course of action.

Lar Harken, seated across the table from Marc, was pluck-

ing experimentally at his harp. A frown creased his forehead.
He was deep within his music. To Marc the notes were random, but he knew to Lar they were an alphabet he was forming into words and phrases. As he listened, a melody
emerged, tentative at first, then stronger as Lar altered one
note, sharped another.

"I hope I can do that."

Lar looked up from his harp and smiled. "I didn't know you
had musical ambitions."

Marc chuckled. "You know I've no more talent than a block
of wood."

"For this," said Lar, indicating his harp, "I agree, but for
other things, no."

"You think I can straighten out this mess, then."

"If anyone can. What I do with music, you do with people.
Find each one his proper niche."

"I don't know if I like that. It's too manipulative."

"That is something you could never do."

Marc smiled. "Not devious enough."

"You have too much regard for human dignity. But people
like me, who would wander aimlessly through life, find in
you a man they can trust and respect."

"That's flattering . . ."

"Not really. It's a fact. You can't help it any more than I
can help a talent for this." Lar plucked a deep note on his
harp. "The difference is you'll wear your heart out over those
who follow you. Like Chor."

"Chor died. Can you blame them for hating us?"

"No. But without us more than Chor would have died."

"Without us there would have been no disturbances and
therefore no reason for death. Corbin is not one to waste time
or energy on unnecessary displays of power."

Lar looked around the room. "And we can't afford any
display at all."

"We can barely survive. Corbin is warned of our subterfuge. We can no longer masquerade as free traders. Corbin
will shut them down. No one will be allowed to operate without the king's sanction. Black market traders will be ruthlessly
persecuted."

"They're going to hate us for that. The traders."

"Yes. And we're not exactly wallowing in popularity now. We won the battle. We checked Corbin's fleet, but the cost was high. We lost our credibility. It will be harder and harder to find help."

"The armor is tarnished. But there is one thing Corbin didn't count on: you."

"You mean the crown."

Lar nodded. "Do you know what Corbin is calling you?"

"I'm afraid to ask."

"Oh, it isn't that bad. 'The pretender.' "

"Questioning my legitimacy."

"Even to the extent of circulating rumors of unsavory parentage."

Marc's hazel eyes took on an amused light. "Then he knows more than I do."

"There'll be worse," Lar prophesied grimly.

"No doubt."

Lar ran a finger idly over the harp strings. "What you need," he said, "is to fight Corbin's tactics with fire."

Marc made a futile gesture. "How can I fight rumor? It spreads on the wind and lodges in the corners of men's hearts or the secret places in their minds."

"There is only one sure way. Rumor will sink to its knees before legend."

Marc laughed, really amused for the first time in days. The dancing lights in his eyes leaped with the laughter. "Legend? Me?" he said and dissolved into another fit of mirth.

Lar waited patiently, letting Marc enjoy the joke, but his eyes were serious.

"You don't mean it," Marc managed.

"I do," returned Lar. "It's a brilliant weapon," he added modestly, "and one that you are ideally suited for. Raised by a legend herself, in obscurity, to become heir of all Dynt. From slave to master. It's blindingly romantic."

"It wasn't romantic to live."

"It never is. It's the storyteller who makes the difference."

"You?"

"Me. One haunting song will destroy Corbin's paltry attempts to discredit you. But there are disadvantages."

"I would become even more isolated. Less human and more fiction."

"Yes. I would not do this without your knowledge. It is a powerful tool, legend. It might serve the king of Dynt well."

"It might. It seems he has few others. Pavis is all but helpless, a prisoner in his palace. I do not think I could live such a life. Go ahead with your legend, only let me hear what you write."

"Of course. It concerns you."

"Do not turn me into a god."

"I was thinking more along the lines of warrior for the people."

Marc grinned again.

"The truth usually makes the best story." Lar's voice was innocent.

"Lar, you are a scoundrel."

"I have been called that."

"How do you propose to explain Chor?"

Lar touched the harp strings. "Simple as a, b, c," he answered, striking the notes. "Chor was Foxxe's engagement, not yours. I think I will begin with a noble, rollicking song of Foxxe's last stand. It will be heroic, it will have a stirring melody that sticks in the mind, and it will give Foxxe full credit for the defense of the outer colonies. Step one."

"Step two?"

"A plaintive melody to tear the heart, mourning the lost. A mother's lament, I think. It will sue for peace and plead for a leader who cares. Then I'll start on you. Subtly, of course."

"Of course. Lar, you should have been a senator."

"Too tame, too slow. I like excitement. It's a flaw, I know."

"Not to me. I'm just glad you're on my side."

A serious note crept into Lar's voice. "Eban Foxxe gave me a chance to amount to something. When he declared open war on Corbin, I followed him because it seemed worthwhile and I felt needed. Corbin doesn't care who gets hurt in his drive for power. Innocent people pay for his greed. And I loved Foxxe as the only father I can remember."

"Good reasons."

"I thought so."

"And now?"

"Now I realize there is no place to run from evil."

"Neutrality doesn't work. I learned that as a slave." Marc looked up as Suzerain placed a bowl of stew, thick, crusty slices of bread, and a jug of pale gold ale on the table. "My thanks," he said, and Suzerain nodded wordlessly.

"This slavery thing," ventured Lar as he relinquished his harp in favor of food.

"You're asking me? An abomination."

"You'll free them?"

"If I get the chance, but it's complicated. They will have to be prepared to live on their own. Some will even prefer the safe life of bondage."

Marc sat musing. Slowly the light of an idea grew in his eyes. Lar, piling stew on a piece of bread, did not see it.

"Lar, you are a genius."

"I know." Lar managed to reply with insouciance even through a mouthful of food.

"You've given me a wonderful idea. We can begin educating the slaves right under Corbin's nose if you will give some thought to a series of teaching songs. If you're clever you can cloak the alphabet in popular music. Then a spelling song. What a triumph to teach them to read!"

Lar was caught by the idea. It appealed to his sense of humor.

"You've already shown me how history can be converted to music. What about counting songs?"

"It can be done."

"I never doubted it. And they will serve to camouflage the songs you write of me."

"They would indeed."

Marc sank his spoon into the stew, feeling he had accomplished something. He ate with relish, but he was not concentrating on his food. The problem of how to safeguard his forces consumed him. Denied their cover as traders, they were an unwieldy body. He had to find a way to hide them and still maintain communications and easy access.

A chair scraped back from the table, breaking his concentration, but Marc looked up with a smile. His old friend and teacher Gisarme stood beside it.

"May I sit down?" he inquired.

"Gisarme, don't be so deferential. Am I to be denied the companionship of those dearest to me because of an accident of fate? If so, I will throw the crown into Lazur's ocean. Sit down!"

"I wouldn't call it an accident of fate. I think you would have been a ruler under any circumstances, and I was merely showing you the proper respect before these ruffians." His glance swept the room and did not exclude Lar. His eyes twinkled.

"First a scoundrel, then a genius, and now a ruffian. I seem to be a man of diverse parts," Lar said mildly.

"I would not underestimate you," answered Gisarme.

Lar put on a most innocent look. It did not wholly eliminate his rakish devil-may-care charm.

"Lar, you fool no one," Marc chuckled.

"Perhaps not here. I do fool them on Dynt—even on Chor."

"For that I am devoutly grateful. If you were under cover before, you must now become legitimate—you and Stella. You can do more good than ten fighter pilots. If you set your music to work for me and keep your ears open, you will be invaluable."

"And, because he is an artist, he can move in any society," said Gisarme.

"Eccentricity does seem to go unnoticed in the arts."

Marc nodded. "You can run the gamut from royalty to the criminal element and no one will think a thing about it."

"Royalty?"

"It's not impossible. And if you have the chance, it would be an advantage to be able to contact Pavis."

"It might be done." Gisarme's voice was speculative. "Provided, of course, you become popular enough."

Lar registered Gisarme's dig with a haughty eyebrow, and Gisarme chuckled.

"Still," he continued, "it might be a better job for Stella. A beautiful woman is sometimes less suspect, and it is well known Pavis has an appreciative eye."

"Whatever you do, Lar, from now on you must be doubly careful."

"Some of these men don't know how to be careful," said

Gisarme. "They're too simple and open to be devious. They'd drop out of character at the first Gardesman's trick."

Lar chased the last of his stew around the bowl with a piece of bread. "Some of them are too stupid," he added. "The only logic they understand is a right cross. You'll never be able to hide them."

Marc sighed. "I know. The only solution I can come up with is to split our forces. Those of us who are known—myself, Coryelle, and Gisarme—will form the command nucleus. You and Stella, and the rest of those clever enough to maintain a cover, will go underground as our eyes and ears. You will maintain escape routes."

"That will be difficult and dangerous now Corbin is alerted."

Marc agreed. "The last group will be split into bands of two to five ships and set to harrying Corbin's forces as Foxxe did for so many years."

"They won't work free," Lar stated.

"I know. They have always been pirates. If they can be used against Corbin, so much the better for us. As incentive, they will be allowed to despoil the *goods* they capture."

"Do you think they'll stop at that?"

"No. Not at first. Not until the consequences of betrayal become known."

"You'll strip a traitor."

"Of everything he's won."

"And banish him?"

"Oh, no. He'll do the drudge work for a year with no pay. He'll be watched. Then he'll be given a new start."

"If he'll take it."

"Such a man," said Gisarme, "will either try to kill you or follow you forever."

"I know."

"It's a kinder solution than most."

"It has to be. Even if it's more dangerous than Corbin's way. He would kill the man and have done with it."

"Neat, but not inspiring of confidence," commented Lar.

"He cows his followers and they fear him. They obey because of the fear and because of the rewards he offers. You ask for more," said Gisarme.

"Yes. More than most of them know how to give."

"There will be failures."

"Always. But there may be success as well."

"One success can be made into a wonderful tale. It will establish you as an honorable man," said Lar.

Marc grinned. "Grist for the mill," he said.

"Definitely. I can see you're going to provide me with a wealth of material. I will not lack for subject matter."

"We shall see."

Suzerain materialized behind Lar's chair and adroitly removed empty dishes and discarded cutlery. Not a piece of silverware clinked against a plate.

"Thank you," said Marc. "Suzerain, you've seen what is left of the forces Foxxe gathered at Chor. You've heard them talk. What do you think of them?"

"Not my place to say," returned Suzerain. There was no insolence in his reply. It was a flat statement.

"But I am asking you. And I would appreciate an answer."

Suzerain remained quiet. His lips compressed as he considered his reply. When he spoke it was terse and to the point.

"Most be dregs. Maybe ten be honest and true."

"So few."

Suzerain's nod was imperceptible.

"Get used to it now," said Gisarme. "There will never be more than a handful you can trust, and even of those, some will betray you."

Suzerain melted into the background. Long practice as Eban Foxxe's slave enabled him to seem invisible. He cleared other tables with the same speed, moving through laughter and talk like a ship at sea. The alien elements surged around him as he continued on his way.

"Gloom and dooooom!" cackled a voice above Lar's head. He jumped, then relaxed, deceptively quiet.

"Some people," he remarked conversationally to Marc and Gisarme, "deserve to be spanked."

"Or kissed," answered Marc, his eyes twinkling.

The suggestion appealed to Lar. Marc could see it in the dangerous light in his green eyes. Lar half turned in his chair, slipped an arm around Stella's waist, and dragged her across his lap. Before she could utter more than an outraged squawk, her lips were occupied with a thorough kiss. She came out of it blushing and sputtering.

"People," said Lar, "should think twice about sneaking up on someone."

"Cad! Taking gross advantage of a lady!"

"Always," said Lar blandly.

"Shameless!"

Lar accepted the epithet with modest dignity.

"And you!" Stella's finger stabbed in Marc's direction. "Don't look innocent and don't think your high and mighty destiny will save you from my tongue!"

Marc choked on his laughter.

"Go ahead, laugh. But I wait for the day. Then I'll laugh. When you're so besotted over some poor, unsuspecting girl you can't see straight. I wait!"

"Pax, pax!" Marc sputtered.

Stella straightened but remained where she was. Her composure had returned but the blush still painted her cheeks with a becoming pink bloom. She smirked.

"I did it," she said complacently.

Marc and Lar gurgled, and Gisarme's smile broadened.

"You did succeed in disrupting things," he said.

"As usual," returned Lar.

"At least you're not all glowering like sleepy cave cats."

"Stella, you're good for us," said Gisarme.

"I know," she said.

"Humble, too," remarked Lar.

"If you would occupy your hands with the harp we could have some music. I feel like singing."

"Whatever madam commands," he replied sardonically.

Lar grasped Stella around the waist and set her lightly on the table. He reached for his harp as her rich contralto voice rang out in a lively ballad. She made the room resound with it.

Marc watched as the throng turned to listen. In many eyes he saw sparks ignited. It was as Lar had said. Touch a man's spirit and you touch a great reserve of power.

CHAPTER 2

The soft glow of an old-fashioned oil lamp sculpted Coryelle's face. It flushed her skin with gold and glittered on the wealth of hair spread on her pillow. Her eyes were bottomless black wells. The dim light obscured their deep blue color, but it could not hide their anguish. Faint echoes of music and laughter from the common room below failed to soften them. She was grateful for the long and twisting staircase separating her from the throng.

She had been a child. She had thought they were safe. The flight to find her uncle was the faded memory of a five-year-old. She had not thought Marc would leave her, but the matter had been lifted out of her hands. Tenebrae handed him freedom with the papers that proclaimed him her adopted son. Without that, Coryelle might have forbidden him to go. He was her slave. Her thoughts were tantalizing, tempting, but in her heart she knew they were toys, played with, but not to be taken seriously. Marc had risked his life, and the possibility of freedom, for her. He ceased to be her slave when he hid her from Corbin. She had clung to him then as the secure foundation of her life. When Marc had told her of his desire to leave Adyton, the foundation cracked.

Coryelle rolled over on her narrow bed and stared at the thick, intricately woven vines which formed the headboard. They were worked in a knot with no visible end. It was a circle game, like her decision to let Marc go, for he had come back to her. He had given her himself, handed her back his freedom and pledged himself to her. It had been sweet, but the kernel of the fruit was bitter. He spoke to comfort a child, with no thought beyond her security, no knowledge of what his gift meant to her.

She lived on that pledge for three long years. She survived on the meager news of him Gisarme had been able to collect, and she ruthlessly extracted from Gisarme and Tenebrae anything they would tell her of him. Attitudes and opinions she had been too young to understand clarified in the recounting. Every twig of information fed the fire within her. Always she dreamed he would come back to her. Never did it cross her mind he might find someone else. Until Stella.

Isolated as she had been, Coryelle did not comprehend society. Most of her memories of Dynt were hazy and the sheer numbers of people were a revelation to her. But it was Stella, with her murky, soft eyes, voluptuous mouth, and hair like a dark halo, who made Coryelle realize the world was full of beautiful women. Terror one of them would reach out and claim Marc drove through her heart like a sword. Every note of laughter, every affectionate gesture on Marc's part twisted that sword in the wound. He treated Coryelle as he always had—with amusement, affection, even love—but with no indication of her years.

It haunted her he might always think her a child for whom he had taken responsibility. She longed to pull down that barrier but did not know how to begin. Tenebrae taught her many things, but the art of playing the social butterfly was not among them. As she watched the coquetry and games of romance going on around her, she knew she did not have the skills to compete, nor did she want to. Her love for Marc was no game.

There was another stumbling block. Marc hated slavery. Even as a child she grasped this fact. Now she knew hatred of his own condition had broadened to a loathing of all injustice. It might be he would always secretly despise her for having owned him. She railed at her own stupidity, for the hundredth time cursing the blindness of her youth. She might have freed him, and earned his gratitude. To have even that would be something.

A burst of laughter, topped off by Stella's warm professional voice, drifted up the stairs. Coryelle twisted angrily into a sitting position, every nerve irritated. The laughter paused, then rose again. She could picture the scene. Stella would be perched on a table, her slender legs crossed audaciously, her face and figure displayed to full advantage. The circle of men around her would be attentive, appreciative, hanging on her every word. Coryelle had seen it all before. That Marc would be part of the crowd gave her a cold, hollow feeling.

Coryelle threw the pillow across the room, doing her best to send it straight through the stone wall, futile though the attempt might be. It was not Stella's fault. She knew that. Stella was familiar, but never intimate. She was one of those women who held the masculine eye. Marc liked her, admired her talent, appreciated her beauty. Jealousy boiled through Coryelle in an angry, overwhelming tide. She sent a second pillow after the first. It struck the wall with a soft whump and slid to the floor.

Feathers against stone. It was apropos of her love for Marc. No matter how she tried he would never see it. Tears of frustration overflowed and trekked slowly down her cheeks. She brushed at them impatiently, but they continued to flow.

She knew, better than anyone else, the problems before Marc. As prince of Dynt he took upon himself the burdens of his kingdom. He was in a precarious position. Though his claim to the throne of Dynt was legitimate, the Seneschal would use any means at his disposal to repudiate it, claiming a regency for himself. The remnant of Foxxe's resistance was undisciplined and for the most part unprincipled. Holding them together would not be easy. Caught between his men and his enemy, he must know pain. Responsible for his people, educated in the royal tradition, Marc was heir to the concept of a life spent in the service of others, every free moment aimed at solving the kingdom's problems. Coryelle knew he had no time for a silly girl, and it would hurt him to reject her love. She could spare him that. Better, much better, to help him achieve his goals, to see Dynt bloom into a land of peace and freedom.

This was a dream she could share, one for which she was educated. She would sometimes be near him. She closed her eyes. She could feel his voice on her skin like warm fingers. He touched her depths, the axis of her thoughts.

She opened her eyes to vanquish his image, but it remained, undaunted, to haunt her. In the privacy of this room
she could surrender to herself and love his every feature,
thought, and movement. She might never touch him physically, but her mind felt the satin and steel of his arms around
her. The clear depths of his eyes flooded her body with
warmth, and the broad strength of his shoulders enfolded her
with safety. It was not real, but it was what she had, and she
clung to it. Stripped by her emotional storm, she sank back
upon the bed. Fatigue added to the languid grace of her limbs.

Though nothing like the slim, stylish Stella, Coryelle possessed her own elegance. Even at seventeen she was a voluptuous beauty. Her figure escaped the whims of fashion and
held to the classic ideal that a woman should be constructed of
curves. The short green tunic, with its flared shoulders and
fitted waist, accentuated them, and the close-fitting green leg-
gings she wore outlined shapely, muscular legs and dainty
ankles. Even her high sandals followed their contours. It was
a most becoming style of dress, but one she had worn so long
she was not aware of the impression it created.

Her dark gold hair was thick and fine, reaching past her
waist. She wore it bound up with a leather thong to keep it
from the grasping branches of trees and brush. Loose on the
pillow, it framed her oval face in light. Her clear peach-col-
ored skin was flushed with health. Her upbringing on Adyton
had given her more than usual physical strength, but she was
no more aware of it than she was of her clothes.

Her thoughts centered around Marc. She tried to achieve
excellence for him. In the last year, seeing him often, she had
become so obsessed with him he filled her life. She put him
aside only for work, and even then he was at the back of her
mind, spurring her on.

She sighed. Tenebrae, she knew, would not have been
pleased. "Never," she once told Coryelle, "make a man the
center of your life. He will be human and he will fail you."
Her words carried no threat for Coryelle. Marc had not failed
her. He never would. She was as sure of this as she was of
breathing.

The oil lamp guttered, its light flickering dim and allowing darkness to overwhelm the room. It became a single point of light that glinted and went out. Sleep stole on Coryelle with the same inevitability. As her breathing deepened and slowed Marc's image blurred, but the thought of him held her safe. Her tears dried as the music of Lar's harp drifted up the stairs in a love-song lullaby.

From the narrow corridor the entrance to the common room was a rectangle of golden light. Lar's harp and Stella's throaty voice sang a duet that invaded the hallway. A dark figure stood listening to it, then quietly shut the hall door.

Rushlights illumined the passageway at regularly spaced intevals. Their light did not touch the face of the man striding down it. Presently he paused, reaffirmed the hall's emptiness, and slipped into a room. Closing the door tightly, he lit a smaller version of the hallway rushlamps. The lamp shone upon boxes and crates of supplies. Cured meat hung from the ceiling, and wax-coated cheeses lined the shelves. Pungent dried cooking herbs were tied in bunches and hung on every available projection. Barrels of winter vegetables lined the walls.

It was to one of these barrels the figure moved, lifting the top and pushing it to one side. He removed tubers from the center of the barrel and brushed sand up against its rim. Deeper digging unearthed a metal object six inches square. Sure hands brushed away dust and sand before unfolding the device.

It proved to be a miniature communication station, even to a microgenerator. The man pushed a single switch, and it came to life. Preset to a stationary home base, the screen showed a room full of computers. The man entered a number code which sent an insistent and annoying beep to the home computer. A man wearing the Garde's dashing blue uniform appeared. His face was sharp and cold, as if he dealt perpetually with unpleasant information.

"Verify," he snapped.

"Code raven blue," answered the figure in a low voice.

"Blue, raven, blue," responded the Gardesman. "Verify."

"Raven twenty."

"We have not heard from you in some time, Raven Twenty. We had begun to wonder if you had been found out." The Gardesman's voice held a threat.

"No."

"You should keep in more regular contact."

"When I can."

The Gardesman shrugged, plainly not interested. The threat was de rigeur ritual. "What have you?"

"Lazur."

"That far out? Surely it can't be a base."

"It's thought of."

"That would be unexpected. How are the resistance forces distributed?"

"All here."

"All?"

"Yes."

The Gardesman's eyes showed a spark of interest. "For how long?"

"Not decided."

"What are the prince's plans?"

"Use this as a base. Split his forces. Go underground."

"Specifics."

"Not yet."

"Contact me as soon as anything develops. I want to know his mind." The spy's silence goaded the Gardesman to threats. "Otherwise your payment might never arrive. After all you have risked I would hate to see you lose everything."

"You will pay."

"Do not hold yourself too high. You can be replaced." The spy's silence was a cynical answer. "At any rate, I have no say in the matter. That is between you and the Seneschal."

"Ran Corbin gave his word."

"The Seneschal keeps his promises."

"Blue, raven twenty, black."

"You will contact me oftener." The Gardesman sighed at the stubborn silence. "Black, raven twenty, black."

The screen died and the spy dismantled the station. He replaced it in the root barrel and returned the storeroom to its original purpose. He extinguished the rushlight, and the room sank into darkness.

The lieutenant of the Garde saluted his captain with punctilious correctness.

"Yes, Tatelen."

Tatelen handed him a slip of paper with a single line scrawled across it.

"What is this?"

"The location of the new resistance headquarters."

The captain stared. "You are sure?"

Tatelen nodded. "This is a reliable contact with the prince's forces."

"What!"

"Your pardon, sir. The pretender." Tatelen's answer was immediate, the words almost tumbling over each other. He had made a mistake, and he was in haste to correct it.

"See you remember the facts, Tatelen."

"Yes, sir."

"If you wish to advance with the Garde you cannot afford errors. Now about this." He waved the slip of paper under Tatelen's nose. "Do you know where this is?"

"Yes, sir. Lazur."

"Lazur is on the outer edge of the colonies. That is not an optimum place for a base."

"The informant has never been wrong."

"Surely you can handle this. The usual surveillance equipment and undercover patrols must be in place at once."

"Sir, I do not think we will need them."

"You might tell me why." The mild tenor of the captain's voice was dangerous.

"The entire resistance force is now on Lazur."

"For how long?" The captain's voice cracked.

"Nothing definite has been decided, but at the moment they are all there. Including the Dynteryx."

"How many ships are in the area?"

"There are three full squadrons at station G-13."

"G-13? I thought that outpost was abandoned."

Tatelen shook his head. "Proposed for termination because of inactivity. As yet unconfirmed."

The captain's eyes glittered. "G-13 is three hours from Lazur."

Tatelen allowed a small light of triumph to show on his face. "Yes, sir."

"How many others know of this?"

"No one. I was alone when Raven Twenty reported."

The captain's voice was cold as ice. "You will be silent as death—or meet it. Do I make myself clear?"

Tatelen nodded. "I have no mouth. However, I do have a record—and a purse."

"Both will be augmented if you follow orders."

"That I have done from early youth. You may count on me."

"I hope so. If one breath of this gets out you will no longer be a member of the Garde. You will wear a traitor's brand on your forehead and be persecuted wherever you go."

"Perhaps it would be best if I were suddenly taken ill, confined to my bed for a period of, shall we say, two days?"

The captain considered Tatelen's suggestion, and found it favorable. "I wish you speedy recovery," he said. "In two days."

"With double pay."

Annoyance crossed the captain's face, and Tatelen held his breath lest he lose everything by pushing his superior too far.

"You are a grasping puppy, however, you are due it. Yes, yes, with double pay! Now be gone! I have no time for this haggling."

Tatelen saluted smartly and turned on his heel in time to hide the smile pulling at his mouth. He had gained ground, particularly if the captain kept his word about a commendation. The captain was not a man of honor and he had made the mistake of allowing Tatelen to confirm it. Tatelen knew it took only a glass of wine to loosen his tongue. Were he to betray the captain, he had more than enough ammunition from the most impeccable source: the man himself.

Tatelen was pleased. He might not get the credit he deserved for the destruction of the resistance, but he had advanced a step. Later, he could make sure his part was known. The right word dropped to the right person would build his reputation. In a way, he was sorry to lose the resistance forces, and the reliable spy with them. They were a solid vehicle for advancement. He would miss it, but he would see, in the years to come, a career built upon its demise.

CHAPTER 3

The moon washed Coryelle's tower room in white light. It leached color, and flushed the atmosphere with silver. Deep black shadows made dramatic contrast. Coryelle was still asleep. Her long lashes lay dark and wet against her cheeks. Her hair was a mass of silver love knots. The shadows accentuated her narrow waist and curving hips.

A rumble of distant thunder echoed in the room, and she turned in her sleep. The thunder kept up a low grumble, growing steadily in volume. A frown creased her forehead, and she flung one arm up to ward off the noise. The thunder roared in a crescendo, and the moonlight was suddenly obliterated.

Coryelle sat up with a start. She was thoroughly awake. The rumbling thunder was the voice of fighters flying low. Corbin had found them.

She blinked the sleep from her eyes and moved. She must sound the alarm. She swung her legs over the edge of the bed, glad to have fallen asleep in her clothes. Every second counted. She reached the door as the first charge struck.

The stone tower shuddered under the impact. Loose rock, dust, and mortar fell, and Coryelle choked on the congested air. She grabbed for support, clutching the heavy brass door handle as one of the stones under her feet gave way, plunging to the room below. A second charge hit, and the room rocked. She clung to the door. A spent blast grazed the tower wall, sending fragments of stone in all directions. They pelted her like a swarm of stinging insects, and she gasped in pain, inadvertently loosening her grip. The door was wrenched from her grasp and she fell headlong into Lar's outstretched arms. He gave her a quick squeeze.

"Come on!" he yelled above the noise.

She nodded, running at his side like a flushed deer. The wooden stairway swayed, groaning under the impact of explosives. It was hard to balance on it. Coryelle risked one backward glance, and saw a jezail blast punch through the walls of her room, sending a shower of debris after them.

Lar jumped, avoiding a block of stone that would have crushed his legs had it connected. His movement pulled Coryelle off her feet. She rolled and slid to the next landing before she was able to stop herself. Lar was right behind her. She grabbed for his hand, pulling herself upright.

"All right?"

She nodded.

"Then let's go!"

As they started down the last flight of steps there was a louder explosion, followed by another shower of dirt and stones. The blast destroyed the landing at the top of the stairs. The staircase was unsupported now and wavered sickeningly. Coryelle and Lar leaped for the last step as its timbers gave way and it crashed to earth. Two strides saw them through the creaking doorway. Flattened against an outside wall, they caught their breath.

"Where?" Coryelle managed, gulping for air.

"The reserve ships."

She nodded, knowing Corbin's first shots had destroyed the space dock and the ships anchored there. Lar raised the hand he held and kissed it, pausing long enough for a smile. She was suddenly glad he was her escape partner.

"We'll make it. We'll all make it," he said.

Coryelle flashed him a brief smile, so like her brother's sudden bursts of charm. It was an affirmation, not hope or belief. Lar took a firmer grip on her hand. "Run!" he said.

Coryelle matched him stride for stride as they skirted the

new-made ruins of the inn that had been their refuge. Lar was making for an outcropping of rock which sheltered the five ships in his assigned escape squad. The path was open and straight. They were totally exposed to enemy fire, but there were no alternatives. Ahead they could see someone disappearing over the rocks. For a moment it looked as if the attacking ships might ignore them, but luck failed.

One of the wedge-shaped fighters broke away from its formation and started after them, spitting blue fire as it came. Where the quick fire touched the earth it clung, then raced forward, sending icy streaks of molten flame after them, growing as it ran to the height of a man. A wall of flame streaked after Lar close enough to singe his hair. Coryelle felt it cold against her back and put forth another burst of speed.

As she ran, she saw three ships rise beyond the rocks and speed away, low over the land to confuse the sensors of their pursuers. The ship above her saw them too, and abandoned Lar and Coryelle for larger targets. The rush of its passage nearly knocked her flat, but before its backlash ebbed Lar was urging her forward. Already they could see their companions lifting off from the other side of the hamlet.

"Now!"

Lar's voice cracked like a pistol at the start of a race. He and Coryelle jumped into the open, sprinting to the rocky face of the hill where the village overlooked the sea. They were immediately and ruthlessly pursued. A fighter swooped after them, sending a barrage of jezail fire before it. It was firing by sight, its sensors scrambled by a rare mineral in Lazur's igneous rocks. Once under the protection of the scrubby trees, the jezails' effectiveness would be halved.

The trees loomed ahead, their twisted gray trunks bent by the wind. They were not tall and they were not luxuriant, but they were shelter. The fighter was dogging their footsteps, the orange fire of its jezails licking at their heels. Coryelle felt it burning at her back as she and Lar ducked into the copse and sank beneath the trees. Through their sparse foliage they could see the fighter sheer off, to come whirling back in a strafing run.

"He's going to run blind." The quiet certainty in Lar's voice echoed Coryelle's thoughts.

"We've got to get out of here!" she answered.

"We've got to trick him. If we head for the ships now, he'll be able to destroy them before we can get to them."

"How?"

"I don't know. I don't know. Think!"

Coryelle's head lowered in thought. "Look," she said, "there's another knot of trees farther down the hill. It isn't in a direct line to the ships. If we made for that, it might give us some time."

"It's better than nothing," Lar muttered. "Let's go."

The fighter was upon them a second time, sending short bursts from its jezails into the trees. Coryelle led Lar through them in a twisting run that seemed to him an endless detour, but he knew it was not. Her woodcraft was far superior to his own, a fact he acknowledged willingly. Though their route dodged and turned they were never faced with an obstacle of any size. In seconds they had reached the edge of the copse.

Lar drew up beside Coryelle, his sights on the next little wood. There was an agonizing stretch of open ground between their haven and that distant refuge. He reached out and grasped Coryelle's shoulder.

"Coryelle, promise me."

She looked up at him in surprise. "What?"

"No matter what happens, you'll keep going."

"Of course."

"Even if I fall."

Her eyes softened. "Yes, Lar. I promise."

He smiled whimsically. "You are much too important to lose, you know."

"So are you."

Behind them the engines of the fighter whined in pursuit. A tree exploded in fire, holding its shape as it burned fiercely. Then it was gone. The fighter sheered off to make another dive at the trees. Lar knew it would not be satisfied until it had destroyed them all and flushed its quarry.

"Now! Run!" he yelled, and they shot into the open.

Coryelle could hear the whine of the fighter's engine as it executed a diving turn and followed them. Explosions punctuated her footsteps as the jezails struck the earth behind her. As she and Lar reached the bottom of the hill the blasts ceased, the ship's engines throttled down: There was a moment of terrible silence, silence more dreadful than any sound, silence in which the labored gasps of their own breathing bore testimony to the futility of their flight. She heard Lar's oath above the popping explosion of blue flame.

"Quick fire! No hope. Run!" Lar shouted and pushed her away from him.

Coryelle stumbled on, but she looked back to see Lar turn and stand perfectly still. The flames roared toward him, spitting and hissing as they came. Quick fire would follow its prey inexorably. It was deadly but impossible to control. Even Corbin used it as a last resort. That it was being used now showed Coryelle how desperately Corbin wanted the resistance destroyed. She saw the flames rear up as they closed on Lar, surpassing his height by a span. They cackled wildly, throwing off showers of blue sparks.

In spite of her promise, Coryelle stopped in her tracks. He meant to die to save her life. She started to turn as the flames lunged for him. Lar dropped under the blue inferno without a sound.

Coryelle took one step toward him, her hands outstretched in an involuntary gesture of appeal, but there was no hope. Lar's body was covered with flame, hungrily licking around his limbs. She turned and ran. His sacrifice would not be empty. She would do her best to reach the secreted ships.

As she skirted the base of the hill, rocky outcroppings became numerous. She was within sight of the overhang that sheltered the five vessels in her escape squad. The overhang was fronted by a high stone wall. The settlers had constructed it to pen livestock, but it was a convenient dock for small vessels. Along the top of the wall Coryelle could see two large stones. Three of the ships had already taken off. Two remained.

The pursuing fighter was back, but it was harder for him to track her among the rocks. She could hear him tacking back and forth to pick up her trail. She smiled. The mineral these rocks contained not only scrambled the finer channels of sensors, it was the basis of laser reflectors. It diffused a laser blast, making it as deadly to the pursuer as the pursued, forcing the Garde to abandon their lasers for the less accurate jezails.

She slipped from boulder to boulder like a shadow, the years of survival training standing her in good stead. She was nearing the man-made cave when she stopped short, then sank back against the nearest rock and closed her eyes, breathing deeply.

One of the rocks on the stone wall would never be pushed off to signal departure. Three blackened, fire-eaten bodies lay before her. Their faces were devoured by flames, but a silver knife with a twisted hilt identified the three. Coryelle turned away from the corpses. She shuddered, gagged, and stumbled on.

Revulsion slowed her steps and made her careless. She was in the open one moment too long, and the fighter pilot saw her. He came after her with a whine, a metallic wasp intent on its victim. Again orange fire pounded around her, but now it blasted rock, sending igneous shrapnel everywhere. A shower of lead pellets could not have been more devastating. Coryelle felt them sting her back and shoulders. She sprinted faster, dodging and rolling to elude the blasts.

An alley of loose flat stones lay between her and the cave. She knew she could not keep her feet on it, not at speed. Instead she threw herself down on the shaly stones, allowing their instability to be her slide. Once started, they rolled beneath her as if they were oiled, building speed as they moved. It was a rough, bruising ride, though faster than she could run. The cave loomed closer and Coryelle suddenly realized that if she could not escape the stream of stones she would be swept by the hidden dock. It would take hours to scale the treacherous rocks, and she would be exposed most of the time. She searched desperately for a handhold.

The fighter was directly above her, taking leisurely pot-shots. In toying with his prey her enemy did her a mortal favor. As she neared the cave he delivered a shot to her left directly into the rushing stones. The earth jarred beneath her, throwing her to the side. As she flew through the air she curled her arms above her head and went limp. She landed on a pile of rocky debris with a dead thump and lay still.

The fighter hovered above her for long moments. Finally, with a petty spurt of short jezail blasts, it roared upward and was gone.

Coryelle allowed herself to relax. Her heart slowed its beat and her breathing quieted as she relished momentary safety. She closed her eyes, concentrating on recuperating as quickly as possible.

"Coryelle! Coryelle!"

Her eyes flew open at the familiar voice.

"You were dead! You had to be! Oh, Lar!" Coryelle wrapped her arms around a very much alive Lares Harken, tears of happiness welling in her eyes. "Lar, I thought you were dead. I would never have left otherwise."

"I told you to run. You promised."

"You know it is a promise I could not keep. The flames enveloped you and I could see no hope."

"That is a little-known fact about quick fire. It does not follow body heat or vital signs, it follows movement. It can be fooled. If the timing is right, you can drop in its path and it will jump you if you remain still."

"But you were covered with fire."

"It looks that way. Actually it jumped over me, and because you paused, there was no movement. That confused it and it roiled around, consuming itself. I had only to wait until the flames died."

"If I had known!"

"There was no time to tell you. I am sorry for what I put you through, but I'm not sorry we're both alive."

"What if I had done as I promised? Run?"

"I admit I banked on your hesitation, and if you had obeyed me implicitly, I would be dead, but I didn't want you to come back to me, and I figured you would remember your promise if you thought there was no hope."

"You take fearsome chances, Lares."

Lar smiled roguishly. "I live with luck. Besides, you are much too softhearted to leave a companion in danger. It was no chance at all, merely an astute estimation of character."

Now the danger was past, Coryelle was becoming angry at Lar for risking himself. Her voice was tart. "Your pride is insufferable."

Lar grinned again. "I know."

"Push that stone off the wall, and the other as well. We cannot stand here gawping all day. Racque will be waiting for us!" Coryelle ordered.

Lar meekly obeyed her. "What about Hawk's ship?" he asked.

"You saw them, then? There were five in that party. I saw three bodies. Perhaps some managed to escape."

Lar skirted the stone wall as Coryelle picked herself up from the ground.

"The ship is gone. I wonder why they did not remove the signal rock?"

"Maybe they were too closely pursued to worry about details."

"Probable."

Lar shoved the rocks from the wall and watched as they cascaded down the hill, creating a landslide of stones and dirt. Coryelle had freed the hatch and was examining their ship when Lar appeared at her side. He made a stirrup of his hands and boosted her into the hatchway, then vaulted aboard himself.

"Check the supplies while I warm her up," he said.

Coryelle went over the cache of food, water, and extra fuel. It was all in order, enough to see them through two weeks in space. She strapped the fuel containers down tight and went to the cockpit. The ship's engines were alive, whining in anticipation of exercise. Coryelle felt them quiver beneath her feet.

"Activate the sensors. We won't be able to check for enemy fighters until we're about two hundred kilometers up. You'll get a lot of echo, but I want them ready as soon as we're clear. We're not out of this by a long way."

Coryelle clipped a safety harness across her waist. She turned the sensors on and the screen exhibited gray snow. It would clear once they were away from the rocks. Lar hit the boosters, and the ship rose slowly. He retracted the landing struts and sent it over the top of the stone wall.

"Look sharp. Corbin's crew won't give up until they've accounted for all of us."

"Nothing yet. It's going to take some fancy flying to get us out of here."

"Don't remind me."

They skimmed the ground, heading away from the settlement. Once out of sensor range, they would leave the planet to rendezvous with Coryelle's brother Racque at prearranged coordinates.

"I'm picking up fighters around the settlement. They don't seem to be going very far afield."

"Any count?" asked Lar.

"At least two full squadrons."

"That means they're fairly sure they've accounted for everyone."

"I know."

Lar turned a quick smile on Coryelle. "They've been known to be wrong. More than once."

"I borrow trouble."

"It's safer that way. Anyone seem to be aware of us?"

"No. I can't even detect enemy sensors in this direction. They're concentrating on the tavern."

"Lucky for us they're so sure of themselves."

"Sensor interference fading. We should be free in another hundred kilometers."

Lar adjusted his course and sent the ship up into the atmosphere. He knew he might be flying into a nest of Corbin's fighters. "Nothing ahead?"

"Not yet. Do you suppose they only left scouts, and all the main force hit the planet?"

"They'd have to be awfully cocky to do that."

"I'm still not reading anything."

"This is too easy. It's making me nervous."

"What we went through wasn't enough for you?"

"So I worry!"

The ship was skirting atmosphere, and space loomed in sparkling darkness. Lar adjusted his course again, sending the ship in an arc toward the rendezvous coordinates. Still the sensors remained clear of enemy vessels.

"Four ships off the starboard bow. It's Racque!"

"Here we go!"

As the ship scampered to join its companions, one of the vessels came to meet it, chivvying it into the group like an overprotective mother hen.

"What took you so long?" Racque's voice blared from the communications link, slightly broken by static.

"We had a little trouble getting away," said Lar.

"We're going to have more than a little trouble if we don't move—now!"

"I'm right behind you," Lar said mildly.

The five freighters moved out in a loose wedge, their various designs making the maneuver a parody of the military perfection of Corbin's fleet.

CHAPTER 4

The ragged wedge of ships skirted Lazur's atmosphere and rose into the star-dusted darkness. They would rendezvous with other survivors at a space station even more remote than the isolated planet of Lazur. Racque glanced back at Lazur's blue beauty. He was sorry to leave it. It had promised haven. There was peace in its loneliness, and its primitive wilderness touched him. Regret changed to alarm as the ship's sensors called raucous attention to a spacecraft dogging its path. In seconds the sensor panel confirmed its identity. The ship was one of Corbin's fighters, following the slightest alteration in course like a shadow stuck to his heels. Racque smiled wickedly.

Normally such a display of precision flying might go undetected, even by sophisticated sensors. It would be easy to ascribe its movement to a sensor shadow, some reflection of the mechanism's beams, considering Lazur's mineral deposits. All of this was possible, were it not for Inspi. His computer genius gave the resistance advantages. He refined sensor probes to detect the chemical composition of tiny objects thousands of kilometers distant. It was a convenience that had often saved their lives.

Racque sent his voice over the communications link to the rest of the party. "Hang on, everyone. This is what we expected. We'll let him follow beyond sensor range of Lazur. Then we'll lose him."

"One ship is less of a target," responded Lar. "Also harder to follow."

"I'll keep that in mind," returned Racque. "For the moment, stay close."

The wedge of ships drew together, bunching like sheep. The lone fighter left Lazur's atmosphere and followed them into space. If it could keep them moving and occupied, it could drive them, at the right moment, into a trap. Racque knew the strategy, but he intended to circumvent it. First, he wanted to draw the fighter as far as possible from his compatriots.

They streaked toward open space, and the fighter closed the distance between them with imperceptible care. He still labored under the delusion he was undetected, and he meant to maintain his cover as long as possible. As carefully as the pursuer crept up on them, so Racque slowed his ship. In moments quarry and prey were within hailing distance of each other. The fighter made no move, and Racque knew it would soon drop back as carefully as it had advanced. "I'm going after him," he said. "Make the rendezvous. I'll meet you there."

"Take care!" It was not Lar, but Coryelle who answered.

"I will, little sister. Never fear."

Racque's words were still crackling through the link as he sent his ship in a twisting back flip that placed it on a collision course with the fighter. The pilot was plainly nonplussed. He supposed himself invisible and safe, only to have his supposition shattered by abrupt and violent action. He froze. Racque's ship kept its course, fire spitting from its forward guns. The blasts turned the fighter into a rocking inferno, but her shields held. At the last moment the pilot came to life and pulled his ship away. Racque missed him by points.

Once flushed, the fighter took off on a skittering zigzag course, trying to shake Racque's tenacious pursuit. Racque stuck to him like a burr. He knew the ship had extra shielding, or it could not have withstood his attack. Layered shielding consumed immense power, yet the pilot flew as if he had fuel to waste. Racque fought a momentary qualm. He was probably pursuing a scout. Such ships were always equipped with greater protection and faster engines than normal.

The fighter lined out and flew straight, turning on the speed. Racque trailed him—too closely. When the pilot stalled his engines and his ship drifted in space, Racque overflew him. Their positions were reversed again, but Racque did not intend to leave it that way. He drove his ship's nose down in a pivoting dive that went beneath the gasping fighter. Before the stalled engines could build power, he was under it.

The fighter pilot slammed his craft forward, leaving a burst of expelled fuel to burn in Racque's face, blinding him. He closed his eyes and flew through the mess to find the fighter waiting for him, its wicked triangular nose spurting fire.

Racque's ship did not have his opponent's shielding. He hit the starboard landing thrusters, and the ship flipped up on one wing to avoid the stinging charges. The fighter's nose turned, following him. It moved in close behind Racque as he swerved across space, its jezails blazing. Racque activated his rear guns and their fire smacked into the fighter's in a spectacular blinding explosion. The fighter, directly behind the blast, had no way of avoiding it, and Racque hoped for the best.

He growled as the ship emerged from the explosion, blue flame licking along its hull to die out as he flew. Abruptly Racque changed course, haring off at an oblique angle. His pursuer followed doggedly.

"Give up your flight, star scum."

Racque's head jerked up in surprise to hear his enemy's voice. He opened his link and responded. "I am not in the habit of taking orders from illegitimate subordinates," he said, sending his ship into a series of serpentines. The fighter stuck grimly to his tail.

"You are a fool. You waste fuel and risk death for nothing. In the end you will be mine."

"Nothing?"

"Running, hiding, scraping along in poverty. It is no way to live and nothing to die for," responded the fighter pilot.

"Are you offering an alternative?" questioned Racque, curious.

"There is no need to die. Ran Corbin is always looking for men of talent."

Racque was amused. "Somehow, knowing Corbin as I do, I do not think he would accept my services."

"How can you be so sure?" queried the pilot.

Racque thought hard. It was completely out of character for one of Corbin's pilots to engage the enemy in conversation. He was being decoyed, and the purpose of that decoy must be the remaining ships in his squad. He had to shake this troublesome whelp and get back to them.

"Perhaps," answered Racque, "I am better acquainted with the gentleman and his methods than you know." He sent his ship on a quick starboard foray, only to have the fighter cut him off.

"I'm afraid I can't accept that. How can a rebel dog presume to predict the Seneschal?"

Racque sent his ship on another short run to the port side, to be cut off again. "Perhaps because I once worked for him."

"Then you ought to be aware of the advantages."

"On the contrary. I learned the disadvantages. You will forgive me if I do not seem eager." He tried dropping back. The fighter pilot flew a frantic tacking course to prevent this maneuver.

"I am authorized to offer you a commission with the Garde."

"Sight unseen? That is generous. Especially for an organization that screens its applicants with such an eagle eye."

"We were authorized to offer all leaders a similar position."

"Indeed." Racque tried a slow turn to starboard, so imperceptible it was scarcely an arc. The fighter moved to his side to circumvent it. Racque straightened his course. "I am afraid," he replied, "that position does not appeal to me nearly so much as concrete benefits."

"That, too, can be arranged. As a matter of fact, reward is our method of incentive."

Racque was well aware of this. He had firsthand experience to prove it, but he let the man talk. "That is encouraging. Personally, I could not think of joining any organization unless it could offer me a substantial incentive—initially and immediately."

Racque could almost hear the Gardesman licking his chops. He had given the man the impression he was a mercenary in the hopes he would report to his superiors. If Corbin believed resistance leaders might be bought, it would be an advantage. Attempts to do so would waste considerable time, giving the resistance a breathing space to regroup.

"I am authorized to offer two thousand dyntares as an induction bonus," replied the pilot.

Racque sent his ship to port in another lazy arc. Again the fighter nosed to his side, preventing a change in course.

"It seems," commented Racque, "you wish me to continue dead ahead. Why?"

The Gardesman chuckled. It was not a pleasant sound. "My orders are to bring you in—voluntarily or under duress. Personally I do not care which."

"And once I am brought in?"

"Then you are to be allowed one choice: you may join the Garde or die."

"How generous."

"We think so."

"Then why waste time?"

Racque's ship jumped forward at top speed. The fighter responded immediately, but his reactions were not so quick as they had been, and Racque smiled. The fast pace was beginning to tell on the ship's resources. If he could play with it for a little while longer, he might leave it behind. The extra fuel he carried would take him to the rendezvous.

There was no time. The V-shaped gateway of one of the Garde's portable space stations gaped for him. Racque's high speed and the fighter nipping at his heels made it impossible to veer off. The station was too close. As he shot toward the portal, possibilities clicked through his mind in rapid succession. He might veer off, risking a pileup on the station's metal supports or a burn by its security system. He might stall, allowing the fighter to ram him, destroying them both. He might take his chances inside, hoping for an opening. The first avenue was foolhardy, even for a man with a reputation for taking chances.

As he approached the gate, he heard the fighter pilot identifying himself. The shimmering golden security wall blinked and faded just as the prow of his ship reached it. One second sooner and he would have been disintegrated. As he shot through the inverted arch he determined to leave as he had come.

Racque dropped the nose of his ship and sent it in a one-hundred-eighty-degree turn back through the gateway, hoping he could complete his stratagem before the shielding was activated. He heard his adversary bark a command and his heart sank. The golden screen shimmered to life. He pulled up desperately, sending the ship in a surging climb against a blast of light. He was blind, his sense of direction confused, and his enemy saw it.

Quicker than thought he sent a holding beam toward Racque's incapacitated ship. It bounced harmlessly off, ricocheting toward a steel support. The beam deployed its golden net around the inoffensive strut.

"Well, well, well," came the pilot's voice. "So you have a shield we have not seen before. We shall have to investigate it—when we dissect your ship."

"You presume."

"Never. I am a practical man. I deal with facts. You, sir, are captured."

Racque laughed softly. He had absolutely no plan, but he knew his open defiance would do more for his cause than anything else. It would make the man cautious, and caution could be turned to good advantage.

"I am beginning to think your ship may be a technological prize. It is something I would not have considered," commented the pilot.

"Why?" Racque was buying time, but he was also genuinely curious.

"Your forces are obviously inferior. It is a valid assumption you must have inferior equipment."

"The military machine doesn't make the war."

"What then?"

"The men. Personnel. Individuals."

"One man or woman can accomplish little. Strength lies in numbers."

"In one sense true, in another, the foolish reasoning of a child."

Racque dropped this insult as he scanned the station for a means of escape. A force field enclosed the bottom and sides. The top was open, but he saw the security net begin to grow from the perimeter. He had missed once before, but if he could push his captor off guard he might escape before it was completed.

"You are the child," responded the pilot. "You refuse to accept defeat. Give up while you still have the opportunity. I could have you gassed, you know. Then it would be easy to study your ship."

Racque's mind clicked. The pilot was alone. The orders he overheard went to a computer system, not another person. He was bluffing.

"Can you now?"

"You are tempting me, swine."

Racque's voice became mocking, light. "And you degenerate to name-calling. Temper, temper."

"You try my patience."

The pilot's voice had an edge, and Racque smiled. "To set your mind at rest, little one, I do not think you should kill me. It would not go well with you should Corbin find out."

"Your boasts are idle."

"Are they?" Racque's tone was condescending.

"I will no longer bandy words with you!" answered the pilot, the edge on his voice sharpening.

"Before you dispose of me, wouldn't it be wise to find out who I am? Or had you thought of that?"

"I suppose you are about to tell me."

"But of course." Racque fed coordinates into his weapons computer so he would leave a trail of fire when he made his move. "You would be most wise not to kill me. Corbin wants me, with all my information, even more than he wants my head on a platter. I am Racque Foxxe."

"You think I trust such nonsense?"

"You don't dare ignore it. Because, in the end, it just might be true."

Racque called up the navigational charts of the station and took a chance. He picked a spot in the exact center of the open roof, gambling the center of the canopy would be the last thing to close. He could feel the pilot's anger building. He pushed harder.

"You really are lucky. Think of the kudos. Though if you kill me, you'd better think of the consequences. I hear Corbin's followers do not make mistakes. It's unhealthy. You really have no choice."

Racque's voice was so patronizing even he gagged on it. He knew it would infuriate his captor. He sent his engines on emergency implode, knowing the risks but preferring them to capture.

"I have had enough of your chatter. You will surrender or die." The pilot was fuming.

Racque made his move. With one hand he flipped both the automatic weapons system and the implosion charge. His ship roared to life, shooting upward at full speed. "School's out!" he called.

The fighter pilot cursed. He barked orders at his computer. The security net around the edge of the station grew faster. Overconfidence had deceived him. The net consumed power, and he needed every ounce to stay with Racque.

He tore off in pursuit to be met by a blinding barrage from Racque's stern guns. They slowed him down, causing him to fall back. The security net was drawing power. His extra reserves were no longer available. It was the disadvantage of being closely tied to a stationary computer. He switched to his own fuel tanks and closed on Racque.

Racque drove for the center of the converging net. The purple threads were building inevitably, and they glinted gold. Sharply etched against the blackness of space, the net reminded him of an exotic fabric. Racque pushed his ship to the limit as the purple threads licked toward him.

He cleared the station one second before the opening closed and the security net was complete. The fighter pilot, flying in his wake and partially blinded by Racque's fire, was not so lucky. He crashed head-on into the net, ripped a jagged tear in its shimmering fabric, and extinguished.

Racque let air slide between his teeth in a conscious expression of relief. He was free. His companions might not be as fortunate. He took stock of his position, and realized he was far off course from the rendezvous point.

He plotted a new course and set out, ever vigilant for the
Garde. His first concern was to reach his friends, but he could
not help puzzling over the bizarre circumstances of the attack,
and the even more odd maneuver he had just been through.
Corbin's men did not talk to their enemies, they eliminated
them. He had been decoyed in an elaborate and risky operation, yet the man seemed to have no idea of his identity, certainly not of his alter ego, Blazon. Such knowledge would
have explained the trap, but there had been no knowledge.
The Gardesman had slipped the fact all squad leaders were to
be captured if possible.

Could Corbin have guessed the large percentage of mercenaries and rabble in their ranks? Could he also have thought to
buy them off? It was out of character. Corbin would have
planned the attack so well not a tree mouse would have
escaped. An officer, on the other hand, with his eye on pro-
motion, might do well if he could produce some highly placed
turncoats. Racque considered these questions and more as he
flew.

He reached Lazur with no incident. There was not one patrol ship on guard, which was unusual. He proceeded along
the projected course with extreme caution. Danger tempered
his thoughts, making him uneasy. As he cleared Lazur's solar
system, his sensor screen lit up like the main street of Pteron
on holiday. The computer calibrated the craft it detected, and
pronounced the greater percentage to be enemy fighters. It
counted twenty small freighter or pleasure class ships.
Racque's heart sank. They were captured. He knew it, but he
made sure.

His computer held the exact specifications of the ships in
his squad. He had it check them against the vessels in captivity. There was a moment's hesitation as the computer sorted
through the vessels, then the single word "confirmed" flashed
on the screen.

Racque groaned. They were lost. His sister, Lar, and the
dynteryx knew who else. If he tried to free them, he would
sacrifice his life as well. There was one immediate course of
action. He must proceed to the rendezvous at once, hoping
against hope that Marc had escaped. If he had, together they
would formulate a plan. If he had not, Racque would do what

he could alone. For the moment, he must outfly Corbin's squadrons. He fed his auxiliary fuel supply into the tanks and set off across space, giving the squadrons a wide berth.

The squadrons' sheer numbers would make tracking them easy. Racque set his mind on ways and means of freeing the prisoners, and forced it from the possible treatment his companions might receive at the hands of the Garde. For once in his life he was sorry he had an intimate knowledge of their methods.

CHAPTER 5

Lar pushed his ship into the lead as Racque went to meet the fighter. The squad reorganized behind him, and they moved toward their destination with unhesitating confidence. Nevertheless, Coryelle was uneasy. She watched her brother's ship depart with a quiver of foreboding. The ship's faint trail of splintered light was a tenuous thread between them. When it died she felt cut off, alone.

"Lar, I don't like this."

"Me either," replied Lar tersely.

"It looked like a decoy."

"Or a scout."

Lar adjusted his course and turned to face her. "You are worried. Why?"

"A nameless feeling, it's nothing ... but it would do no harm to be extra careful."

A red light flashed from the control panel, sending a staccato beam over Lar and Coryelle. Tracking purposefully across the screen's dark surface were the closely formed ranks of Corbin's squadrons. As they watched, the formation opened to enclose a handful of ships, their motley specifications a blemish on the squadron's uniformity.

"They'll be here before we can breathe. Still, we're going to give them a run!"

Lar sent the order to the three ships in the squad, and settled his vessel on a steady course away from the rendezvous point. With so great an adversary and no shelter in sight, capture was inevitable.

"Lar, I can handle the ship." Coryelle's voice was tense. She was thinking fast.

"I see no reason . . ."

Coryelle cut him off. "We cannot evade them. They are too many and there is no shelter."

"Granted," said Lar shortly. He was concentrating on gaining as much ground as possible before the squadrons discovered them.

"I cannot hide. I will be recognized. You, on the other hand, are not known to be an active part of the resistance. If there is no cause to think so now, they might free you."

"And you want to knock me on the head to ensure my safety." Lar chuckled recklessly. "I think there's something wrong with that."

"More or less. I'll lock you and your harp in a storage compartment. When they find you it will be as a hapless entertainer caught up in a dangerous moment. If you're free, it will give us all a chance."

Lar handed her the controls. He dropped a kiss on the top of her head and squeezed her shoulder. "Keep her straight on course. I can pull the lock shut myself. I hate leaving you to face them alone, but you're right. Keep heart."

He was gone before she could reply. She sent the ship forward, dividing her concentration between the sensor screen and the viewport. The sensor blips moved in deadly order, engulfing all in their path. Coryelle was afraid to encourage the three ships following close behind her for fear that her leadership would cause dissension. Two of the craft were manned by mercenaries with little respect for authority and no respect for women. Racque and Lar could keep them in line, but she knew they would not obey her. If they decided to sheer off and head for the rendezvous, they would lead the Garde straight to the others.

The sensor blips were converging on them. Coryelle was

aware of an eerie feeling of being sucked in, inevitably drawn inside a voracious maw to be digested alive. Out of the corner of her eye she saw the blunt noses of enemy fighters as they drew up beside her. Though there was no escape, she did not surrender, pressing forward to the last and forcing the Garde to surround her. It was an expenditure of time and fuel she hoped would help the chances of others.

The first enemy ship crept past her starboard wing, pressing dangerously close. To maintain control she was forced to veer to port where another fighter opened the way for her. The first ship closed in beside her, urging her on. She knew she was being run in a circle so the squadron might surround her. She tried diving but found her movements checked by six space-craft. She was boxed, surrounded. She flew one desperate, angry circle around her enclosure, like a caged beast testing the bars of its prison. When she brought her ship to rest it was with the conviction she could do no more.

To Coryelle's surprise, the fleet stopped. The squadrons swallowed other quarry on the move, absorbing them as they went. Since they had stopped, it was probable she and her companions were the last of the fugitives.

The fighters made a threatening circle around the four vessels. They were quiet, like the audience at some barbaric cockfight before the entertainment begins. A shiver passed over Coryelle's shoulders, but she, too, waited. She did not relish being played with, but time was time. She had a feeling she would be playing for seconds before the encounter was through. Finally her communications link sputtered to life.

"The Garde orders you to surrender!"

"The Garde has left me little choice."

"A woman!" The Gardesman sat back in surprise. Women were excluded from his service. He did not wish to deal with this one, obviously a leader and certainly no weakling from the sound of her voice.

"Sir," he ventured to his commander, "I have the leader for you."

"I do not waste time with these peasants," replied Commander Ydre, his jaded expression unchanged.

"Sir, it is a woman," answered the Gardesman.

A flicker of interest came into the commander's lazy eyes.

"So, a spiteful little vixen come to taunt me. I shall enjoy teaching her some manners."

The commander bent over the communications panel, one arm resting on the console. The Gardesman shrank out of his way.

"This is Commander Ydre. You will prepare for boarding." He managed to make his words, in spite of the coldness of their tone, sound suggestive.

"I shall await your arrival."

Coryelle's voice was cold in return. Ydre did not miss the twisting of semantics that brought him to her. He smiled sleepily.

"My dear young woman, do not expect to see me. A detachment will bring you to me—at my pleasure. Be assured you will await me."

"I shall not hold my breath. Good day, Commander."

"I could order your termination. Or hadn't you thought of that?"

"Termination would be infinitely preferable to submission. However, I have a command to think of. I cannot indulge my own whims."

"I had not thought to find you so solicitous. You will disengage all security locks and leave your ships open for boarding. If you resist, we will take you by force."

"The locks will be opened, Commander."

Coryelle disengaged her own security locks, and ordered the remainder of the squad to do the same. Surrounded by the ships of Ydre's squadrons, there was no alternative but annihilation. Coryelle could see no advantage in self-destruction.

She felt a jar as the expanding boarding hatch of Ydre's command ship probed the hull of her vessel, searching for means of ingress. An indefinable tautness, a sense of suction, announced the consummation of its search. She heard the probe pressurize, flooding with atmosphere, and tried to control her instinct for flight. The throbbing footsteps of Gardesmen traversing the length of the probe matched the pounding rhythm of her heart. She waited for the opening of her vessel's hatchway. When it came she faced an unexpected shock.

Coryelle had not been in the physical presence of the Garde since the age of five. She was not prepared for the resurgence of the paralyzing fear she experienced so long ago. Whether it was the anonymity of their uniforms or the flat, expressionless faces, she could not say, but fear silenced the words of surrender in her throat. Two of the Gardesmen stationed themselves at either side of the open hatch, while the rest lined the passageway. An offensively young man with lieutenant's insignia on his shoulder approached her, closely flanked by two battle-scarred veterans. Coryelle surmised the young man had attained his post through some brilliant and ruthless act or by bribery. Looking at his face, she suspected bribery. A lack of respect in the attitude of his two attendants supported her suspicion.

"Commander Ydre claims you and this vessel for the crown," announced the young man.

Coryelle, with the power discipline gave her, pushed her emotions aside and answered the young toady. "I doubt the crown has any part in your actions. I serve its heir and I do not recall you among the companions."

Her voice was cool and impersonal, so flat any accusation of sarcasm or disrespect was hard to level. The man flushed with anger.

"You are an upstart and your leader is a pretender! Surrender now!"

"I believe I have already done so." The lieutenant choked on his next expletive and Coryelle continued unperturbed. "Your lack of courtesy does your Garde no honor, sir. You have not identified yourself—indeed I have no proof you and your uniform are legitimately related. So be it. Yet I will not answer your rudeness with my own." At these words Coryelle saw one of the escort's lips twitch. "I am Coryelle Foxxe, daughter of Senator Foxxe, niece to Eban Foxxe."

The young man's face faded from red to gray. Coryelle Foxxe was a dangerous prize. He did not dare offer her further discourtesy, though her fate might easily be death. She was Corbin's quarry, and that struck terror into his small heart. He almost fell over himself in answering her.

"Your ladyship, your ladyship is most welcome. I am Lieutenant Jabot. Commander Ydre awaits you."

Coryelle regarded him, her wide blue eyes innocent. "And

now you overreact again. I am your prisoner. I must follow
you."

Again her words made him flush, and Jabot knew in her
dignity she had made him ridiculous. He thought of her death
with pleasure. A muffled thumping interrupted his thoughts.
He fixed Coryelle with an accusing look as he gestured one of
his men to discover the source of the disturbance.

"What are you trying to hide?"

"Actually, nothing," replied Coryelle. "That is an unwanted
nuisance. I had almost forgotten it."

The Gardesman approached the ship's storage bay cau-
tiously. The steady thumping was coming from within it, and
the Gardesman rested a hand on the hilt of his short sword as
he studied the lock. "This lock requires a computer code, sir,"
he said.

Coryelle looked at Jabot and smiled. "I had no time for
niceties," she replied. "I jammed it."

The Gardesman nodded and reached for the door handle.
He was not a tall man, but he was broad, and the ropy muscles of his arms showed clearly through the uniform tunic. He
grasped the handle, the muscles of his broad back bunching
with effort. There was a metallic tearing sound as he ripped
the door from its frame.

The storage compartment was small. Lar was wedged inside it, his hands tied and a gag knotted in his mouth. His
clasped hands showed how he had alerted the Garde to his
presence. The Gardesman grasped him by the arms and
dragged him from the compartment.

Lar hit the floor with a crash and rolled, to come up against
Coryelle's legs. She pushed him disdainfully away with one
small foot. "As I said, a nuisance."

The Gardesman picked at the knot of Lar's gag. When it
loosened, Lar spat it out.

"A thousand thanks! I was nearly suffocated!"

"Who are you?" Jabot's voice snapped in annoyance.

Lar rubbed his throat. "I can hardly speak," he croaked.
"Water, please."

"You are lucky to retain your head! Your name!"

"I am Lares Harken, jongleur, at your service."

Jabot regarded him with a disapproving frown. One of his Gardesmen spoke.

"He speaks the truth, sir. I saw him a leave back with his partner, Stella Choraula, in the Black Bird on Dynt."

"What were you doing in the storage compartment, minstrel?" demanded Jabot.

"Um, that was a miscalculation on my part. I was stranded on Lazur by an ungrateful freighter commander. When the Garde appeared, I am afraid my judgment became clouded. In short, I ran. This woman was even less understanding than the freighter captain." He rubbed the back of his head. "She knocked me on the head when my back was turned and when I awoke, I found myself in this uncomfortable position. You gentlemen have my undying gratitude, but that is little payment. A song, perhaps . . . where is my harp?"

Lar's subservience was drowned in righteous anger. His eyes swept the cabin. "Woman, what have you done with my harp?"

Coryelle's tone was cool. "Do not distress yourself, harper. You will find your instrument in the compartment above the one you occupied. It is unlocked."

Ignoring the Gardesmen and the young lieutenant, Lar turned to the storage compartment with the ardor of a fanatic. He extracted his harp from the wealth of oddments stored there and ran his fingers over its frame, checking its strings.

Jabot regarded him with exasperation. "You, minstrel."

Lar looked up inquiringly.

"You will be assigned quarters on Commander Ydre's ship. You will not annoy him or any of the crew, and you will keep to yourself. Archos, take him!"

The Gardesman who had freed Lar grasped his arm. Lar allowed himself to be dragged into position behind Coryelle and Jabot. The luck of the lares was in full force. He trod gently lest he break it.

The passage to Ydre's command center traversed a good part of the ship, and Lar made the most of the opportunity to study it. Ydre's flagship was constructed much like the fighters, but larger. Where the fighter housed its engines in a compartment, Ydre's filled a deck. They passed the interior docking bay, and Lar noted it was capable of holding a double complement of fighters.

He searched the walls for signs of his location. He meant to use his freedom to free the companions, but he could formulate no plan. His mind refused to function. He watched Coryelle, walking before him with the same self-possession she might exhibit in her own home. She was game. She had nerve. He was slowly coming to know this girl Marc had risked his freedom and his life for, and to appreciate her quality.

Stella was a woman who attracted men, a siren whose beauty was sometimes a tool, often a curse, but Coryelle possessed a different charm. He loved Stella with all his heart and would do so until he died, but his feeling for Coryelle eluded him. He wanted to call her a little sister, but some quality of reticence behind her openness prevented this. He knew he was bound to her, as deeply as he was to Stella, if for different reasons.

Coryelle, walking beside Jabot, felt the solidity of Lar's affection. It supported her on the arm of a friend. She knew her position now, knew her probable fate at Corbin's hands. She was even more aware of the slim chance for escape. All this she knew, but she held hope fast in spite of logic. The overwhelming odds now facing her were no more monstrous than those facing a child and a slave in their flight from Corbin so many years before. Somewhere in the back of her mind lurked the certainty that Marc was not dead. If he lived, so would she, against the odds.

"The strumpet, Commander."

Coryelle's concentration broke at the contemptuous words. She lifted her eyes to the face before her with cool indifference.

"This is the squad leader, Commander. She is . . . ," Jabot faltered, "that is, she says she is Coryelle Foxxe."

"Coryelle Foxxe indeed." A smile drew the corners of Ydre's mouth unpleasantly. His lowered lids gave him a sleepy expression that deceived Coryelle no more than the feigned repose of a tree snake.

"And you are . . . ?" Coryelle let the sentence hang, but

Ydre remained silent. "You have no more manners than your lieutenant, Commander. No less than I expected."

Ydre's eyes flicked to another Gardesman. "Take her to detention—security one. She will await my leisure and the Seneschal. No one else is to be permitted access to her." His eyes flicked back to Coryelle. "I am not in the habit," he remarked mildly, "of introducing myself to a peasant wench." All interest in his eyes was veiled, and he dismissed her with a gesture.

Lar watched the proceeding from the rear of the party. With Coryelle's dismissal he faded into the background and out the door. Archos was waiting for him. His powerful hand gripped Lar's shoulder. Lar cringed, relaxing the muscles of his arm, trying to make them soft and flabby.

"You come along with me, minstrel."

"I was just coming to look for you," Lar protested. "About my quarters . . ."

"That I will see to, and payment from you besides. Tune your harp, minstrel, for we'll want a song this night."

"Delighted. Happy to oblige," Lar muttered, twisting under the man's grip. He spoke the truth. He was delighted. The ruse was working. It looked as if he might soon have free run of the ship. He allowed himself to be dragged down a corridor, his height and physical power eclipsed by a cowering posture.

Commander Ydre walked into his quarters and locked the door. He wanted privacy for this communication with Corbin. After all these years he was in a position to ingratiate himself with the Seneschal. Coryelle Foxxe would make his fortune and perhaps his career as well. He had no doubt Corbin would reward him for his capture of her. He would be doubly grateful to have her alive. Ydre savored the riches he foresaw.

He savored his prize also. He had not thought the girl would be so beautiful, so voluptuously compelling. She was Corbin's and forbidden fruit, and he wanted her more desperately than he had wanted anything for some time.

Women were Ydre's playthings, of little consequence and easily forgotten. He was unprepared for the force with which Coryelle attracted him. He was appalled he could consider this temptation in the face of Corbin's claim. Yet there were ways to bring her down and wipe her mind clean of memories. He was an expert in such torture, inflicting agony and degradation, wiping out the memory of them, and inflicting them again, the terror fresh in the mind of the victim. The thought of the pleasure he might feel, over and over again before her mind wore out, literally made his mouth water. He was drunk with it. His communications link flashed, invading his solitude, and he answered it automatically. "What is it?"

"Sir, I have the Seneschal's aide," said Ydre's communications officer. His voice was carefully diffident. He was well aware of Ydre's uncertain temper.

Piqued at dealing with an underling, Ydre was curt when he responded. "This is Commander Ydre, master of the *Ravening*."

"Lathric Rupya, at your service, Commander."

Lathric's answer was smooth and courteous. It grated on Ydre's nerves. "I have just completed a strike run against the resistance. We were able to catch them off guard and we destroyed two-thirds of their force. I have captives that will interest the Seneschal."

"Their leader?"

"Not the pretender. An old piece of business the Seneschal would finish—Coryelle Foxxe."

Lathric was quiet, his brow furrowed. At length he answered. "I will inform the Seneschal of your captive. I am sure you can expect a visit. What is your present course?"

"We are en route to Dynt, down the old slave trail."

"Good. Expect the Seneschal's ship at any time. And, Ydre, the Foxxe girl had best come to Corbin unharmed. It is not wise to make free with his possessions."

Ydre brushed Lathric's threat aside. "It is an honor to see the Seneschal. We await him with anticipation."

"I am sure you do," answered Lathric. "I am sure you do."

Ydre turned away from the viewscreen and switched it off. Corbin was well known for the rewards, as well as punishments, he meted out to his followers. Ydre could see riches in the shadows of his room and perhaps a small estate on Dynt itself. He rubbed his hands together and pushed the thought of Coryelle's beauty to one side. With the reward for her capture he could buy many women. It was even possible that if Corbin decided to dishonor rather than kill her . . . she might become anyone's slave. Money could buy many pleasures, and he intended to sample them all.

CHAPTER 6

The space buoy filled Racque's viewscreen. Though it looked like an old-fashioned straw beehive, it was an automated booster station for sensors and communications, one of the outposts Eban Foxxe outfitted as an emergency refuge for his resistance forces. Outwardly innocent, its interior had been revamped to accommodate up to twenty small vessels, placing a protective security screen between them and the prying sensors of Corbin's fleet. Stocked with food, fuel, and weapons, it made an ideal meeting place.

Racque set his course for the flattened bottom of the beehive, and punched a number code into his computer. As he did so, the bottom of the buoy opened into curved, triangular sections that slid back to form a central circular entrance. Like a trick coin purse held in a miser's hand, it remained open until Racque's ship had passed through its portals, then snapped shut upon its treasure.

Once inside the station, Racque drew a long, relieved breath. Clustered to one side were five ships he knew at a glance. If their occupants were unharmed, Marc, Stella, Gissarme, and Suzerain were among the survivors. Eager for the sight of his own, he sent his vessel nosing in among its friends. As its prow touched the improvised dock, his communications link crackled.

"Racque! What happened?"

The ship's hatch slid back and Marc lept aboard, his eyes alight with both relief and apprehension. Racque closed the hatch. "What was that for?" Curiosity and worry vied for position in Marc's voice.

"I want you to hear this first, and alone."

Marc slid into the copilot's seat, watching Racque's cold profile with appraising eyes.

"My squad is taken by Corbin's Garde."

"But not dead."

"I believe not. Not when I last saw them."

"Tell me." Marc's voice was soft. Despair hollowed him out, evicting feeling.

"I was decoyed by one ship. Elaborately decoyed. He almost got me. When I shook him, I went back, but they were captured, surrounded by two squadrons at least. There was nothing to do but hope you were alive. I came in." Racque's voice was empty of the sardonic wit and bravado that were characteristic of him. His icy blue eyes were expressionless. Marc reached out and grasped his shoulder.

"Racque."

Racque was silent, but Marc could see the words piling up inside him. He waited.

"I have failed her again."

Racque's voice was so faint it was hard to hear, but Marc had been waiting for this statement. "You have failed no one. Coryelle would never think so."

"She is in the hands of those swine. She would be better off dead. They will torture her until she cannot help revealing all she knows. They will humiliate her. They will put her on display, and bargain for her. Then they will use her as they would not the lowest house slave, but they will not kill her. They will be most pleased when she goes mad."

"They will not have the chance."

"You would go after her? All of them?"

The ghost of a smile pulled at Marc's mouth and touched his eyes.

"But you risk yourself—through you, all of Dynt. Millions willl have no hope if you are taken."

"It is for all of them I must try to free the captives. Right now, Racque, I have a very small kingdom. It consists of a handful of followers. From a purely political standpoint, if I refuse to defend them, if I choose to save myself at their expense, I am not fit to be their leader. If I am not fit to lead those who are loyal to me, I am not fit to head a nation."

"Flawless, if emotionally charged, logic."

The old sardonic lilt was back in Racque's voice. Marc smiled.

"Have you not learned I am an emotional man?"

Racque looked at him through narrowed eyes. "You hide it well, you know. Most people feel your warmth, but they do not realize it motivates you. For years I tried to live alone, for my selfish ends, loving no one. It was death—suicide, for it was voluntary. Corbin's ruthless destruction of my family roused something in me, and when I found Coryelle, I finally realized what it was. My heart had come to life."

"Then she finished it."

"Yes. She loved me in return—a man reputed to be a paid assassin. She gave me my life back. I think I would trade it in her service. I think I would actually die for her and count myself satisfied."

"Coryelle is like that."

The supreme lightness of Marc's words caught Racque like a flash. His eyes became placid pools of blue as he studied his prince. Marc's clear hazel eyes, so revealing of his thoughts, were a serious gray, the whole cast of his face thoughtful, yet it was his mouth that betrayed him.

"I forget myself. You have been more a brother to her than I," Racque hazarded.

"Never that. First, a slave, then protector, and sometimes, I thought, a friend."

"If you had not been willing to rescue her, I would have gone myself."

"I know that."

"I would have betrayed my pledge to you to go."

"I know that also."

Racque read his face. "You would not have blamed me."

"No."

"To break a pledge is no small matter. I must know why."

"I do not say I would not be hurt, hurt especially at your loss, but I would understand. Each man must follow his own heart in the end. If he does not, he betrays himself."

"Even the evil man?"

"An evil man cannot be turned to a better way by force. He must come to it on his own or it will never be a part of him." Marc's smile was calculated to turn the subject. "Now," he said, "we must find a way to free our friends."

"Not before I ask one final question." Racque's smile was mocking. "I admit my selfishness, but I cannot let this pass. I must know."

Marc's eyes narrowed. "I think you are being hard on yourself."

"Perhaps it is deserved. Marc, do you blame me for this?"

"You blame yourself. No, no, I will not make a quick answer to cover my feelings. Racque, I am angry. I am frightened. Those feelings lash out. Yet there is no blame. You are to blame? I am to blame as well. Lazur was not a secure post. We were caught like ducks in the ice. Men died. They died because they followed me. Responsibility is something we all share. We do our best. I know you, Racque. You are reckless and daring and you convince the world you are sophisticated, deadly ice, but I have seen deeper, living waters. I know in the depths of my heart you did your best."

Racque's silvery fair head was bent. Marc watched as he digested the answer to his question. "I know also," he said, "how you love your sister."

Racque raised his head, his blue eyes transparent with light. "I was right when I pledged myself to you," he said. "It was an affirmation of the worth of all mankind, including myself." Marc's quizzical expression made Racque smile. "About that escape plan," he said, "I think I might have an idea."

His words were punctuated by a thunderous pounding. Deep in their conversation, both men started. Mechanically, Racque opened the hatch to reveal Gisarme, his arm upraised for another blow, his face a mixture of concern and annoyance. Marc beckoned to him, smiling at his affection.

"You're not dead, then," said Gisarme as he stepped into the ship.

Racque closed the hatch, and Gisarme was taken by surprise. He half-turned to see the doors close, and then raised a questioning eyebrow at Marc and Racque.

"You lost your squad?"

"Yes."

"And?" This question was directed at Marc, not Racque.

"We are going to get them back—and any others the Garde might have captured as well."

"What are the chances of success?" Gisarme was quizzing him in his concern.

"I suppose I could compute them. Would it serve any purpose?"

"Not likely. Nor, I suppose, would any arguments as to your value as crown prince?"

"Racque has already tried that tack. It proved fruitless."

"I could have told him. A leader cannot stand in the shadows. He must do more than share the risk, he must face it first. It is a lesson you have mastered."

"Gisarme, I want your advice. We must devise a plan to free our friends, one that has the hope, at least, of success."

"I do have an idea," said Racque. Gisarme motioned him to continue. "We have one piece of information Corbin lacks. He does not know that the mercenary Blazon, who was in his employ for years, is actually the prodigal son of Senator Foxxe. I think he must assume Blazon perished when the fleet attacked Chor, or that he was unsuccessful in his search and faded into the background."

Gisarme nodded. "Once Coryelle came out of hiding, his contract with Corbin was null. Though Corbin might also believe Blazon is lurking somewhere to kill Coryelle, then demand his reward."

"It would be like him," admitted Racque.

"You are saying Corbin would accept Blazon. That Corbin's forces would be compelled to offer him hospitality."

Racque smiled, his old sardonic grin. The dangerous mercenary flashed in a look and was sheathed. "Especially," he said, "if he came bearing gifts."

Marc's eyes questioned him.

"Gifts that might tempt Corbin are few and far between," said Gisarme dryly.

"Nevertheless, I think I have one. Almost the first link in the chain of events that led me to Coryelle was a slave boy named Drusillus."

"Drusillus!" Marc's voice was eager. "I have often thought

of him. He was so frightened, subservient, not a fighter. I was afraid he would not survive alone."

"He didn't. When I found him he was in the hands of a particularly dirty little slave dealer. He was ill then. He wouldn't have lasted long."

"I would have been happy to know he had gotten away." Marc's voice was wistful.

"In a way he did. He's still on Dynt—in Pteron, as a matter of fact—and he's free. He's not memorable, so with his freedom and the changing of his name he was safe. I left the warrant out on Drusillus."

"So I might become him." Danger crackled in Marc's statement, danger to himself and to his friend.

"What of the slave dealer's records?" asked Gisarme. "Will they not show the purchase of the slave—by Corbin's assassin?"

"Yes, but the slave dealer never knew Drusillus' identity." He chuckled rudely. "If he had, I would not have been able to buy him. He'd have sold him to Corbin for twenty times the price he extracted from me."

"Can anyone identify him?"

"Only a Gardesman, and he saw the boy from the back, running. The glimpse of his face was not enough for a clear identification so many years later. Marc and Drusillus have the same coloring, and they are about the same height. I do not think there is any possibility the ruse can be traced."

"The biggest problem is Racque's identity. We have not been too careful to cover his alter ego, though we've not paraded it either. If Blazon and Racque Foxxe are ever linked, it will be the end of you," said Gisarme.

"It is a risk," admitted Racque.

"There are always risks." Marc's voice was crisp. "However, it has a chance of working. We might even get out alive. And it is certain Corbin or his men would be interested in Drusillus. It is well known Corbin is obsessed with anything relating to Coryelle's family."

"I wish there could be more of us."

"It would never work. One or two may be lost in the crowd, more . . . ."

"I know it. Gisarme, we are underdogs with a vengeance

now. Worst of all, we have no intelligence on Corbin's squadrons. We don't even know who commands them. Racque and I will be walking blind."

Gisarme smiled wickedly. "You sound like me, cautioning against overconfidence and foolhardy bravery."

"You were a good teacher. Do you know when I left home, I was lost without your counsel? So I played a game with myself. Whenever I decided on a course of action, I'd mentally step to the side and pick it apart. Even if my decision remained the same, at least I was more aware of the dangers surrounding it—and I had a better chance to combat them."

Gisarme's smile broadened. "Why do you think I kicked you out? It was time you became more self-reliant."

Racque pushed himself out of the pilot's chair. "You gentlemen," he said, "may continue this discussion without me. I find I cannot concentrate without food, and I have not eaten in too many hours."

"I am sorry, Racque. I was thoughtless. And we will find Coryelle. In time."

Racque's icy eyes thawed again. "We'll need a ship," he said. "Not one of these."

"We'll find one. Go!"

Gisarme watched Racque leave, noting the weariness in the graceful movements and slow footsteps.

"When I first met that young man I would not have trusted him as far as I could throw a wood bear. He did not know himself, and he posed a danger to others in finding himself out. Now I think he will be there at the finish."

Gisarme's voice was low and his words were for his own ears more than for a listener, but Marc was glad to have heard them. He, too, watched Racque's disappearing figure.

"And I saw only the hardness of his recklessness and sophistication, not what it masked. He must have been terribly hurt and angry to deny love in himself. I think he has known a kind of pain I have been spared. Gisarme, do you think me a fool?"

Gisarme's smile warmed his eyes and he said lightly, "Aren't we, in essence, all fools?"

"Don't be rhetorical. Do you see me throwing it all away?"

"No. You are taking a big risk by going after Coryelle and

the others, but it is not foolish. You are right when you say you cannot lead men while remaining by your fire. And it is unlikely you will come to a quiet end. In the final breath, it does not matter what I think. If you are to be king, you must rule yourself . . . for good or evil. You cannot be a puppet swayed by every new piece of advice."

Marc's eyes darkened. "Evil."

"There have been evil kings, you know." Gisarme's voice was mild.

"I do not wish to be one of them."

"Temptation can be strong. Sometimes to accomplish good through evil means."

"Does it ever work?"

"Not in my experience. Of course, it is a complicated question. Is it better to give up to a ruthless enemy and live under his hand, or fight him, drawing those who follow you to their deaths, but perhaps giving others a chance for freedom? I do not know."

"What choice is there?"

"The only choice I find is to do my best. What do you feel?"

"I don't know. I am in a quandary. When I try to reason it out, I am tied in knots. Yet underneath all my logic and planning, I know I am quite simply compelled to try to free Coryelle and Lar and all the rest. I saw what placing personal desire before the welfare of others did to Tenebrae, Foxxe, and even to Ran Corbin. Perhaps I, too, am following that road, but I do not want to turn aside from it."

"Answer me this, then. Is there any responsibility you flout by your actions?"

"Only that to survive, for the crown."

"And if you survive by betraying those who believe in you, you will also betray the cause for which you are to live?"

"Yes."

"Then it seems to me you betray nothing."

"Then why is my mind running like a squirrel in a cage?"

"Hmmm." Gisarme regarded Marc with a glint of humor. Marc pounded the arm of his chair in frustration.

"Don't just say 'hmmm'!"

"You really are upset about your own compulsion to justify this rescue."

"Of course I am! What did I just tell you!"

Gisarme noted delicate shadows on the young man's face, shadows that accented contours of expression. There was gentleness, even innocence, lurking in those shadows, and a vulnerability he well remembered. He looked into the troubled hazel eyes, and the laughter inside him bubbled to the surface.

"I might tell you its cause, but I do not think you would credit it. I cannot tell you not to let it trouble you, but I can tell you that it does not trouble me."

"Again! Riddles when I asked for an answer!"

Gisarme's laughter spilled over into chuckles. "Follow your heart, lad! It's true, and it holds your answer."

Gisarme's enigmatic reply was no answer, but Marc knew he would get no other. His thoughts turned inward, and Coryelle was an aura of golden light at their heart. He would free her, and her companions, through the transparent ruse Racque offered him. Drusillus' apprehension, carried off with Racque's bravado, would slip them under the Garde's nose. Somehow they would snatch the prisoners from the raven's claws. His fingers closed in a possessive gesture. Gisarme, watching him, smiled.

CHAPTER 7

Ran Corbin, Seneschal of Dynt, sat in his garden. The sunshine washed over the unmarked beauty of his features. His eyes were closed. In repose he exuded tense stillness, but rather than relaxation, his attitude suggested the pause of a deep breath before violent action. His surroundings, however, reflected the most peaceful aspects of nature.

The lush foliage was dew-sprinkled by an invisible irrigation system. Carefully planned ventilator channels sent gentle puffs of air through the garden in a caressing breeze. The cobblestone walkways were touched by a soft patina of lichen and the raised stone pool in the center of the garden was mantled in it. The clear water of the pool was occasionally broken by the silvery flash of a fish rising to the surface. Waxy white water lilies dotted its face, their rich perfume a surprisingly lascivious touch in the otherwise austere surroundings.

The garden's peace magnified every sound. When footsteps intruded upon its perimeter, Corbin opened his eyes. He was annoyed. His moments of rest were few and far between. His dislike of having them interrupted was notorious; therefore the intrusion was important, but this did not lessen his irritation.

The footsteps neared. Corbin did not move his head, but he alllowed his eyes to slide to one side. His slave's sturdy feet in their twisted leather sandals came to a halt. He closed his eyes again in an unconscious gesture of dismissal, but the slave remained.

"You may speak," Corbin said finally.

"My lord." The low voice adapted to the green quiet, hardly disturbing it. "There has been a message from your aide. He commanded I repeat it to you at once."

Corbin waved his hand. "Then do so."

"He says Coryelle, child of Senator Foxxe, has been captured in a recent raid on the resistance."

Corbin's eyes snapped open. "Where is she?"

"Lathric reports she is being held by Commander Ydre of the *Ravening*."

"I will rendezvous with him in one day's time. Inform Lathric."

"Yes, lord."

Corbin cocked one of his arched eyebrows at the slave. The woman's face was devoid of expression. She had been a slave for a long time.

"Do not call me 'lord.' "

"As you wish, sir." She made no excuses, though she had been in his service for a short span of days.

"I will be leaving for the space dock within the hour. See to my needs."

The woman clasped her hands and bent her head in a silent

acknowledgment of his command. She backed away ten paces before turning down the path. Corbin found her quiet submission soothing. He leaned back against the gnarled trunk of a tree, trying to recapture the mood he had forsaken. He wanted to savor privacy before he had to assume the burdens of his office.

Unfortunately, his thoughts strayed to the prize Ydre held for him—and to Ydre's raid on the resistance. Ydre had not informed his superior of his actions. Corbin fully understood the man's desire for spoils and the magnified reputation that went with a dramatic military coup. Still, he did not sanction Ydre's actions even though they had resulted in the apprehension of a long-sought prize.

Coryelle Foxxe was an untidy thread that needed to be trimmed from the finished fabric. Her political importance was minimal, though her name was a morale booster for the resistance founded by her uncle, Eban Foxxe. As far as he could determine, Coryelle's part in the resistance movement was small, yet he savored the thought of her death as he would not that of the pretender prince. The name Foxxe galled the wound in his soul. To exterminate the name from the kingdom was a private, cherished goal.

Long ago he had set a bounty hunter on the Foxxe child's trail, an enigma of a man whose ruthless dedication to his quarry was uncanny. Though the man he called Blazon had searched for years, his prey had eluded him in the end, to rise to the surface in the destruction of the planet Chor in the company of Tenebrae Dynteryx, princess of Dynt. The fox always found a safe earth. The luck of it dug at his vitals, the injustice stung his spirit.

Merit had nothing to do with her safety. The fates smiled on her. In spite of all he could do, she escaped the consequences of her uncle's thoughtlessness and cruelty. To visit the sins of the fathers upon the innocent was a just sentence for Foxxe's viciousness. He would mete it out with the greatest of pleasure, but not before he extracted every minute piece of data she possessed about the resistance and Marc Dynteryx.

Corbin considered Marc's surname with distaste. The boy was heir to the throne of Dynt. In his mind he could say this; otherwise he did not admit Marc's legitimacy. He was the lady

Tenebrae's heir. Corbin's mind dwelt heavily on the fact. It was a bitter irony that the boy might easily have been his own son if the willful princess had followed her father's wishes and her duty to the realm instead of her lower instincts. Though he was not consort to the princess, Corbin held Dynt as surely as if he were its true king—did so, as a matter of fact, in the king's face.

Pavis Dynteryx had been the perfect figurehead, never lifting a hand in the affairs of the kingdom, allowing his seneschal full rein and questioning nothing, until recently. Pavis' belated sense of responsibility was overdue and futile. Corbin's control of the kingdom was complete, in spite of Marc's claim to the throne. The pretender would never rule. He would be either killed or hounded through space like the cur he was. If he were foolish enough to appear in Pteron to claim the throne on Pavis' death, he would be taken and used—as a Judas goat or martyr.

Corbin chuckled, savoring the certainty of power. Inevitably events were playing into his hands. The resistance was becoming a joke, the annoying antics of a spoiled child. They had lost their new base as they lost Chor, and a good portion of their followers as well. This capture of the Foxxe girl might put an end to the entire farce. In the past, the boy Marc had evinced a dangerous loyalty. He had been a fool to risk saving Coryelle in the first place. It was more than possible he might try to rescue her.

Corbin applauded himself and the instinct that prompted him to go to the girl instead of sending for her. It would be much harder to infiltrate Ydre's squadrons than to attack a vessel in transit to Dynt with the prisoner. Once he had questioned her, he would devise a trap for Marc using Coryelle as bait. He would control the situation and take the prince as well as his close followers. The resistance would be broken for good. Only a few scattered rebels would remain, men who would never touch the kingdom's imagination as Marc was beginning to do.

Corbin's eyes hardened as he thought of the slowly growing legend weaving itself around the pretender prince. Tales and songs were finding their way to the surface, stories of loyalty, bravery, and honor. In themselves, they were nothing, but if Marc were allowed to survive, they would give him a deeper legitimacy than even the old king's endorsement might achieve. They would burrow into people's hearts and minds and find root there until Marc became the ultimate leader. When he reached that state, he would be unassailable. If, on the other hand, he did not survive, the stories would be fragments to tease the imagination. They would be harmless tales told to children.

Coryelle Foxxe would lure the man who had saved her life to his destruction. Corbin leaped at the thought. Here was the truest revenge. He would destroy his enemy through a woman, as he had once been destroyed.

Unbidden, the image of Tenebrae Dynteryx rose in his mind. The breathtaking beauty of her youth lived there still, beyond her physical death at his hands. It was a beauty of such passionate, flashing power it still touched him. He did not often allow her to invade his memories, but he found a curious desire to linger over her now. The laughter, the challenge in her eyes, the voluptuous promise of her lips were not for him. This was a realization he faced long ago, yet it haunted him anew. He had deserved her love. He had been everything a royal beauty should want, and all for her. He had excelled in his studies for her. He had become the master swordsman on the planet for her. He would have died for her, and she scorned his honorable love for the back-door kisses of a roué. The bitterness of it galled him afresh, as if it were yesterday and not two score and more years gone, yet his mind lingered over her features.

"You haunt me still," he murmured, "though I cut you out like a disease. Release me to the life I have chosen, and do not bring back the days when I believed in you."

Corbin's words were soft, scarce ruffling the air. He squeezed his eyes tight to blot out Tenebrae's face, but still it lingered, lovely, laughing, a mockery of his years of discipline.

Lar leaned back in the heavily upholstered chair and idly strummed his harp. His eyes were sleepy and the melody his fingers extracted from it deceptively simple. One had to watch

Lar's fingers as they flew in an intricate, repeating pattern to realize the harper was not half asleep. Fortunately for Lar, he was surrounded by gross inattention. Not one of the men in the officers' lounge seemed aware he was drinking in their conversation like spiced wine.

Frustrated by the streams of meaningless chatter, Lar was driven to the complicated notes he fingered. It was the only outlet he could allow himself if he wished to remain inconspicuous. His ears were tuned to the smallest reference to Coryelle and the other captives, but Ydre's officers seemed much more interested in games of knucklebones and the outcome of tomorrow night's fencing match. Occasionally someone would make a crass comment on Ydre's coarser indulgences and the ease with which a junior officer might rise in the ranks if he could secure the right type of pulchritude for his commander. Lar was playing his waiting game with less and less patience when Ydre's second-in-command stalked purposefully into the room.

Captain Sphaleros was a man of medium height and military bearing. He tolerated no nonsense. In the short time Lar had been aboard *Ravening* he had overheard comments suggesting Sphaleros was the reason Ydre maintained his reputation as a disciplinarian. There was a sudden influx of tension into the normally relaxed lounge. Sphaleros paused in the center of the room and swept a comprehensive glance over the assemblage. He wasted no words.

"The Seneschal will be arriving at any time. From what the commander said, I judge we have approximately two hours for preparations. If your stations are not ready for a high-level inspection, I suggest you remedy the situation. There will, of course, be a preinspection and an honor inspection by the Seneschal himself."

There was a bustle of activity as men departed to check their already flawless stations. Lar ground his teeth as he swallowed fear. He had hoped Corbin would wait for the captives to be brought to him, thereby giving the resistance time to formulate a plan of escape. Corbin had not taken that chance. With the whole ship on alert, gossip would be cut in half. The chances of learning anything valuable were smaller than before. Lar felt events slipping out of his hands and into the raven's claws.

Sphaleros watched the men depart, noting their stations and mentally organizing the ship's readiness. As the chief of the engineering deck departed he turned away from the door and crossed to the one occupied table in the room.

"Ydre coming down hard?" asked the man with the blue and white insignia of a ship's doctor.

"Ydre doesn't know what hard is," answered Sphaleros as he sank into a chair with a sigh. "I am not looking forward to the Seneschal's visit."

"Those prisoners?" questioned the doctor sympathetically.

Sphaleros nodded. "I wouldn't mind if it weren't for the Foxxe girl. She's too pretty by half."

"Ydre wouldn't try anything with Corbin's prize?" The doctor sounded shocked.

"Probably not, though I can see the temptation in his eyes. What he will do is try to convince Corbin the girl should be given to him when he has no more use for her."

"I am surprised Ydre would take even Corbin's leavings. He usually prefers fresh meat."

Sphaleros cocked an eye at the doctor. "Where have you been, Shem? It's well known Corbin cares nothing for women. If he amuses himself, it is not something that intrudes into his life."

"I begin to see your point."

"Yes. The situation will be tense if Ydre thinks of nothing but the reward he thinks he deserves. He is foolish when he allows his passions to override duty."

Lar's ears were burning. He had heard of Ydre's lascivious tastes, but Sphaleros was confirming them. He gave Lar a concrete weakness to exploit. He was also an unknowing ally in keeping Coryelle from immediate harm.

The doctor regarded Sphaleros quizzically. "Why do you protect him? Surely you cannot count him any real advantage to your career?"

Sphaleros smiled, his expression pleasant even if the look in his eyes was not. "If I had not already scanned this room for eavesdroppers I would wonder if you were trying to lead me into an incriminating conversation."

"Haven't you already been incriminating enough?"

"Forgive me, Shem, my nerves are on edge. We've helped each other before. I have no reason to suspect you."

The doctor waved the reply aside.

"I am afraid, if you want to know, of the consequences should Ydre push too far. Ran Corbin does not often lose his temper, but I once witnessed the results of it. The Foxxe child is close to his heart. If any attempt is made to thwart his intentions—even if it is a mistake—I am afraid he will show no mercy. It is easy for a second-in-command to share his superior's fate in such a circumstance. I have no wish to die."

"How in the world will we control him?"

Sphaleros shook his head. "I don't know. We have no time to be clever. We must come up with something."

Lar played a lush run on the strings of his harp. The music penetrated the men's absorption and Sphaleros looked up, searching the shadowy corner of the room for its source.

"You will pardon me," interposed Lar softly. "I did not wish to intrude on a private conversation, but it occurred to me I might be able to offer you a solution to your problem."

Sphaleros fingered the hilt of a short knife he wore in his belt. "What is your solution, minstrel?" he asked smoothly.

"The more public a situation, the less time for private business. If Ydre were to be continuously on display for Corbin, he would not have time to get very far with the girl. He would not even be able to do more than insinuate with the Seneschal."

Sphaleros' fingers closed over the knife hilt, the spiral of jewels around it hard against his fingers. "That is true. Such negotiations need privacy. Corbin would never discuss his plans in public."

"What do you propose, minstrel?" asked the doctor.

"I understand," responded Lar, "that during the day Ydre must maintain the ship. The Seneschal will not interfere with that duty, it is not his way. That leaves the evenings free for intrigue."

"You speak lovingly of intrigue," said Sphaleros. "I would warn you intrigue can lead to trouble."

"All jongleurs are gossips at heart. It makes them useful to their friends. Yet you will find their mouths remain shut except to sing."

Sphaleros' thumb rubbed the delicately engraved initials on the base of the knife's hilt. "Out with it, then!"

Lar played another glissando. "I was thinking of a dinner. In Corbin's honor. It would keep him amused for an evening at least. Will Corbin be here long?"

"No," answered Sphaleros absently, totally unaware he had given Lar a vital piece of information. "It is a good idea," he said abruptly, "one Ydre will like, and it will keep him occupied." He withdrew the knife from its scabbard. The blade flashed white under the glare of light panels. "Now I think it is time to keep you occupied."

Lar continued to pluck the strings of his harp. "Aren't you forgetting something?"

"I cannot imagine what," snarled Sphaleros.

The doctor's low chuckle broke his concentration. "I am afraid you have, Captain. Such a celebration requires entertainment. Do you wish to kill the one source provided by the gods for you?"

"I know only one way to ensure his silence."

"Who would believe anything he might say? He is a minstrel. They are all liars and not one of them would hesitate to slit a throat much less a purse if it served their interests. If he spreads rumors you can simply say he tried to buy his way into Ydre's harem and you prevented it. Do you think anyone would contest your story?"

"No." Slowly the captain's hand lowered and the knife resumed its place in his belt. "Know that as long as you remain on the *Ravening*, my knife will be at your back. If one word of this conversation surfaces, I will have no mercy."

"Pax!" said Lar, a note of real desperation in his voice. He did not want the man's enmity, yet it had been a chance to safeguard Coryelle.

Sphaleros sent him a glance of withering scorn intended to shrivel the minstrel in his tracks, and departed. The ramrod straightness of his back was a wordless reminder he did not make idle threats.

"Don't worry," said the doctor, "he will have so much on

his mind in a few hours he won't even remember what you look like."

Lar had reservations, but he was glad to hear the man would have little time to check on his whereabouts.

"How about a song, to wash this down?" asked the doctor, raising his glass of amber-dark beer.

Lar smiled and struck his harp in a rollicking drinking song. The doctor tapped the rhythm with his heel, his swallows punctuated by the beat of the melody. All the while Lar's mind was running like a stag through the forest, searching for a way to contact Marc and reach Coryelle. He could see no plan for escape. It was as if a curtain descended, separating his thoughts from inspiration.

CHAPTER 8

Pavis drew a hand across his forehead and stared at the reading glass on his desk. His hands shook. He propped his elbows on the dark, polished wood and rested his head on them. He was tired.

"I am sorry to be the bearer of such news, my lord," said Stella in her soft, rich voice.

"It cannot be helped. Nothing is to be withheld from me ever again. I am old. Pain can no longer touch me."

Stella's eyes filled at the dry acceptance in the king's voice. The stately old man was growing frail, but his immense dignity dismissed weakness. She noted the enlarged knuckles of his hands and knew how difficult it was for him to scribe, yet the pile of neatly written paper at the corner of his desk had been done recently. Pavis might live in a secure cocoon, but he was no less courageous because of it. Many a muscled warrior succumbed to the ravages of illness. Pavis would not do so. He fought his disabilities and age with a quiet determination that was awesome.

"So the child Coryelle is in Corbin's clutches," he said.

"Yes, along with approximately twenty others."

"He will be interested only in her."

"I know."

"You will attempt a rescue." The king's statement was positive.

"You seem to understand Marc well."

"In this, perhaps better than he understands himself. Yet I do not think he would leave any of his followers in Corbin's grasp if he could think of a way to free them." Pavis sighed.

"You are distressed?"

"No. This boy is a continual lesson to me. He is what I should have been, but now it is too late."

"You are proving, my lord, it is never too late."

Pavis aimed a raking look at Stella. "I cannot hope to atone for the anguish I have caused by my laziness, apathy, and inattention. Do you know, that among other mistakes, I signed the death order for Coryelle's family?"

Stella nodded silently. "She has never blamed you, lord. She knew it was Corbin's plan."

"I am grateful for the generosity of her heart, yet even her forgiveness burns at the heels of my guilt. Stella, I must manage these last days well, for the good of Dynt. I cannot erase my name from the orders that condemned the kingdom to slavery under Corbin's hand or from the unjust edicts that resulted in suffering for my people, but I can try to secure an heir of my choice. I tell you now, Stella, I will do all I can to help Marc Dynteryx."

"When I approached you and trusted you with my involvement in the resistance, I hoped for such a pledge."

"I would like to know, Stella, how you feel about the young prince. Not facts and figures—I have done enough research on his activities to fill a scroll—but how you regard him as a person. I have never been able to ask that of someone who knows him."

Stella's eyes narrowed as she considered her answer. "That is a good question. I have followed the resistance because it answered my own need for freedom. I followed Foxxe because he offered me a better life. Marc . . ." Her words trailed off as she searched for her answer.

"He commands your loyalty," ventured Pavis, "and perhaps your love?"

"Love? Not, I think, as you mean it. That part of my heart lies elsewhere. Yet I do love him, and I think that is the reason I am loyal to him."

Pavis' question surprised her. Stella had not thought to question her alliance to the resistance after Foxxe's death, for Lar was there, and committed to his mentor's cause. When it became known Marc was heir to Pavis' throne, she had accepted his leadership without question. She was now, for the first time, wondering why.

"He is not a usual man," she said slowly. "His powers of concentration are immense, and his self-discipline is almost uncanny. I have seen him work thirty-six-hour stretches efficiently. He is thoroughly educated in the classics and he has a flair for diplomacy that has kept our motley forces together. In arms I do not think there could be a better man, yet in spite of his position, he does not take himself seriously. He can laugh at his own absurdities."

"You have recited a catalog of virtues, yet I think you have not yet touched the heart of the matter."

"No." She paused. "To a student of history like yourself, it might seem silly, but it is his heart that draws men after him. He cares, really cares, about all of us."

"That will net him enough heartache to twist his spirit."

"I hope not, at least not away from the choices he's already made."

"If that is the choice he has made—to care for his kingdom and his friends—then he has chosen the road I did not follow. In that alone he has outstripped me. He will not, at least, make my mistakes."

"A friend of mine says we can only make our own mistakes, never another's."

Pavis smiled at her. "Nevertheless, if one possessed a speck of wisdom, one might learn from the lives of others." He gestured to a pile of papers. "That is why I have recorded my story, including what I know of Corbin and of Tenebrae. When you come again I will have transferred it to a scroll for you to take with you. Should Marc ever claim the throne, he will need to know what has and has not been done. I will do my best to help him."

Stella reached out impulsively and kissed the old man on his finely drawn cheek.

The king squeezed her hand. "You are kind to an old man."

"I am kind to someone I love."

"My sister followed her heart and abandoned the kingdom. If Marc follows his he may betray it as well."

Stella's eyes grew wide and she leaned back, trying to get a better look at Pavis' eyes. They were sad. "You don't want him to rescue them!"

Pavis lifted his hands in a gesture of impotence. "I do not know! If he is killed, the last hope of the kingdom is dashed. Yet if he turns his back on them, is he fit to rule? I do not know! There is no easy answer. In the end he must follow his own destiny and accept the consequences. I would wish the choice were not so desperate, and so many lives would not be touched by it."

Stella reached out for the king's hand, clasping it in her own. "If it is any reassurance," Stella said, "I think it would be hard for him to love selfishly. He has spent his life caring for others. Even as a slave, his duties were to attend someone else's children." Stella smiled whimsically. "Perhaps that is his destiny—to tend the children of the kingdom."

Pavis patted her hand. "With that I must be content. Like any fond parent, I wish my child to avoid the mistakes I made, and to have a better life than I have built. I must learn to let go. Marc's life is his own, not an extension of my rule, but I cannot help my anxieties."

"Marc would be touched you regard him so highly. May I tell him that? That you look upon him as a son? It would cheer him, I think."

"Marc is my heir, the child who will follow me. He was chosen as a son by my sister. I have heard much about him, and it has prompted my respect. You may tell him I would be honored to call him son."

"Thank you. There aren't many pleasures in his life. I will be glad to be able to give him such news."

Pavis' eyes misted and he patted Stella's hand absently. He

was lost in thought. Stella traced the veins in his stiff but still
beautiful hands and noted the transparent quality of his skin.
He was failing. She wanted to give him hope for the land he
had ruled so badly.

"Speaking of pleasure," said Stella, "I was summoned to
sing for the king."

"So you shall, my dear. You have no idea how your voice
soothes me."

"Royal favor has given an indecent boost to my career as a
singer."

"I am glad I can do that for you. You are an uncommon
talent and you deserve praise. I am a connoisseur of the arts,
you know, and I have sponsored more than one deserving
talent. It is one of the few things in my life I am proud of."
He leveled a finger at her. "You disparage your ability too
often. I well remember your father and his keen instinct for
phrasing and drama. He taught you well. You are a credit to
him and to yourself. You will remember that."

The king's voice was stern and Stella bowed meekly. "Yes,
my lord."

"Don't you 'yes, my lord' me! In this I am an authority.
There are few things so desperately needed in this world as
the joy of song. Your duty, to yourself and to the world, is to
use your talents! I command it."

Stella's eyes were twinkling, but she bowed again, this time
making it plain she was taking him seriously.

"Now, I would like a song. Especially one of those original
pieces I hear you've built your career on."

"The songs are Lar's, and I am happy to sing them for
you."

The king settled back in his chair, lacing his fingers across
his belt. Stella perched audaciously on the corner of his desk,
her shapely legs crossed. She knew her physical charms, and
displayed them to good advantage, aware the king was a connoisseur of the feminine form as well as the arts. If her beauty
gave him pleasure, she was glad.

She launched into a love song, her voice caressing the
words Lar had written, but her mind was otherwise occupied.
With each passing day the king was growing weaker. His bat-

tle against his own infirmity was brave, but he would lose it. As his body weakened, the spark of his spirit shone brighter against the approaching dark. He was placing himself between Corbin and Marc like a shield. As long as Pavis was alive, Corbin would feel secure of the kingdom, for the king had not opposed him in decades. By fostering this complacency, Pavis was giving Marc time, time to gather his forces, and to formulate a plan against Corbin.

Stella saw the half-smile her song brought to Pavis' lips, and was glad she could bring him a moment's peace from the struggle. Pavis had been isolated for so many years he was an unknown quantity to the people of Dynt, a faceless name and title. There were a scant handful who actually knew Pavis personally and a smaller number who were his friends. It was a shame so few people would ever know the man's stature. At an advanced age he had turned his back on a grave mistake and was fighting a quiet battle to retrieve it. The moral courage of this was something a military commander would not understand. She resolved to make Lar see this quiet battle so Pavis would not be remembered as an ineffective dolt. Lar's songs had a way of sticking in the mind. She knew one of them could do more for Pavis' memory than a thousand history books. Her voice rose in earthy sweetness over the climax of the ballad.

Pavis felt the rich notes resounding in his soul and marveled he was capable of such feeling and apppreciation. As a youth he had been told advancing years would rob him of sensitivity and eradicate physical stimulation. He had not found it so. Instead, his capacity for enjoyment enlarged. He learned to enjoy life with an open hand. He no longer grasped at moments. Instead he savored them.

As the melody of the love song died away and Stella took up the simple strain of a traditional lullaby, Pavis' thoughts strayed to his beautiful, passionate sister and her final gift to the kingdom. She had died to save Chor. Though her information proved an adjunct to that already in Foxxe's possession, her gift was no less profound. She had signed her own death sentence when she faced her lover. In the end, as he was doing, she put herself aside and acted for the good of others.

More than that, she had trained Marc to succeed him, giving Dynt the hope of freedom.

The pain of Tenebrae's life, the loneliness and frustration of it, were offset by the joys, for she had known joy. Her love for Foxxe had been a shattering thing few people ever experienced. Her love for Marc and Coryelle had provided her with children. Pavis suspected Gisarme's presence had given her more real comfort than anything else, in spite of the fact she could never return the love he bore her. His own life could boast a few high points. It had been uneventful, and in retrospect, dull.

He married a woman he was expected to marry, produced children who died young, and of whom he had seen little, mourned their loss, the subsequent loss of their mother, and immersed himself in studies. Only Chevie had penetrated his insular world. Now, at the end of his life, he was discovering she was all that truly mattered to him. It was through Chevie he had come to touch the pain of his kingdom. He could never repay her for that, nor the courage that prompted her to challenge him into awareness of it. She would not accept her freedom, but he had his own plans for her. Through the years Chevie's beauty had warmed him, her body inflamed him, and her spirit comforted him. She was his true consort, and a woman whose honor was far beyond his paltry attempts. That he had been graced by her love was a miracle beyond price.

Pavis' wandering thoughts were abruptly terminated. Heavy footfalls sounded in the corridor and he recognized the tactless interruption of one of Corbin's emissaries. He gestured to Stella. "Though they know you sometimes entertain me, it would be better if the Garde did not find you here."

"Where?"

"Behind the hanging there is a door. The chamber is a private library. Hurry."

Stella slipped behind the tapestry as the door opened. She scarce dared to breathe, afraid the Gardesman would detect her presence. Though, as Pavis said, it was no secret she entertained the king, Stella did not want to parade her connection with the crown in front of an underling who could be relied upon to gossip. Besides, from the security of her hiding place she might overhear something of importance.

She pulled the door of the hidden chamber shut, careful to control the catch so it made no sound, and settled herself in the king's overstuffed armchair. With her legs drawn up beneath her, she looked like a child. As the Gardesman's words filtered thorugh the open screening of the chamber's door, Stella relaxed. The man had come to get Pavis' signature on yet another stack of edicts. He was annoyed because the king insisted on reading them. It would take hours. Pavis' curt command interrupted him. The shuffling of the Gardesman's boots told Stella he had been ordered to sit. She waited, her thoughts straying.

For all her talk of Marc and news of Coyrelle, Stella's heart was revolving around Lar with frantic impotence. She knew he and Coryelle had escaped together, but that was all. News of Coryelle's capture filtered back to the resistance not only through Racque's report, but in the gossip of the fleet. Corbin's obsession with Coryelle was no secret. She was therefore an object of interest. Lar, on the other hand, was a traveling musician whose popularity was of secondary importance in comparison to a prize for the Seneschal. There had been no word of him.

Stella knew he was flying the ship when he joined Racque on the perimeter of Lazur. It was rumored Coryelle had been flying it when the squad was apprehended, and that it was she who had surrendered to Ydre. Stella could think of no reason for Coryelle to fly if Lar were not injured or absent. Her mind whirled helplessly around unknown events.

She had come to the king with news of Coryelle's capture because access to the royal house was easy for her. To update Pavis on Marc's activities was originally Gisarme's idea, and it had proved to be a sound one. Pavis was acting as an ally in ways that would be invaluable to Marc once he ascended the throne. It was expedient for her to come, but it had also been a happy circumstance for Marc. With a flash of intuition she realized she had been conveniently sidetracked to give Marc a free hand. He would attempt a rescue, and not entirely for Coryelle. She also had a suspicion he would try to accomplish it from the inside. A shiver ran up her spine as she realized her position.

There were so few of the companions left, and of those even fewer were trustworthy. Now, split as they were, each must help himself. Stella squirmed in her chair. Every inch of her body itched for action. It was torture to sit still. She knew without doubt to remain passive would drive her stark staring mad. She stretched, trying to ease her restlessness, but it persisted. There was one remedy: immediate, decisive action.

Very well. She had fulfilled her duty to the king. She would find out about Lar herself. She was adept at disguise and there was a certain class of woman who was at home with the fleet. A ship of any size had quarters for a few house slaves. It had been one of Corbin's concessions in building the fleet. By maintaining the slaves aboard ship, Corbin was able to keep his men in space for longer periods of time without mutiny. As one of his officers once remarked, he'd do anything to squeeze an extra tour of duty out of his men.

As a house slave she would have free run of the ship, as long as she was careful not to interfere with its operations. Ydre would be feeling especially smug, sure of himself. It would not be impossible to infiltrate. Besides, there was the commander's well-known taste for women. Stella proceeded to concentrate on the disguise that would best submerge her identity and decided on one of the nomadic tribeswomen of Modos. Their coloring was similar to hers and she understood their customs, having grown up in close proximity to them. She was mentally rearranging her face when she heard the Gardesman rise to his feet. There was a shuffle and the door closed behind him, muffling the sound of his heavy footfalls.

"All clear," said Pavis.

Stella pushed herself out of the chair and went to join the king, her footsteps quick and purposeful now she had made a positive decision. "You are tired," she said, concerned over the pallor of Pavis' face.

"Everything is an effort now," he answered, "especially managing an interview with those coarse Gardesmen. It seems Corbin sends the most vulgar specimens to me. I think it is his way of torturing me."

"Save your strength, my lord."

"For what? Another day? There will not be many more of those."

Stella opened her mouth, but he silenced her with a weary gesture of his hand.

"This is something you must tell Marc. He does not have long. Soon he will be king. I am trying to hold on, to give him time to fight Corbin, but I know it cannot last much longer."

"My lord, your courage is humbling."

"It is nothing. I have nothing left to fear. Stella, you must come again. Soon. Promise me."

"Of course, my lord."

"I have something to give you. You must come."

"I promise, my lord."

Pavis ran a gentle hand across her cheek. He smiled. Stella saw again a glimpse of the charm that once won Pavis friends and still kept them.

"You are a good child, but a reckless one. Do not take foolish chances."

Stella bowed her head, afraid he could see her thoughts. A blush of guilt mantled her cheeks as she thought of her plan. "I think, my lord, sometimes one must," she replied.

CHAPTER 9

The *Ravening*'s docking bay loomed large and empty, its ceiling support beams arched like the ribs of a whale. The ship's fighters were out on maneuvers, prowling like a pack of hunting wolves, and driving any unmarked independent vessel before them. If they found the spaceways empty, they returned surly.

Their ground crews were enjoying the only real peace of the day. With the ships all out, there was no work for them, and no way to inspect work previously done. They lounged around the perimeter of the chamber, making a pretense of repairing worn equipment as they talked or rested. Lar was amused to see the finesse with which some of the crew managed this. One man seemed to be industriously employed in cleaning baffle filters, but when Lar studied him, he could see the man's eyes were closed, his fingers operating automatically.

Lar approached the largest group, his harp slung over his shoulder. He sauntered around the outskirts of the bay, heading obliquely toward a knot of men splicing cable. It was handwork they could do while they rested, and there were always miles of it to be repaired. The companionable group with their deft fingers and easy camaraderie reminded him of fishermen mending nets, but the nets they flung trapped men and women. He reached the edge of the group and found a convenient place to lounge, cocking one knee and lacing his fingers around it.

A mechanic looked up from his work. "Give us a song, minstrel, since you'll not dirty your hands with work," he jeered.

"Does the commander allow such frivolity?" Lar queried. "I assume you are on duty."

"None of your affair," replied the man. His regulation clean-shaven jaws bulged with muscle. So did his arms and chest beneath his short-sleeved work shirt. Lar calculated the largest and densest muscle was located firmly between his ears. "We run things as we like down here."

Lar shook his head sorrowfully. "I must disagree. The preservation of my own skin interests me. Obviously you have no such preoccupation."

A man to Lar's right snickered. "Clon, you blew your fuel." He jerked the spliced cable he had been working on to test it. "Now me, I'd really like a song. Been too long since we've been in port and entertainment's only for the officers. We're lucky the minstrel here comes down to our level. Most of 'em just candy after the commander. And you had to be rude."

"No offense, no offense," said Lar mildly.

The man jerked the cable again, and satisfied, reached for another broken piece. "It really is true we can do as we like as long as no one notices," he said. "A song would do none of us any harm and might even speed the work along."

Lar laughed and shrugged the harp from his shoulders. "That is a lesson most people learn early," he said. "It is one of the reasons I have a job. This one, now, should go with the rhythm of your hands."

Lar drew his fingers across the strings, sending a rush of sound into the huge cavity of the docking bay. It was swallowed by the sheer size of the area. His fingers began to pluck an infectious rhythm and he smiled as he noticed the men's hands beginning to move in time to the music, a few seconds faster than before.

The sea chanty he had picked up in his travels lightened the men's spirits. These men were not members of the Garde like the rest of *Ravening*'s crew. They were civilians who found the constant employment and good pay enough incentive to endure the rigid discipline of life aboard one of Corbin's ships and the enforced isolation from the more frivolous city life. Many of the men, like Clon, were not overly bright. Even more had rough backgrounds, and found a safe haven from the Garde in serving them. Lar was once again amazed as he watched the magic of his music turn such contrary individuals into that momentary unit, an audience. He finished the song, allowing the notes to die away before he spoke. "I don't suppose you'd have a flagon of ale for a thirsty throat?"

The man who had rebuked Clon nudged a youth next to him. The boy dropped the cable he was working on and flinched. "Get the minstrel some ale, boy," he said kindly. He made a point of not noticing the clumsiness with which the boy fumbled to his feet.

Lar could see most of the company were not so gentle. He surmised the boy sat close to this man for his own protection. The others did not seem to cross him. Lar put on his most winning smile. "My thanks," he said.

"Ours to you, minstrel," the man replied.

"I am Lares Harken, lately caught in circumstances I wish only to escape."

The man chuckled. "Not unlike the rest of us," he said. "I am called Brun Wini."

"Would that I had escaped both the resistance and the fleet, but it was not to be. I stopped on Lazur for a change of scene. My welcome had grown thin with the captain of an ore freighter."

"You mean your money ran out," Brun guessed shrewdly.

"I admit it," answered Lar. "I hoped to pick up some cash on Lazur. As far out as that post is, they're starved for entertainment. I was just congratulating myself on the inn being full and anticipating the bulge in my purse when the fleet appeared." He spread his hands expansively.

"You ran?"

"Like a rabbit. But it was no use. If I hadn't been recognized by one of the Gardesmen I'd have been sitting in a cell instead of singing for you."

Brun looked up with a knowing eye. "I've heard tell minstrels are rare hands with the ladies."

Lar arched an eyebrow, inviting further comment. "I admit to some affinity for them."

"Heard tell you were captured with the Foxxe girl."

"Yes. For the life of me I can't see what Corbin wants with her. She's too temperamental for me, and he could have any woman on Dynt."

"There's always talk," answered Brun, "but the Seneschal has his own reasons, I'm sure. And having him here will be a boon to us. I've no complaints."

"I'd think you'd dread a visit. Doesn't Ydre go into a spit-and-polish fit like the rest of Corbin's officers?"

Brun grinned. "Sure. But that's before he arrives. While the Seneschal is here, Ydre's attention is on him and not on us."

"Aren't the prisoners a nuisance?"

"Not to us. It's the maintenance crew who get stuck with them. Besides, they won't be around long enough to become bothersome."

Lar's eyebrows lifted in a question.

"The Commander finds his prisoners a great source of entertainment. Unfortunately the entertainment is hard on them. They do not survive long."

"But he hasn't touched them!"

"After the Seneschal has looked them over, Ydre will move in. He sometimes accepts a slave in place of the financial bonus Corbin allots to those who distinguish themselves in the service of the state."

Lar ran his fingers idly down the strings of his instrument. "When is the Seneschal due to arrive?" he asked.

Brun was instantly suspicious. "Why do you want to know?" he asked.

"So I will know how long I can enjoy peace and quiet," Lar replied. "Unlike you, my work begins when a celebrity appears on the scene. I will be instantly summoned to provide entertainment."

Brun chuckled, his hands balancing a heavy piece of cable as he searched for the right size splice. "Minstrels are a lazy lot," he commented. "Their work consists of enjoying themselves and they complain. Me, I'd be happy for such an easy life."

"No doubt," returned Lar. His mind was racing ahead. Coryelle and her companions were safe for the moment, but their safety would not last beyond Corbin's arrival.

"I doubt if even the Commander knows the exact hour of Corbin's arrival. The Seneschal keeps his plans to himself. From past experience, though, I can say you probably have five or six hours of peace before you'll be pressed into service."

Lar laughed, still strumming his harp. "Let us put the time to good use," he said, and launched into another rollicking ballad.

Brun smiled and nodded, again matching his movements to the beat of the music.

Coryelle paced the confines of her cell, her footsteps soft on the unyielding deck. The narrow enclosure was bare and spotlessly clean, antiseptic in its atmosphere, untouched by transient human habitation. As she ranged up and down its length, she counted the fourteen paces her stride measured off with each circuit of the room. It was monotonous, wearing, and meant to be so. The hypnotic precision of her steps dulled her mind, numbing it against the moment.

After hours of fruitless searching for possibilities, she concluded she must await an opportunity, but her mind raced onward, hammering away at her circumstances, giving her no rest. She must be strong to take advantage of an opportunity when it came. She needed rest. Finally she devised this method of wearing herself out.

The worn leather of her hide boots made little sound on the smooth metal deck. She was banking on not attracting attention. She had no wish to appear a hysterical, caged animal, helpless and frustrated, before the Garde. Unfortunately, her jailer was a man who took his work seriously. He had unusually keen hearing and he was attuned to any change in the condition of the people he kept. She was not more than mildly tired when she heard the computer lock on her cell door whir to life.

The panel slid back to reveal the Gardesman standing in the coffin-shaped opening. His dark uniform made him a faceless silhouette against the bright light of the corridor. Coryelle was in the act of turning when the door opened. She regarded the man over her shoulder with icy royalty.

"Yes?" she inquired coldly.

The man slouched against the doorjamb, resting one forearm on it with a negligence that suggested he found her no threat at all.

"What are you running from, rabbit?"

Coryelle regarded him with disdain and did not reply.

"Couldn't be from me, could it? Or the Commander? I'd give it up," he advised. "You've got no place to go."

Coryelle's shoulders stiffened. "I assure you it never occurred to me to run from anything, much less an overconfident junior officer," she replied, turning away from him.

"There will come a time when you'll wish you'd been a little friendlier to this junior officer. When the Seneschal is done with you, when Ydre wears you out, you will come to me. As you wipe my boots you will have cause to remember. I will use you up, little rabbit, until you lie down and die."

Coryelle was beginning to realize she had made a mistake

with this man. He was easily influenced and she was antagon-
izing him out of her own pride. She would be better off using
him. She allowed her eyes to widen in alarm. Given the innocence of her look, it was an effective ploy. The Gardesman
smiled, and Coryelle knew he had used the same tactics on a
hundred other prisoners. She hated his bullying and the commander who allowed him to get away with it.

"There, now. All you have to do to make your stay here
pleasant is to remember who your friends are."

Coryelle allowed the defiance to drain out of her stance, to
be replaced by uncertainty and veiled fear. The Gardesman
was entranced.

"We've had word," he announced, "the Seneschal will be
arriving shortly." His smile spread as he noted her flinch. "It
seems he especially wants to see you."

Coryelle could feel his eyes on her, waiting for a physical
reaction. She gave him one. She shrank. She could feel the
pleasure her fear gave him. She came close to cowering, all
the while afraid she was overacting, and he would detect her
deception, but he was not aware of extravagance on her part.
She fed his appetite for terror.

"I can tell him nothing," she said, her voice on the verge of
trembling.

"Now, now, we all know who you are, girl. Your father was
a traitor and your uncle a rebel—you come from strong stock!
And the pretender's prize pigeon. You're going to be a nice
lever in the scheme of things."

Coryelle began to realize the man was a fool. He should not
be warning her against Corbin's arrival, nor should he have
entered her cell without Ydre's command. For the first time in
hours her spirit lifted. Still, he was a danger as well as a
source of information. She sat forlornly on the hard edge of
her sleeping pallet.

"Don't be so down, girl. There's always hope for a pretty
piece. To kill you would be a fool's mistake."

"I am comforted," she said involuntarily, belatedly hoping
he had not noticed the tinge of sarcasm in her tone.

"I would not mock my position, if I were you. The Seneschal has been known to act outside the bounds of ordinary men."

Coryelle regarded her jailer with a stab of fear. She kept her tongue and watched him relax. If she could contain her temper, she might make good use of him. Already she had the distinct impression it would be no trouble to get him to open her cell. She knew he underestimated her.

"I am grateful for my preservation."

The Gardesman actually laughed. "You're learning, girl, you're learning."

Still chuckling, he stepped back from the door and touched the lock. As Coryelle saw the door slide into place and heard the decisive click of the computer's combination lock, she smiled. She had quite a store of information for her encounter. The Seneschal was coming to see her. No one would attempt to harm her until he departed, so she was physically safe until his arrival. Corbin's presence would upset the routine of the ship. It would present opportunities, and she would be ready for them. She stretched out on her pallet, her body relaxing in spite of the hard surface.

Coryelle's thoughts wandered to Lar. She knew he was doing his best to contact the survivors of the attack on Lazur, that he would be seeking out ways and means of escape. He was adept at the role he was playing, and she trusted him implicitly. He was a small comfort at the back of her mind, a development Corbin would not anticipate. She sighed softly, suddenly tired.

She closed her eyes against the stark white walls of her prison, willing darkness. Gradually the light no longer penetrated her eyelids. Her mind drifted. Marc rose in her consciousness like a comforting balsam. She clung to the thought of him, letting everything else fall away. Not for a moment did it cross her mind that he might be dead.

Lar's hand stopped in mid-strum as a bell sounded through the docks. He looked up, to discover a flashing warning light.

"Can't be our fighters," muttered Brun. "They've not been out a half watch."

The airlock doors, invisible from the docking bay, began to

open. The rumble of their movement vibrated through the docks. It was an uneasy feeling, like standing on earthquake-rocked land. Lar was drawing a breath of relief as the vibrations died away when there was a hitch and they resumed.

"Closing," explained Brun succinctly, noticing Lar's nervousness.

"I guess I've never been on the docks of a ship this size when she opened her lock," Lar answered.

Brun grinned. "No need to apologize," he answered. "It's the *Ravening*. She's a sturdy old lady, but nothing works smooth. I doubt if it ever did. You won't find that kind of vibration on the newer ships. I guess I've gotten used to it, but it does give you a turn at first."

Lar nodded, his eyes on the doors of the docking bay. The smaller, upper section was parting to admit an unmarked ship. It was a class II freighter, one Lar had not seen before, yet he had a distinct impression of familiarity. Perhaps it was the dashing way the ship blasted into a strange space dock, executed a sharp turn, and landed exactly in the center of a marked slip. The sense of familiarity niggled at his mind. The vessel's silence was an irritation, and he waited for its hatch to open with rising impatience.

The inflexible sound of marching feet invaded the relative peace of the docks, and the mechanics bent diligently to their work. A detachment of Gardesmen strode through the upper entrance and cut across the landing area toward the new arrival. Lar realized the unexpected vessel had been ordered to remain sealed until a security detachment could be summoned.

Gardesmen surrounded the vessel and formed an enclosed yard in front of the hatch. Like shellfish opening for the tide, the hatch rose. Lar could see a man's feet, worn leather boots reaching to the knee, and the hem of a blue cloak. Certainty settled in his stomach like a lead weight even as hope flashed through his mind. The hatch parted to reveal Racque standing arrogantly on its edge, holding a length of chain. .

His eyes swept the assembled Gardesmen with passing scorn, and he turned his back on them as their leader advanced to demand his identity. Racque jerked sharply on the

chain, and another figure stumbled into view. Cowering in
fear, dressed in ragged homespun, the man cringed back as
he saw the escort Ydre had provided. Racque gave another
jerk on the chain, dragging the man forward by the slave
collar around his neck. As the slave lifted his head Lar was
startled by the expression of fear in hazel eyes he had
looked into many times. He ducked his head lest others
note his recognition of the prisoner, but his spirits leapt like
lightning.

Marc in the guise of a slave! He itched to speak to Racque,
to find out the plan that had brought them here after their
friends. He had half-formed a plan to contact him when Racque turned and spoke to the detachment's leader. His manner
was that of an officer talking to a decidedly junior subordinate.

"You there!" he said, gesturing toward the officer. "Arrange
for secure accommodations for my prisoner. Inform your
commander he is for Ran Corbin."

The Gardesman was full of the pride of his uniform. "And
to whom does the *Ravening* owe the pleasure of this task?" he
asked sarcastically.

Racque turned on him coolly. "It is none of your business,
puppy. You had best learn to mind your elders or you will
soon find yourself in irons. However, I am feeling generous
today, seeing I have a fair prize for the Seneschal. You may
tell your commander Blazon requires lodging for his prisoner
and himself, and a message sent to the Seneschal that I have
brought him something of interest."

At the name Blazon the young man's arrogance disappeared
and he became a fawning servitor. Lar noted disgust on the
faces of his command. Lar quailed at the risk Racque was
running. There was no guarantee his pseudonym was secure.
When Racque left Blazon behind, he had made no secret of
his past, though it was not a thing he paraded. It was more
than possible Corbin knew his bounty hunter's true identity.
Racque was facing death. It was a desperate chance, and it
told Lar reams.

He watched as Racque and his prisoner were escorted from
the docking bay. As the workmen resumed the tasks Racque's

arrival had interrupted, he slipped his harp to his shoulder and followed the Gardesmen up the winding corridor. He was only a minstrel and his movements went unnoticed.

CHAPTER 10

Lar followed unobtrusively as Racque and Marc were escorted through the maze of corridors to *Ravening*'s command center. When they disappeared into Ydre's lair, he turned back down the hall, trying to look as if he came from Ydre, and now dismissed, wandered idly. He moved slowly, killing time. When he heard doors open behind him he ducked into the nearest entryway and found himself outside Ydre's communication complex.

The heavy tramp of Gardesmen's feet followed the sound of the door and Lar glimpsed Marc, escorted by a fierce gaggle of Gardesmen. He was torn between following Marc to the detention area or waiting for Racque. The door behind him was open, and he glanced inside. The technicians were ignoring their instruments, for one wall of their chamber was a window into the control center, and they were entranced by the spectacle unfolding there. Someone had turned the sound on, and Blazon's return was being broadcast in every detail.

Lar's curiosity got the better of him. He slipped inside in time to catch Racque's explanation to the commander.

"... so I knew Corbin would be interested in him. With Coryelle Foxxe the circle of revenge is complete." Racque's voice sounded strange over the amplifiers.

"All but that renegade brother of hers." Ydre bent his saturnine features on Racque. Lar caught his breath, sure the commander knew Racque's identity. "You disappoint me, Blazon. First you miss the girl, and now her brother. Your reputation is tarnished."

"Sometimes, Commander, the fates do not favor us. I regret

losing the child. Even more, I regret losing the prize I might
have gained from her capture. The Foxxe estate is sizable."

"It is reputed to have grown considerably under govern-
mental management." Ydre's features were cold, but they
held a flicker of interest for this man who would not back
down even when he failed. "You may still earn it. The brother
is free. Perhaps the Seneschal will give you another chance.
On the other hand, I have the girl. You have lost, Blazon."
Ydre's tone was insulting and the smile in his eyes was thoroughly unpleasant.

"The Seneschal makes his own arrangements." Racque's
voice was like iron. "Do not assume payment you have not
contracted for."

Ydre's eyes were hard as Racque swept a graceful bow, his
blue cape swirling dramatically, his silvery blond hair a sharp
contrast to the commander's dark uniform. Thank the stars,
thought Lar, he is so blind he cannot detect the confrontation
of fair and foul. Ydre was mercifully oblivious to anything but
his knowledge of Blazon. For the moment Racque was safe.

"I am grateful for your advice." Ydre's voice dripped sarcasm.

"I will lay you odds," said Racque, "I find the brother before you do."

"I never wager with underlings," answered Ydre.

Lar stifled a smile at Racque's audacity, but his adrenalin
was boiling. He felt a dangerous desire to be equally reckless.
Racque and Ydre fenced back and forth, with Ydre trying to
pierce Racque's control. Lar glanced around the communication center, checking his own position. The technicians were
still neglecting their work in favor of the show before them.
The instruments chirped monotonously, relaying information
to deaf ears. Almost under Lar's hand a computer printout
was being disgorged. He traced the edge of the paper with his
finger, idly interested, when a name on the report caught his
eyes. He pressed the paper against a console to flatten it and
read it carefully.

Short and to the point, it detailed Racque's and Marc's
plans for freeing their companions. It was signed with the
obvious code name Raven Twenty.

For a moment Lar was so stunned the significance of the

message did not register with him. His mind grappled with the only fact of any importance: the companions were betrayed. Somewhere in their midst was a spy. Lar prayed this was the first message concerning Marc's and Racque's presence on the *Ravening*. From the wording it was likely.

He reached down and carefully tore the paper from its slot, every nerve tensed against discovery. The sound of the perforated paper tearing was loud in Lar's ears, but the technicians were oblivious to its raucous departure. The sound of the equipment, in all its phases, was so familiar it did not register on their conscious minds. Lar folded the paper and slipped it under his belt. He wanted to get away, to consider his discovery, but the confrontation between Racque and Ydre held him.

"You drive a hard bargain for a man who has failed his master," said Ydre with a sneer.

"I wager high, Commander. I am no slave."

"You are slave to your own incompetence. Still, I will not haggle like a market woman. You have heard my offer. It is more than generous for a tracking hound named Laughingstock."

Racque stiffened. He quivered under Ydre's insult. "I do not dispute you, Commander, but there are those who would not agree with your estimate of my character."

As Racque spoke a knife appeared in his hand, glittering like a wolf's fang in the strong light of the control center. Ydre's surprise at Blazon's temerity registered and blossomed into an evil smile. Racque stood his ground but the Garde did not. They surrounded him, their weapons drawn. Ydre stared at the knife, watching Racque test the blade. Racque looked up and the humor in his eyes nonplussed the commander. Ydre's pride was stung, and he waved his Garde aside.

"I cannot decide, Blazon, whether you are a fool or not, but I admit your audacity. It is amusing. You will make the Seneschal an interesting dinner companion. Tomorrow at the third bell."

Racque chuckled as he flipped the blade back into its scabbard. He made a curt bow to Ydre and whirled between the Gardesmen as if they did not exist. Lar finally breathed. He slipped out in Racque's wake, hoping to catch him, but the corridor was empty.

Lar sought his quarters in the bowels of the ship, avoiding the invitations the crewmen sent after him. The spy's message was burning a hole in his hopes. When he reached the security of his single cubicle, he was shaking. He closed the door and sank down on his cot, thoughts pounding through his mind like the feet of the Garde.

One fact loomed large. There was treachery near the heart of the resistance and it was dragging all of them into a bottomless pit. The identity of the spy was something he wanted to run from with all his heart, but he could not. It had to be someone close to Marc, aware of his movements. Racque, by his position on the *Ravening*, could not have sent the message —unless it had been delayed and the confrontation he had witnessed was an elaborate ruse between Ydre and the bounty hunter. Lar pushed the thought away, feeling certain Racque would not betray the sister he loved. As a poet, emotions were Lar's stock in trade, his area of expertise. He knew Racque's affection for Coryelle was genuine, even if his actions were unpredictable. His identity was well established through Gisarme.

Gisarme, Marc's mentor. Lar knew Marc would trust Gisarme as he did his own right hand, but it might be possible Gisarme now wished to repudiate the adopted heir to the throne of Dynt and establish his own claim. Again, Lar's heart intervened. Gisarme had raised Marc, had educated him. He had had ample opportunity to pick up the crown, and he had never shown the slightest inclination toward it. No, Gisarme had preferred to let the charismatic young man lead the fight. Moreover, he would never betray the trust Tenebrae had given him.

That left Stella. Lar's overworked heart cried out in protest, for to believe Stella a traitor was to destroy it. Could she feel Marc and the resistance were leading him to his death and if she finished them, he would be free? He could not believe it, especially since she knew he had escaped with Coryelle. Unless she had bargained with Corbin for his safety . . . Lar could not accept his premise.

Stella had no world but her music and his love for her. Without either, she had no anchor. If she betrayed him, she would lose him in spite of his love. Lar knew the rampant gossip of her affairs and trysts to be utter nonsense, the inevitable train of falsehoods following any public figure. There was no one else she would trust.

Having eliminated the worst possibilities, Lar gave up. He knew the spy could be as simple a thing as an implant in a person who was totally ignorant of its presence. If they escaped, there would be time to discover the traitor's identity. Urgency drove him, seeking a way to consolidate plans.

Marc was surrounded by a tight knot of Gardesmen. A second chain had been attached to his slave collar and the two men who flanked him held him cross-tied. In addition, his wrists were manacled, the chain between them clanking heavily at each step. There was none of the physical jostling so common to petty soldiery. The Gardesmen stayed marginally apart from their prisoner. The crispness of their uniforms and the unconscious unison of their movements gave them an untouched quality. Marc, human, rumpled, with a day's growth of beard, was unclean, a germ in the antiseptic security of their world.

Long ago he had committed the physical layout of Corbin's ships to memory. Now, in a few short moments' walk, he had to sort out the route he traveled, and coordinate it with the floor plan in his head. He was being distracted by the anger boiling up within him, an anger he had not anticipated. He thought his disguise a clever, somewhat ironic ruse, but years of civil treatment lulled him, eroding the emotional knowledge of the degradation of slavery.

He hated his involuntary confinement. He hated the twisted strap of metal around his neck and the twitching chains that pulled him off balance with every step. He hated the metal bracelets rubbing his wrists raw. He wanted to snap the chain between them with one quick jerk. The temptation was almost irresistible, but he did not rise to it.

His only chance to save his friends lay in the success of the deception he and Racque were attempting. He schooled himself to subservience, to the cringing terror that would have been the real Drusillus' reaction. There were advantages in rolling one's eyes like a hunted beast. It gave him the opportunity to peer down branching corridors and read numbers on doors he passed. He remembered with deep respect the brilliant disguises Eban Foxxe had affected, many of them diametrically opposed to his own personality. Foxxe had maintained his persona in the most trying circumstances. Remembering him, Marc was heartened. He channeled his anger, letting it escape in a physical tremor. An imperceptible smile touched the impassive features of the man on his left as he perceived Marc's distress. He twitched the chain in his hand.

Unfortunately, the man on his right had chosen the same instant to take a firmer hold on his captive and what should have been a painful jerk was equalized. Marc, still trembling and to all intents and purposes terrified, knew a moment of pleasure himself, and it shocked him. Not the emotion, but the fact that the minutae of the incident made him react so strongly. It struck him forcibly that such moments made up the emotional highs of a slave in the kingdom of Dynt. That such a petty incident could become the equivalent of joy ached like an old wound.

The tight blue phalanx swung around a corner and Marc could see a preliminary security grill blocking the passage. The corporal of the security detail raised a hand for his men to halt and proceeded to a keyboard on the wall outside the grillwork. He entered the day's security code and a low hum ceased. The security field had been deactivated.

A Gardesman appeared on the other side of the grill and keyed in a sister code. The grill parted in an elliptical opening large enough for a single man. Marc stumbled as the Gardesman shoved him through the opening.

"Another one for you."

"I'll be running out of cells if the Seneschal doesn't arrive soon," grumbled the jailer as he secured Marc's neck chains and removed the manacles. Marc fought the desire to rub his wrists. Instead he cringed away from the Gardesman. "What's this one, anyway?" the jailer asked.

"Some slave connected with the Foxxes."

The jailer nodded. Corbin's obsession with Foxxe's family would have been laughable if the man had not commanded such fear.

"We'll keep him safe for his Excellency, right next to the little chit."

"That one said anything more?"

"The girl?"

"Umhm. She certainly had enough to say when she was captured."

"Must've worn her out. There hasn't been a peep since."

The corporal's eyebrows shot up. "She's all right, isn't she?"

"Sure. She's just not saying anything."

"She'd better be all right or our necks will be on the chopping block."

Marc's adrenalin raced. Coryelle was still alive, still unhurt, ironically protected by the man who would eventually order her termination. He scanned the corridor for a way to communicate between the cells. Each cubicle was completely sealed from the outside. She would be unaware of his presence.

However, others would not be. At the end of the corridor Marc could see a series of open cells, old-fashioned barred cages for unimportant prisoners. Right now they pressed at the bars watching the new arrival's initiation into their fraternity. He recognized faces among them, and prayed no one would discover his identity. He ducked his head, surreptitiously watching their expressions. No one seemed to recognize in the slave the heir to the throne of Dynt.

Bitterness swept him afresh. The slave collar he wore was a cloak of invisibility. It transformed a man into an object. It was an attitude so deeply ingrained, even in people he knew opposed slavery, that it was truly frightening. As the Gardesmen marched him down the corridor, he kept his eyes lowered, but the precaution was needless. His security was intact.

His jailer paused in front of one of the sealed cubicles. When he opened the door Marc was almost blinded by the stark white interior. He had seen horrible prisons and hiding places that were cold and dark and reeking of filth, but they could not compare to this blinding, sterile capsule for discomfort. Without a word the Gardesman booted him into the room, and rammed a fist against the lock. The door crashed shut behind him. He was trapped.

The panic of a wild creature snared for the table surged through him, and he trembled with the violence of his reaction. He wanted to claw the walls, snarling out his fear and frustration, but he knew a slave like Drusillus would not act that way. Those were the reactions of a free man caged. Instead he crept to the sleeping niche and curled up there, his head buried in his arms. He knew the cells were monitored. His actions had to be in character.

The need to think, to plot some course, was paramount in his mind, but his boiling emotions would not allow him to concentrate. Years of practice in the rigid martial disciplines of *auctorite* taught him how to make his emotions and his mind work for him. He needed peace to think. He sought that freedom in the depths of his memories.

He closed his eyes and concentrated on the color green. A spot of green appeared in his mind, and he held it there, coaxing it into life. Within moments it became the thick, yellowy-green lichen on the trunk of a crinklebark tree. Slowly he drew his thoughts backward, surrounding himself with green: the tree's big, drooping leaves, the thick brush at its base, and the greeny-gold of the filtered sunlight. The forest of Adyton grew around him, rising in his mind with all the grandeur he remembered. He wrapped green peace around like a blanket against anger.

The anger ebbed, faded with the forest's growth, and his mind cleared. As a prisoner earmarked for the Seneschal, it was obvious he would be kept isolated. He had two sources of information from the outside world. The guard might be tricked into dropping something of value, but that was an unreliable variable. His main contact would be Racque, dropping by to check on the welfare of his prisoner. Racque's visits would be few.

Marc's frustration boiled within him. His disguise passed him under the Garde's watchful eye, but the incarceration he now faced hamstrung him. Coryelle was so close he could reach her side in a few strides were there not an impenetrable wall between them. His helplessness drove him. Not until Racque was able to make his report would he be able to formulate a plan. He remembered the disciplines and exercises of patience he practiced as a child. Now he had to sit and wait while lives hung in the balance. To be passive was more torture than the beatings he had endured as a slave.

Coryelle saved him once, when he was defenseless in the hands of a set of bullies, unable to protect himself because the laws of the land condemned any slave who raised a hand against a freeman. Even as a five-year-old child she had been generous and loving. When she claimed him the bullies retreated, afraid of the consequences of injuring a senator's property. Now he came to save her, and found himself caught, like a watchdog whose master is slain as he lunges helplessly against his chain.

Memories of a lifetime with Coryelle Foxxe chased each other through his mind. The stubborn, willful child whose passionate temper turned with blinding rapidity from anger to loving affection had kept his life interesting. The moody young girl whose tears salted his leave-taking had grown, by the time he next saw her, to a woman of compassionate strength. Years of isolation and discipline on Adyton had left their mark on her.

Fond as he was of the vivacious Stella, warm as he felt toward other women, he found in Coryelle an unusual largeness of heart. She had a way of accepting pain and transforming it into something positive which awed him. No matter what life handed her, she loved it back.

He clasped his arms around his knees, an involuntary gesture of restraint against violent action. Again he sought the forest in his mind to subdue a useless anger. As the trees assumed dominance in his thoughts once more, he relaxed. The effort of will to maintain control was exhausting. He needed rest and he knew it would come, cradling him in green thoughts, but the forest was no longer empty. Coryelle walked its paths, the gold of her hair flaring now and then in the dappled sunlight, the generous strength of her body as much a part of the scene as the ageless trees. To think of her so, free in the home she loved, sent a rush of warmth through him.

In the fancy of his mind a flight of dynteryx, their wings beating soft against the unresisting air, followed in her wake. They danced and cavorted behind her back, charging at each other in mock battle, rearing and striking with their tiny hooves, but all in silence. It was a great joke to follow her thus. Marc's last conscious thought was of the clutch of winged horses prancing daintily behind her head, dancing on air, their tails streaming like flags in the wind of their wings. He saw Coryelle duck under them and turn, laughing as they spooked in all directions. When she continued on her way they emerged from hiding and reformed their ranks, beginning the game again.

CHAPTER II

The spy set a wide-range electronic receiver into a nest of circuitry and began to connect it. He worked laboriously, painstakingly. It was evident from the deliberation of his movements that he was not comfortable in the role of engineer. Nevertheless, the communications link grew under his fingers.

It was a smaller device than those he had used. When it was completely assembled it would fit inside the housing which enclosed the air circulation system in his cubicle. It was a good hiding place, one he chose carefully. The cover to the housing was easy to remove for quick access, and it was unlikely to be discovered.

He picked up a pair of needle-nosed pliers and twisted a wire into place. He knew he should be paying strict attention to the microplates he was adjusting, but his mind was rebellious. He was angry. The destruction of Lazur had come too close. He had reported the position and condition of the resistance forces. He had expected action from the fleet, but he had not expected to be caught in the middle of it.

He had been used, and he knew it. He had been a fool. He had expected his contact to safeguard him from the fleet's sweep of destruction. He now knew his safety lay in his own hands, in his own ability to plot the actions of others and avoid adverse consequences. His anger surged inward at himself, for his stupidity, but there was a hard edge of dispassion in his attitude toward his contact. From now on he would not be so quick to report a possible strike. First he would make plans for escape. Never again would he rely on another for his safety. It had been a hard lesson, with dead men at his feet, and he would not forget it.

He slipped a clear plastic cover over the communications device. Safe in its translucent cell, it would be protected from dust and the myriad contaminants that plagued micromechanics. As he popped the cover off the circulator, he reflected there was a certain comfort in the knowledge of treachery. His contact, the Garde itself, Corbin's whole system, was built on a foundation of treachery. The system saved its supporters pain, for they knew in advance they could trust no one.

The ruthlessness and selfishness of his contact's actions in jeopardizing his spy for his own ends possessed a curious honesty. The man made no pretensions of honor. He was out for himself and his career, exclusive of anyone else. It was a reliable alternative to the hypocrisy of the resistance that pretended friendship while it sought power, stepping dispassionately over the corpses of its followers.

The spy's fingers shook with emotion as he replaced the circulator's cover. The Garde called Marc a pretender. The accuracy of the title amazed him. All of Marc's honor, his care for the kingdom, even the reputation for openness and caring he enjoyed, were built on the bodies of his slain followers. All the charisma in the world could not conceal this to the spy's eyes. The vaunted heir of Dynt was a liar who enslaved others to his cause by making them believe he was their friend.

In the end, Marc's only friend was the crown he intended to wrest from the aging king. This latest stunt, going after the captives, was merely an excuse to retrieve the object of his lust. Coryelle was another pawn in his rise to prominence. He and Corbin were cut from the same cloth, but Corbin was honest about his methods. Once he had achieved his goal, and Coryelle was made his consort, to bear children like a brood bitch, he would turn his desires in other directions. Even now he was not averse to cuddling the lovely Stella. With bitter clarity the spy recalled Stella's departure for Dynt and Marc's farewell hug. He had drawn her against his chest, accepting her slender form, blotting out the physical distance between them. His arms had been comfortable around her and the kiss he dropped on her head had been unconsciously intimate. The memory of how Stella had snuggled close to him, completely trusting him, galled the spy. He would betray her trust and affection as the spy had been betrayed.

He sank on his bed and buried his face in his hands. He did not relish the coming destruction. He knew he was sending the whole resistance to its death, but they followed the pretender freely and were therefore liable to his fate. The price he was paying was high. He, too, would have corpses to dodge in his dreams. If the reward for deception were not so high, he could not endure it.

The timer on his light panel activated, subduing the light automatically. He could hide in the twilight. It made everything blurred, indistinct, and easier to accept. Somehow, though, it could not obliterate the face of the man who had died at his feet on Lazur. The spy turned away from the vision, but it would not abandon him.

Stella adjusted her position, grimacing as she did so at the cramped quarters of the shuttle. Ten women were confined in a room meant to house five. She squirmed, trying to ease her cramped muscles in the bed she shared with another woman. Filmy strands of the woman's hennaed hair floated across her nostrils and drove her mad. She blew it away, but it drifted back, and Stella almost choked on her effort to repress a sneeze.

She twisted over on her back, convulsed by the tickling hairs. The woman beside her slept, oblivious to her bedmate's contortions. Stella's dark eyes stared blankly at the ceiling. She was in the process of sneaking aboard Ydre's flagship. Corbin's commanders were given a free hand in their methods of reward and discipline. Marcel Ydre, commander of the *Ravening*, ruled his officers with a twisted iron hand, but he rewarded them liberally, financially, and in kind. As a part of his incentive program he maintained a company of house slaves on board the *Ravening* for the enjoyment of the senior officers. Stella had managed to infiltrate a group of replacements on their way to Ydre's vessel.

She knew a house slave would have free run of the ship. She could appear in odd places at odd times and no one would give it a second thought. If Lar were alive, she would find him. She tried to evade the thoughts of what she might be called upon to do to maintain her cover, but they worried her like the nibbling lips of a thousand tiny fish. Her whole body ached with the longing to be protected, folded in someone's arms against the harsh realities that awaited her. She longed for the gentle fierceness of Lar's presence as he adroitly shielded her from unwelcome advances, for the sanctuary she found in Marc's affectionate embrace. She had neither.

The same men who diffidently chased the flamboyant entertainer would use the house slave like a rag and throw her away. Stella knew she should be on her way back to the space buoy's hidden rendezvous instead of haring off across space on this emotional fool's errand, but she could not tolerate safety while Lar was in jeopardy. That her presence might risk some plan she did not accept. She was safely under cover. As a house slave she was an object, unnoticed except when her service was required.

She must find Lar. She said she loved him. They had been paired for some time, yet she was just begining to realize that without him existence would be out of tune. Her passionate nature flared, flying to his defense with a determination that surprised her.

Stella's eyes grew darker as she considered the company she would be keeping. Rumor whispered Corbin would board *Ravening* to personally interview Coryelle before her termination. Corbin's presence was unnerving, especially if Marc attempted a rescue. Stella was not sanguine about the chances of survival. Once she had stormed at Lar and Eban Foxxe for trying to take on Corbin's fleet single-handed. Now she was doing the same thing. Such impossible actions, so often labeled courage, were the result of that persistent voice inside us all. She now understood that to deny its influence was impossible when it coupled with love.

* * *

Marc jerked awake at the unfamiliar noise. He blinked in the stark white light of his cell, disoriented. The hard voices in his ears brought him back to his ruse and the rough material of the tunic he wore confirmed his persona. He was masquerading as the slave Drusillus captured by Corbin's bounty hunter, Blazon. He shook his head to clear it of noise, but the voices remained, and he realized they were coming from an intercom unit above the door of his cell. He focused his attention on the words. They clanged in his ears after the sealed silence.

"Look, all I know is, I've got my orders. The roster says I work the day shift, I work the day shift."

"I can't take it anymore. I've been on night security for six weeks running. Now Ydre's got me doing double time in the armory to be sure there's enough spit and polish for the old crow. I've got to get some rest. Give me your shift for one day—get sick, whatever, I don't care, only give me one night's sleep."

"You'd better watch your tongue."

"I know it. I'm so tired I don't care. Does that tell you anything?"

"I'd do it if I could, but you know Ydre's policy. Only an emergency changes the roster."

"See if I do you any favors," grumbled the Gardesman.

"You just want to avoid security inspection when the Seneschal arrives," guessed the other man shrewdly.

Marc took the Gardesman's silence for acquiescence.

"Look, nobody wants to stand up to those hollow eyes, but it's your turn. You squealed out of it the last time."

"Another week of this and I'll be dead."

"Hah."

Marc's eyes widened as the implications of the Gardesman's conversation dawned on him. The night Gardesman was exhausted and that made him vulnerable to error. Corbin's visit was causing an upheaval that might support an escape.

"What do you think the Seneschal will do to the Foxxe girl?" The first Gardesman was shifting the subject.

"Terminate her."

The lack of interest in the Gardesman's voice hit Marc in the stomach like a cold fist.

"Maybe the Commander will talk him out of it."

"He killed the rest of her family. Why should he spare her?"

"Corbin likes to keep his officers happy. You know how Ydre is, but he's a good commander."

"Come to think of it, degrading his enemy's kinswoman might appeal to Corbin."

"I wouldn't mind it myself. Ydre hands me his leavings."

"Not much left, is there?"

"You'd be surprised. He's not as young as he once was."

"No, but he's just as vicious."

"Double," answered the Gardesman grimly.

There was a scuffle Marc could not make out as something knocked against the intercom panel.

"You'll catch it for leaving that switch . . ."

The voice was abruptly cut off as the intercom went dead. Marc was sick at heart. The hollow feeling in the pit of his stomach was a pale reflection of the horror of his thoughts. He faced the probability of Coryelle's death, even her torture, but he now realized when he had thought of her capture he thought of Corbin and Corbin's lack of interest in women. Corbin treated man and woman alike. He would kill, might torture them, but he received no twisted sexual pleasure from his actions. They were expedient. It had not occurred to Marc that Coryelle might come into someone else's hands.

It was obvious from the Gardesmen's conversation that Ydre's pleasures were perverted. What he would do to Coryelle was a negation of humanity. Her face rose in Marc's mind in all its untouched innocence. Her isolated youth, with its emphasis on a code of honor, had ill prepared her for the dishonor of others. Stella, streetwise and shrewd, would have no illusions about her fate, and would use her anger to survive to the last possible moment. Coryelle knew only love, and Marc was afraid for the evil that was coming, afraid it would stun her when she most needed her wits about her. He wanted to throw himself physically in front of her, to ward off his danger as he had the small worries of her childhood. For a fleeting moment the temptation to trade himself for Coryelle crossed his mind, but he knew it would never work. Corbin would give up nothing. If he did, there was sure to be a deception in it. He had killed Tenebrae by remote control years after letting her go. The dictates of logic told Marc nothing was to be gained by such an offer, but the temptation was strong.

The vision of Coryelle as a child haunted him, her sturdy defiance and open affection in the face of overwhelming adversity bringing to his days a warmth he could not name. Now she was no longer a child, but a girl whose voluptuous beauty was its own source of danger. He wanted to hold her, protect her against it, but he was separated from her by an unyielding wall of metal. He rebelled against his enforced inactivity. If he could not touch her physically, he would hold her mentally. It might be no comfort, do no good. Then again, it might. There was no way of knowing, but it was an action he could take. He sent his thoughts around her in a loving embrace, molding them around the curves of her body and the intricacies of her mind.

The lock on his cell door clanked as it was released, jarring him from his exercise, and the door slid back into the wall with a thump. The Gardesman who stood in the doorway carried a curled whip in one hand. He was shorter and slighter than the man who received him at the security gates. His sandy hair caught the strong light of the corridor and cast an inappropriate aureole around his head. He gestured with the whip.

"Up!"

Marc dropped immediately into character, shrinking away from the Gardesman and rising at the same time.

"Don't whimper!" snapped the man. "I can't stand sniveling. Now, out!"

Marc edged toward the door, but too slowly for the Gardesman's taste. The man took two impatient steps forward and gripped him by the wrist. With a flip of his arm he tossed Marc into the corridor and followed him out the door. Marc stumbled and rolled, crashing to a halt against the bulkhead on the opposite side of the corridor. The whip snaked out and flicked him on the shoulder, tearing his tunic and stinging like the bite of a horn fly. Marc shivered at the pain.

"Get up! This is your exercise period and you're going to move. Walk!"

Again the whip flicked out, its wicked tongue lacerating his clothing but missing flesh. It was a warning he did not ignore. As he crawled to his feet the whip sang around his head, the Gardesman enjoying his own skill. Marc ducked away from it, blinking.

"Where do I walk?" he asked timorously.

The Gardesman did not seem annoyed by his question. Marc judged him to be a man who wanted no annoyances. If he could accomplish his purpose by answering a question, he would do so.

"Down the center of the corridor. Do not touch the walls. You might as well not bother to look in any of the cells. They're all sealed for exercise of maximum security prisoners."

Marc started forward, and the Gardesman curled his whip. He stepped back and activated a laser field that separated him from the rest of the corridor. Marc could see him indistinctly through it. The Gardesman sat down and leaned back. His posture suggested he had nothing better to do than take a nap, but Marc knew the slightest deviation in the sound of his footsteps would bring the man to his feet. He walked up and down the narrow hallway, catching himself now and then when his footfalls became too firm, too decisive.

As he walked, he noted the layout of the detention area. The first six cubicles on either side of the corridor were single rooms for isolating high security prisoners. Three of these were occupied. Marc could tell because of the blinking green lights over three of the doors. One of the cubicles was his own. Down the corridor the cell doors were farther apart, suggesting larger chambers capable of housing several prisoners. At the far end of the hall were two huge cells where the rabble were thrown together before their termination. It was in these two cells he had recognized other members of Racque's escape squad.

It was obvious the locks on each door were coded to individual computer tie-ins. It would not be possible to sabotage the computer to open all the doors at once, and there would be no time to open even the three that contained the known resistance prisoners. Escape would have to come from the outside, from Racque.

Impatience for contact with Racque gnawed at him. He needed information now. He had a strong feeling Corbin's arrival would throw the *Ravening* off balance and favor an escape attempt. The thought of scooting out of captivity under Corbin's nose almost made him smile, but he caught himself in time, and when he turned to face the Gardesman his expression was the lost look the man expected to see. His meaningless round of physical movement was another ruse. Concealed beneath it was the relentless discipline, of *auctorite*, honing his muscles and reflexes to a sharp edge.

The Gardesman saw nothing but an unimpressive slave who owed his position in security detention to the Seneschal's interest. Slaves were not worth his attention. He failed to notice Marc's exceptional balance and the compact strength of his frame, the nearly perfect proportions that resulted in athletic ease of movement. It never occurred to the Gardesman that a woman might find the slave's softly curling dark hair attractive, or the strength of his features might excite her desire. He never thought to consider the man's intelligence at all. A slave was a slave, useless to all but its master. The Gardesman narrowed his eyes through the laser field at the man he most truly overlooked.

Racque stretched his legs out and crossed his ankles, luxuriating in the comfort of the overstuffed furniture in *Ravening*'s officers' lounge. It was one of the few places on the ship where he did not have to deal with the prying eyes and backhanded whispers of the crew. The officers were at pains to treat him with courtesy, but they did not degenerate into unwise familiarity with Corbin's bloodhound. If they gossiped, it was not in his hearing.

At this early hour, the lounge was deserted except for the maintenance engineer who was readying it for the after-party onslaught of the ship's junior officers. The dinner Ydre was planning for the Seneschal would be paralleled by their merrymaking. Racque accepted a tall golden glass of pear juice with a frosty smile.

"This early interruption must be annoying," he commented. "Nonetheless, I appreciate your trouble."

The man's tired eyes lifted from the glass he placed before Racque to the bounty hunter's aquiline face with little change in expression. "I am happy to serve you," he replied formally, his unspoken reference to the Seneschal apparent in his tone.

Racque leveled his icy blue eyes at the man, knowing as he did so he was adding stones to the wall between them. His words would mean nothing, but he said them anyway. "Thank you," he replied. "I will not bother you again."

The man bowed and withdrew, as was proper.

Racque closed his eyes. His interview with Ydre got him a dinner invitation, but he was no closer to the companions than when he arrived. He had seen Lar across the way, but they had not chanced to encounter each other, and they had no real excuse to seek each other out. That Lar was free on the ship told him there was already some plot afoot, and he hesitated to proceed without knowledge of it. He needed information, and his persona as Blazon, useful as it proved in gaining access to the ship, curtailed his conversation. Blazon had a deserved reputation for reticence he could not alter. He was hamstrung from engaging in the kind of garrulous conversation that so often yielded pertinent information.

Lar was not bound by these restrictions. As a jongleur he was expected to talk—all the time. No one would blame him for gathering the pieces of information that might come his way. He needed to talk with Lar, to find out the circumstances of his capture and to pool their knowledge. There must be an excuse, a way. He demanded an answer from his blank mind. It refused to comply.

CHAPTER 12

"Captain! Ship approaching. Twelve points off starboard bow."

Sphaleros' footsteps rang on the metal floor of the command bubble. "Configuration?"

"A large fighter, sir. Her identification is being processed now."

"Corbin," murmured the captain.

"The *Ravensong*, sir."

"Prepare the docks for the Seneschal's arrival. The honor guard is to meet him. On the double."

Ydre would meet the ship with the honor detail in his wake. There was no need for the *Ravening*'s captain to leave his post. Still, he was curious to see the Seneschal. Corbin's visits were rare enough to make them occasions. Sphaleros raised his eyes to the star-studded heavens, searching them for *Ravensong*. One could tell a great deal about a man by the way he flew his ship. He had no doubt the Seneschal was at the helm. He rarely traveled with more than one pair of security guards.

The *Ravensong* appeared as a tiny point of light in the distance. It grew rapidly into the sleek lines of a fighter, its pointed nose and upswept tail streaking straight for the squadrons. The ship altered course for *Ravening*'s starboard docks, but it never ceased its driving flight. Within fifty kilometers of the dock's doors Corbin throttled down and allowed the ship to drift in. Its speed as it came into the hold was fast enough to make Sphaleros nervous, but it settled to earth precisely in the center of the fifth landing pad. *Ravensong* was scarcely down before the engines ceased their vibration. It was the work of a master who flew with such skill it had become unconscious.

As Sphaleros watched the space doors close behind the vessel, he paid tribute to that skill. On the landing pad, Ydre was preparing to pay tribute to his position. Ydre strode at the head of the honor guard. His blood-red uniform was in sharp contrast to their austere blue. As they neared Corbin's ship, twenty of the honor detail advanced beyond Ydre, marching in columns of two. At *Ravensong*'s hatchway they halted. Metal clashed once as they drew their curved dress swords and raised them in salute, the points of the blades touching in a shining arch. There was silence.

From his position at the end of the archway, Marcel Ydre awaited his seneschal's appearance. Though he had appeared undisturbed by Corbin's visit, more concerned with the excuse it offered for diversion than politics, he quailed now. His own reputation as a ruthless commander was deserved, but he knew Corbin to be his superior. He did not like to match wits with Corbin, he did not like trying to impress him, but most of all he hated looking into the opaque wells of the Seneschal's lifeless eyes.

A low whine signaled the opening of the hatch. It sank into the cargo hold like a slab of stone, leaving a dark opening. He heard Corbin's deliberate, quiet footsteps before he saw the man, and each footfall revved the panic he was trying to keep under control. Corbin's trim form in its dark blue uniform was almost an anticlimax. The expense, the perfection of its design and cut made Ydre feel overdressed.

Corbin walked down the short ramp, not bothering to make an impression. He did not need to. He was perfectly at home under the respectful arch of weapons, absolutely unafraid that one of them would descend upon his unprotected head. He had the reins of Dynt firmly in hand, and no man here would dare to cross him, not at the height of his power. The two Gardesmen who trailed him were an unnecessary frill.

Ydre awaited his commander, showing his nervousness in the defensive tension of his posture, though he bore gifts he knew would be welcome. Corbin was quick to note his fear and it gave him pleasure to confirm power over the man. His heel was squarely on the adder's neck, and the man writhed, powerless, beneath it. Corbin wasted no words.

"The Foxxe girl?" he questioned.

"Secure, Excellency. She has given no trouble."

"You have questioned her?"

"Very little. I was sure the Seneschal would prefer to interview her."

Corbin nodded and began to walk toward the command center. Ydre followed him, behind his left shoulder, hovering like a blooodstained vulture. Swords clashed once again as the honor guard sheathed their weapons and fell into a tight phalanx behind the officers.

"Any attempts at rescue?"

"None." There was dismissal of the issue in the Commander's voice, but Corbin was not about to close the subject.

"What measures have you taken to ensure the prisoner's security?"

"She is being held in security detention. The rest of the upstarts are in temporary holding, awaiting disposal."

"Have you deployed a scout team around the squadrons?"

"There has been no need. The resistance is broken. There is nothing left."

"I did not see, on any of your reports, a notation of the death or capture of Marc, who calls himself Dynteryx."

Ydre looked uncomfortable. "We did not find a body, but no one escaped Lazur. It is a dead settlement. Not more than a handful of ships cleared atmosphere, and most of those were captured."

"Most?"

"There were a few escapes, but where could they go? They could not have supplies or fuel for any great journey. They drift in space, empty hulls with failed life support."

Corbin's voice was dangerously soft. "You have scanned such vessels?"

"There was no need . . ."

"What you have told me, Commander, is that you have been guilty of negligence."

"I tell you, Excellency, there is no possibility of retaliation. The resistance is no more."

"Where there is one man, there may be retaliation. Where

there is one man, there may be an army. Never underestimate your opponent, Ydre. You have become soft with the security of the fleet."

"Only a madman would attempt rescue. They were vastly outgunned. There would be no chance for survival." Ydre's voice held a pleading note, and the saturnine quality of his features was in abeyance.

"Eban Foxxe did not let the impossibility of the task he set himself deter him from it. He died, but he prevented the military action I planned, though without Foxxe's leadership, that action is no longer necessary."

"But, Excellency, we have the girl. Surely the pretender would not jeopardize her safety."

"As for that, Ydre, I'm sure the boy has few illusions about her safety here with the Garde. You are to institute widespread security measures immediately, search for the escaped ships, and make sure all incoming vessels are monitored."

"Immediately, Excellency."

They walked in silence. Ydre knew no detail of the condition of the ship or its crew was escaping Corbin's eyes. He knew he would receive recommendations for improvements from headquarters soon after the Seneschal's visit.

"Excellency, we have another prisoner as well. One you will be interested in."

Corbin cocked his head. "Why was I not informed?"

"You were en route when he arrived."

"Communications have been known to contact a ship in flight," Corbin remarked softly. Ydre knew the danger of the Seneschal's thoughts could be gauged by the gentleness of his tones. In Corbin, anger and softness went hand in hand. Ydre cleared his throat and continued, hoping the news of Drusillus' capture would offset his oversight.

"The slave Drusillus, of Senator Foxxe's household, was brought in by a bounty hunter."

"Drusillus. The name did appear on the list of household goods. Unaccounted for."

"He is here, also in security detention, also awaiting your interview."

"Drusillus. The slave probably has no knowledge of the resistance, but if his memory can be forced, he might yield

some details on the character of the boy." Corbin was murmuring to himself, and Ydre did not wish to disturb him. The
Seneschal looked up at his subordinate, a flicker of interest
passing through his empty eyes. "You said a bounty hunter."

"Yes, Excellency."

"Blazon."

Ydre nodded, surprised. In any other man, the tone of voice
would have meant affection. Corbin was incapable of affection. Such inconveniences of the heart did not sully his life.

"I will meet with him later. Inform him, Ydre."

"I had planned a small gathering in honor of the Seneschal's visit. He is among the guests."

"Satisfactory. I will see him there."

As Corbin entered the command center, the tenor of work
snapped. Captain Sphaleros turned from the authorization he
was signing and advanced to the Seneschal, hand raised in
salute. Corbin returned the man's courtesy and motioned him
to continue his work. Sphaleros nodded curtly and turned
back to the scanning computers. Corbin's eyes swept the
command post.

"Your efficiency levels seem adequate."

Ydre relaxed under his words. "We have had good results
from the new in-ship scanners. Their clarity allows us to pick
up more detail."

Ydre moved to the viewscreen and activated the scanners in
Coryelle's cell. He could not resist showing off.

Corbin examined the screen, apparently interested in the
technical quality of the picture. He did not ask who the prisoner was. He knew Ydre well. There was a marked resem-
blance between this girl, who must be Coryelle Foxxe, and
the blond good looks of the late Senator Foxxe.

"The installation seems to be adequate," replied Corbin, but
he did not take his eyes from the girl.

She stood in the center of her cell, her straight, strong car-
riage indicative of life in an earthly wilderness, not the insular
world of a star cruiser. The full, female contours of her figure
were not in fashion, but they gave her a timeless appeal
beyond the dictates of society. She was no carbon copy of
some mandated standard. The determination of her expression

was something he had not faced in some time, and never in a woman.

Not since Tenebrae had Corbin met a woman he could not cow. He might make this girl afraid, even break her mind, but in the depths of her spirit there would be an island he could not touch. He turned abruptly away from the screen.

"My quarters," he snapped, and Ydre ushered him down the corridor. "I will speak with you this evening. My Gardesmen will report the status of your ship. I will inspect it at my leisure. You may go," he said at the door to his luxurious apartment.

Ydre withdrew, and Corbin's men took up their posts at either side of the Seneschal's door. The honor guards deployed themselves down the hallway at regular intervals.

Corbin, alone, sank into the unfamiliar luxury of a sumptuous divan. Coryelle's face, with its wide, innocent blue eyes, disturbed him. It recalled another face, long buried under the rigid regimentation of his daily life. Tenebrae's flashing, bewildering beauty was fighting its way to the surface, freed by the sight of a girl so like her in quality. The oval perfection of Tenebrae's face, surrounded by waves and braids of shining dark hair, fought against the knowledge of her death, and his responsibility for it. It did not seem to matter. Tenebrae lived in his mind. He could not exorcise her. She was beyond his power to control, for she had become memory.

No. Corbin did not accept that. His eyes lost their shadows of pain and hardened. He was in control of himself. He would not allow her her freedom, not even in memory. She had been beautiful, yes. He had loved her, with all the passion of his youth, with the best instincts of his mind and against all odds. She had been flame to his body and food for his soul, and she had betrayed his love by not returning it. Worse, she made him an object of ridicule. He had not accepted that, either. Now there was no cruel laughter in Dynt, no laughter at all.

He began by controlling himself, and ended by controlling the world. He would not abdicate that control. He dug a mental pit, shoved the unprotesting memory of the one woman he had loved into it, and covered it over. He dismissed it, he put it out of his mind, but still, on the borders of consciousness, the elusive beauty lingered.

"S'blood!" snarled the Gardesman, picking himself up from the *Ravening*'s deck. "Clumsy oaf! Take your hands off me!"

Lar was bent solicitously over the man. He put a hand on the Gardesman's elbow, but the man twitched away.

"You've already done enough damage," he said. "I'll thank you not to add to it."

Lar ignored him, murmuring apologies as he brushed imaginary lint from the Gardesman's spotless uniform.

"Stop playing nursemaid!" the man roared. "Just get away from me!"

"Yes, sir. I'm terribly sorry, sir. Your pardon, sir."

"Quit 'sirring' me. I'm a technician third grade. Now get out of my way!"

The Gardesman shoved aside Lar's helping hand and stalked down the corridor, muttering under his breath as he did so. Lar caught a few expletives that made him grin. He watched the man until he turned a corner, checked to make sure the corridor was deserted, and unfolded the crumpled piece of paper in his hand. As he thought, the communications technician had been in the act of ferrying information from the resistance spy to command.

"Received no reply last message. Marc Dynteryx and Racque Foxxe attempt rescue. Please answer," he read. At least this time the spy would be less suspicious. Presumably communications had acknowledged the message.

That information from the spy was hand-carried to someone in command was interesting. As far as Lar could see, it meant the spy was a personal contact for one man, a power play. Ydre was the most likely candidate for such a maneuver, and he was also the man most easily able to secure sufficient reward to motivate the spy's betrayal. Lar stuffed the message into a disposal slot and had the satisfaction of hearing it disintegrate before he walked on. He had no desire to meet the Gardesman on his return. The message was truly lost, for it came through the decoding computer link. The machine decoded, printed, and sealed high-security messages between prearranged contacts. Once the link expelled a message, its memory was wiped clean to prevent any security leaks. If the Gardesman did not discover and cover his loss before he reached command, his life was in danger.

Lar strolled down the corridor, looking as if he had not a care in the world. He was tempted to invade the officers' lounge again, but he knew there was a good chance he would meet Racque, and it would not do for them to be seen in close conversation. He needed a ruse, a way to disguise the contact. In the meantime he was hungry. The general mess would satisfy his appetite, both for food and information. By now he was sure the whole ship knew of the proposed evening's entertainment. The party was a further departure from routine. There must be a way it could be turned to advantage. The nonchalant ease of his gait divulged no hint of the turmoil of his thoughts.

The ship's galley was empty except for kitchen drudges and the mess officer. The spicy odor of roasting fowl sent Racque's stomach into a chorus of involuntary murmurings and he realized it had been a full day since his last meal. The cook looked up from the vegetables he was flaying and laughed at Racque's expression.

"Hunger is the great equalizer," he chuckled. "You, Blazon, look like an old hound on the trail of Sunday dinner."

Racque's quick, flashing smile held all his charm. "And I came nosing you out, to beg for a leftover bone."

"I think we can find something more substantial than a bone."

The man swept the vegetables into a pot, then wiped the scarred wood of the counter with a wet cloth. He removed the top from a simmering pot, and the smell of smoked meat and onion and basil filled the room, the steam nourishing Racque's senses. His stomach rumbled in complaint at being overlooked. The cook ladled thick soup into a bowl. He reached for slices of black bread and cut crumbly wedges of white cheese, extracted cold meat from a storage chamber, and pushed the food toward Racque. He wiped his hands on his apron and indicated a table with a nod of his head. "I'll bring hot ale and join you. I could use a break."

Racque accepted the food gratefully and carried it to the table, but he was mulling over the cook's friendliness, wondering at it. The man placed a steaming mug of ale in front of him and slid into the opposite chair. The cook leaned his elbows on the table and circled the ale mug with his big, strong hands. He seemed oblivious to the heat.

"My compliments," said Racque, diving into his soup, "and my thanks."

"It is my work. I am very good at it."

"And humble," said Racque through a mouthful of bread and cheese.

"That is something no one ever accuses me of."

Racque's eyes twinkled. "I am surprised," he said, "you have the freedom to socialize with a passenger."

"I am not one of Ydre's military morons. I am an artist, and I am paid well for my work. The commander values his luxuries, and I am one of them."

"He is forced to coddle you as you would an egg, and this superb food is the result." Racque sputtered with laughter, nearly choking on his soup.

"We are all willing to pay a price for something of value," returned the cook.

"You have the advantage of me, sir," answered Racque when he managed to control his amusement over the spectacle of the dangerous dragon sitting up and begging like a puppy for a treat. "You know my name, but I have not heard yours."

The cook extended one of his huge hands and Racque accepted the offering. "I am Sithe Fedan, master of the hearth. Your name preceded you in the mouths of the rabble I feed."

Racque dipped a spoon in the rich soup and swallowed slowly. "I take it cooking for the ship does not interest you."

"Is an artist interested in a plumber's praise?"

"That depends," answered Racque, "on the plumber."

"A point, bounty hunter, I find easy to lose sight of in this sea of indifference. They could be eating pig swill for all they notice."

"Then why are you here? Surely it cannot be solely money."

"The ship's officers are a discriminating group, and Ydre is a continual challenge. There is nothing so difficult to please as a jaded roué."

"Surely there are few opportunities . . ."

"On the contrary. Ydre loves to entertain . . . himself. You are no doubt aware of tonight's soirée."

"I will be there."

"A personal invitation from the Commander? I thought so. He gathers his audience, heading his table with the Seneschal. He requires an audience for his diversions."

Racque bit into a piece of cheese, careful not to seem too interested.

"My dinner will be superb, a roast fowl with a new blend of herbs and a vegetable hash to tease the palate. Fortunately it will be enjoyed and praised before Ydre starts the revels."

"Revels?" asked Racque.

"You mean to say you have not heard of the Commander's entertainments?"

"I spend most of my time in isolated areas, hunting the hidden. I am an infrequent visitor to an officer's court."

"Even so . . ." The cook waved his ignorance aside. "Ydre uses his prisoners as a diversion. They are made to perform for him . . . according to the whims of the moment. It is quite horrible—something I try to avoid, since there is nothing I can do about it."

"He would not use the Seneschal's prisoner . . . ?"

"No. He is not so foolish. But he will make her watch."

"He risks security for a moment's pleasure?"

"There is little risk. Many do not survive, and the banquet hall is swarming with armed Gardesmen."

Racque swallowed the last of the meat, glad of a decent meal. He would not be able to eat much this evening, knowing what Ydre was serving for dessert. He wondered at Corbin, for such sadistic torture was not his style, but reminded himself the Seneschal seldom interfered with his commanders as long as they followed him. "It will be an interesting evening," he commented lightly, maintaining his persona as an empty-hearted bounty hunter.

The cook shook his head, gathering up the dishes. "More

power to you, hunter. You've a stronger stomach than I have."

"Very interesting, indeed," Racque murmured again. One golden fact emerged from the information he had gained: All the prisoners would be gathered in the banquet hall at the same time, including Coryelle and perhaps Marc.

CHAPTER 13

Gisarme leaned back in his chair, his broad shoulders overlapping its frame. He stretched and yawned, flexing the muscles in his arms and across his chest, then stared glumly at the computer panel. The space buoy's computer system was primitive compared to Inspi's complex programming, but it would serve his needs in extremity. Gisarme mourned the computer wizard's absence, but was glad Inspi had escaped the destruction on Lazur. His services would be urgently needed when the resistance secured another base.

Gisarme sighed. Searching the computer for a likely headquarters was not his forte. Nevertheless, it was necessary, and positive. It was profitless to dwell on calamity. If he went on, if he looked to the future, he could evade for a time knowledge of disaster. The resistance was likely to die, with Marc and Coryelle, at Corbin's hands in the coming hours.

He folded his hands behind his head, his neck cracking in the process. His mind told him he was too old to fight idealistic battles, but his heart brandished a sword. He smiled grimly at his own idiocy.

The computers chirped away, hunting for a likely hiding place, and Gisarme closed his eyes. He needed rest. His muscles, used to more active occupations, were cramped in the confined quarters of the buoy. He ached to be gone, to roam a wilderness with the wind in his face. He reached into the warm recesses of memory and returned to Adyton, ranging its mountain peaks beneath the fresh winds of a spring night sky. His muscles eased as he wandered.

An almost inaudible creak piqued his delicate hearing. His curiosity was aroused. He remained in a deceptive state of somnolent relaxation. The creak was repeated, and the soft sounds of hands on the metal floors followed in its wake. Gisarme waited. There were two sets of hands, he decided, matched by an equal number of feet—small ones. They did not move in sequence, so he judged they belonged to two individuals.

"You can't get off the station, you know," he said, and the movements stopped, presumably as the creatures froze in their tracks. Gisarme cocked one eye and allowed his chair to pivot slowly. What met his eyes roused a quick rush of pity.

Crouched at his feet were two children. The boy was approximately ten years old and the girl two years younger. Their eyes were wide with terror. The little girl hid behind the boy, peeking out from a thatch of auburn hair. When Gisarme leaned forward she hid her face in the boy's shoulder.

"I won't hurt you," said Gisarme. The softness of his voice brought the girl's eyes up and he smiled reassuringly. "How did you get here?" he asked.

The boy swallowed, but he could not speak. Gisarme waited, knowing any movement on his part would send him into headlong flight.

"We hid on the ships!" the girl blurted.

"Sh! Elianor!"

"Come now. You are well caught, and there is no place to run. Why don't you tell me your story?"

The boy moved in front of Elianor, his protective stance making it plain he did not trust Gisarme. Gisarme was hard put to it not to smile.

"She is right. We hid on the ships."

"But why?"

"We were curious. Our father said the ships were off limits, but we were curious."

"You hid when the crew arrived?"

The boy nodded. "In the storage compartments."

Gisarme shook his head. Only in an emergency situation would the storage chambers go uninspected. This time laxity had saved two young lives. "Do you know where you are?" he asked.

The boy shook his head.

"You are with the last of the resistance on an intermediate station."

"Can we go home?"

Gisarme's voice was gentle. "No."

The boy lowered his head and then raised it, trying to read Gisarme's face. Gisarme made it easy for him. "There is nothing left," he answered.

"Then where will we go?"

"If you wish, with us—or, perhaps, with me. It all depends on who's left."

"Is there a choice?"

"Little. It will be some time before I can make other arrangements."

"My family died because of you."

Gisarme considered his reply carefully. "Partly. They died because they were in the way and Corbin's fleet did not choose to save them."

"How can we stay with you?"

"I, nor any other member of the resistance, wished your family harm. It preys on my conscience that my presence brought their deaths. I offer no guarantees of safety. No honest man can do that. But if you stay with me, you will have my love and that of my friends. It is more than some offer."

The boy drew a deep breath. "We stay," he answered.

Gisarme allowed some of his warmth to show in his smile. "Good. I know your sister's name, but I am ignorant of yours."

"I am Dev."

"And I am Gisarme. When was the last time you had food?"

The boy clutched at dignity, but his eyes spoke his hunger. Gisarme turned from the computer and extracted a sack of dried meat and cheese from the storage chamber. He pushed it toward the children and opened two bottles of spring water.

"Hardly a banquet," he said, "but it won't be long before we'll be eating computerized pellets."

Gisarme watched the children with shadowed eyes. They were victims of a conflict they did not choose and their defenselessness saddened him. Too many times it seemed one's intentions did not bear fruit in action. The innocent were dragged into the battle with no chance to defend themselves. He knew he would sink into deeper melancholy if he followed his thoughts.

If Marc succeeded in his audacious attempt to free Coryelle and the other prisoners, he would need a place to flee, a place to regroup and to make plans. The only profitable move he could make was to pursue that question. He eyed the computer's blinking lights as possible locations appeared on the screen. A bleep sounded the termination of the program, and Gisarme regarded the list of possibilities with resignation. There were five of them. He would consider each in turn. He punched the printout key and the printer began to chuckle.

Marcel Ydre was listening to the Seneschal with half an ear. He knew this was dangerous, but he could not help himself. The Seneschal's physical presence distracted him. He much preferred to deal with his superior long-distance. There was an illusion of safety in it.

". . . and we will rendezvous with Fafnir two points off Dynt. The prisoners will be transferred to *Dragonet*, and you will return to the mundane pleasures of border patrol."

"I understand, Excellency. However, I request a change of technicians before resuming patrol. These have been with me too long. They grow restless and they know too much."

"A reasonable request. I will see to it Fafnir brings your replacements."

Ydre regarded Corbin out of narrowed eyes. He could never quite tell what the Seneschal was thinking. He did not know, for instance, whether Corbin was pleased or not by his high-handed move on the unprotected resistance. An abrasive fear he should have informed the Seneschal of his intentions ate at his confidence. Corbin's austere patrician face and bottomless eyes gave him no answers.

"Now, Ydre, about Blazon's prisoner."

"You wish to speak with him? He just left the galley. I have been kept informed of his whereabouts."

"I will see Blazon later. His prisoner I would speak with now."

"At once, Excellency. Security. Bring the slave Drusillus to my quarters under priority guard. Immediately!" Ydre received no verbal reply, but the green acknowledgment light flashed and he leaned back in his chair.

"How considerate of you to anticipate my wants," commented Corbin mildly. "I was about to request he be brought here."

Ydre actually flushed under this mild rebuke. His officers would not have believed their commander capable of it. "As you wish," he answered, vainly trying to save face.

Corbin smiled his frosty smile. Ydre's military acumen was valuable, but it would never do to let him get out of hand. He had a reckless streak that went looking for trouble.

"Security ten reporting, sir," interrupted the monitor on Ydre's door.

"Enter," replied the Commander, canceling the door lock with his voice.

The door slid open and two Gardesmen marched through it, then moved to opposite sides of the door. Marc entered the chamber flanked by two more Gardesmen. He was followed by the rest of the patrol. The six Gardesmen deployed themselves around the room to protect the two officers from the criminal. Marc stood in the center of the room, his homespun clothing rumpled from being slept in, a day's growth of beard roughening his features. His hands were bound in front of him and his shoulders were hunched. He escaped cowering by a hairsbreadth. As the silence lengthened, an uncontrollable shiver crawled up his back. His eyes were dark and frightened.

"Stop twitching!" snapped Corbin, and the shock of his voice jolted the slave out of that physical expression of fear.

Marc, intent on maintaining his character, studied Corbin avidly. Here was Dynt. Ran Corbin controlled the kingdom, held it in his closed fist. Marc could sense Ydre's fear of his superior. The subliminal impressions he picked up from Corbin were a sense of complete self-mastery, the subtle tension of a watchspring ever adjusting to its situation with cool, perfect precision.

"You are the slave Drusillus."

Marc ducked his head at Corbin's words. They rustled like dry leaves across the floor.

"Are you mute?" The sarcasm in Corbin's voice was cutting. "The right words might save your life. Better yet, they might ensure your freedom."

Marc's head came up with a jerk. "Free?" he quavered.

"The possibility exists. If you answer my questions."

Marc nodded vigorously.

"You knew another slave of the estate, called Marc."

"Yes, Excellency." Marc's voice was unsteady, but he answered readily.

"Describe him."

"It was many years ago. He was of average height for a fifteen-year-old boy, dark hair and changing eyes, quick to learn."

"No better than I already had. What were his duties?"

"He was watch slave to the children."

"Have you seen him since you were slaves together in that house?"

"No."

"Do you know he is making claim to the throne of Dynt?"

Marc allowed his eyes to widen in surprise, praying they would stay dark. "But how can he? He is a slave."

"Not anymore." Corbin's voice was dry as sand.

Marc gulped and made no comment.

"It would serve my purposes to know about him. Any small quirk you might remember would add to the picture. Of course, I could have your memories extracted, but that is a painful, time-consuming process. It would be so much easier if you would simply tell me."

Marc shuffled his feet before he answered. "I will tell all I know, all I can remember," he managed.

"Good. Where did the slave Marc come from?"

"We were the same age, so I do not really remember, but the story was he was part of a legacy to the senator. He was a very small boy at the time."

"A legacy from whom?"

Marc's brow puckered as he played the game of trying to recall events he had not thought of in years. "An uncle, Excellency. Some sort of eccentric, I think. He left a library, a horse, and the child."

"There were no hints of the child's origins?"

Marc shook his head. "I never heard of any."

"Then it is unlikely any attachment to a prominent family could be proved. All he has is Tenebrae's proclamation." Corbin's words were for himself. "What have you heard of the pretender prince?"

"The lady Tenebrae's heir?" Marc's eyes widened another notch. "You mean he is the same Marc who belonged to Senator Foxxe?"

The look Corbin bent on him was sarcastic in the extreme. "You have answered my question," he replied. "Now tell me all you remember of the slave Marc's personality. Was he quick-tempered, placid, stupid, bright?"

"To tell the truth, Excellency, at the time I did not notice. To look back . . . he had a temper which boiled under the surface. I never saw him lose it, though the air was sometimes black with his anger. He was educated. The senator allowed him access to the library."

"So Foxxe broke the law there, too. Was he an athletic boy?"

"He thought so, but I could beat him in a swimming race."

"I am uninterested in your abilities. Had he any deformities or markings?"

"Not to be seen."

Corbin lowered his head, thinking. His predatory profile made Marc think of an eagle at rest. Though from his words it seemed Corbin did not suspect Marc's identity, shivers chased each other up and down his spine. The fragility of his deception was nerve-wracking, yet it was a magnificent opportunity to study his adversary.

"Describe the last time you saw Marc."

Corbin's voice was dry. As Marc recounted his last meeting with Drusillus, he probed Corbin's face. It was a closed circuit, touched by no outside influence. He read in the impassive features a man apart from the world of the living. It struck him like a sledge that this man who held the reins of the kingdom in his own hand, this man who ordered the lives of a whole string of planets, was himself dead. It was ironic this soulless creature should spend his life administering to the living.

Marc searched the man's face again, unwilling to accept his own verdict. This was the same man who had once loved Tenebrae with such passion he was williing to kill for her, a man of such violent reactions that in the end he had killed her. No violence showed on his face. It was as if he had erased all memory of those days, freeing himself from the enslaving clutches of emotion.

Marc barely kept his eyes from lighting in excitement. He had found a key to a deadly adversary. Corbin placed emotion outside the sphere of his actions. Somewhere there must still be a spark of feeling, deeply banked and ignored. For the most part, he would react like a machine. Sympathy or pity would never play a part in his plans. And like a well-engineered computer, he would be ruthlessly efficient. Whatever stood in his way would be destroyed. He might kill for recreation, but never something that was beneficial to him. His raids on independent traders had all the earmarks of a stag hunt, but the maverick traders stood in the way of the prosperity of the crown trading company. He was destroying vermin.

"And you have not seen him since?" asked Corbin as Marc finished his story.

Marc shook his head. It was the truth. He had not seen Drusillus since that day. No matter that the ex-slave was now living in Pteron, a free man with another name.

Corbin flicked his hand and the Gardesman closed in on Marc. "Take him back to his cell. Blazon can sell him for whatever he'll bring."

"But, Excellency, you said if I helped you I would be free," Marc whined, fawning.

Corbin regarded him with impersonal coldness. "I said I would consider it. You had nothing of importance to impart. You have earned nothing."

"But, Excellency, I told you all I know!" Marc's voice was desperate, pleading.

"That is of no consequence. Take him back to his cell."

The Gardesman grasped Marc by the arms and turned him,

dragging him from the room. Marc twisted his head around, pleading with the Seneschal for his freedom. Corbin ignored him. He was borne sobbing into the corridor where he collapsed.

"Get to your feet!" snapped a Gardesman as Marc lay huddled on the floor.

When he did not move, they picked him up by the arms and dragged him back to the detention area. As they flung him into his cell and slammed the door, Marc's hysteria vanished. He lay where he had been thrown, aware the cells were visually monitored at all times. He had passed the computer viewers on his way to Corbin's quarters and every screen had been activated, even those to empty cells. However, his quick eyes had detected no light indicator for the audio monitors. It seemed they remained off unless the Gardesman on duty chose to listen in on his charges.

He lay where he had been thrown and closed his eyes, letting the interview sink into his subconscious mind, aware that if he let it go, his impressions would surface again, clearer and stronger than before.

Corbin, on the other hand, showed no such patient passivity. He was thoroughly irritated. He had learned nothing from Drusillus. The man had parroted back known facts like a walking computer chip. Admittedly, Drusillus had not seen Marc in years, but Corbin found it hard to credit the man's total lack of personal information on someone with whom he lived and worked. He had threatened to extract the thoughts he wanted from Drusillus' mind. He toyed with the prospect. There was something about the cringing little beast that did not track. Corbin's contempt for the man's cowardice and readiness to sink under threats prompted him to dismiss Drusillus as an unprofitable source of information. He was the kind of man who would say what he thought would save him in a given situation. That he was practicing a deception Corbin considered, but did not credit. Drusillus did not have the imagination for a convincing lie.

The Seneschal pushed Drusillus to the back of his mind. He would always be in his cell, available for further questioning.

He turned to the subservient Ydre, who was patiently awaiting his master's whim, and resumed a discussion over a new security air-lock system for the command center which the interrogation had interrupted.

CHAPTER 14

Stella craned toward the porthole, trying to catch sight of *Ravening*. A portion of the ship's nose was visible, blunt and dark. Beyond it ranged the four squadrons that had destroyed Lazur. She shivered. There were ten women in the shuttle, all of them slaves. They were the cream of a select crop and it was with difficulty Stella had managed to invade their ranks. Their slave collars were elegant twists of copper and gold. They wore uniform white tunics clasped around the waist with a copper and gold belt that was a more intricate variation of the slave collars. The tunics were short, filmy, and revealing —the uniform of Ydre's stable of house slaves. The women wore heavy makeup, each with elaborately painted eyes and mouth. Their complicated hairstyles were dramatic and oddly flattering. Stella wore a red wig curled and plaited into a lover's knot on top of her head. Her eyes had been painted to resemble butterfly wings in black and green and gold.

The shuttle moved along *Ravening*'s side and the port was filled with its sleek dark body. Stella alone took notice of it. The shuttle moved closer to the belly of Ydre's ship, and the airlock slipped into place with a thump that rocked the shuttle. One of the women uttered an involuntary cry of fright.

She was a small girl with a flat, round face like a rose petal and huge, uptilted violet eyes. The makeup and layered curls of her black hair could not disguise her youth or her fear. A

flaming anger, red as her false hair, flashed over Stella. The
girl was Ydre's pleasure, and he would destroy her.

The airlock hissed as it was pressurized. The hatch opened,
and a Gardesman entered the cabin. He motioned the slaves to
their feet with a gesture, the looped plaits of the whip he held
coiled like the gleaming scales of a blacksnake. Stella could
feel his eyes on her. She cursed the necessity for a disguise
which made her subject to the whims of men. It was something she had sworn she would never do, but for Lar she
donned a house slave's garb without a moment's hesitation.
She knew also the advantages of her position. Once aboard
the *Ravening*, she would have almost unlimited freedom to
roam the ship. Control centers and the engine room would be
off limits, but no one would give a thought to a house slave
wandering down any other corridor on the ship at all hours of
the day and night. It would make contacting Lar easy.

The airlock door opened, and they were hurried down the
short ramp between the two vessels. Their arrival on the *Ravening* was noted by a solitary Gardesman who presided over
the shuttle dock. Stella knew the ship had a huge docking bay,
but the shuttle had avoided it. Instead it docked on the side of
the ship at the third level. This made it possible for the
Gardesmen to move the new house slaves to their quarters
without marching them through hordes of curious workmen.

As the corridor stretched out in front of her, Stella studied
the construction of the ship. The branching corridors they
were hurried past led down halls lined with smooth closed
doors. The markings on the walls were numerical, obviously
meant to identify one's position on the ship, but, without a
point of reference, she had no idea where she was.

They turned down a hallway which terminated in a rounded
cul-de-sac filled with, of all things, live flowers. The lead
Gardesman pushed a sensor lock, and a door parted in front of
him. He stood back, gesturing with his whip that the women
were to enter the cabin. Stella found herself in a comfortable
foyer furnished with opulent overstuffed couches. Doors
ranged around the room like those in the story of the lady and
the tiger. The Gardesman threw a sheaf of papers on the nearest chaise.

"These are your quarters. You each have your own room.

You have the run of the ship, except for control and engineering."

"Even security?" asked a dark-haired girl with a hard, coral-tinted mouth.

"Security also. I have provided scans of the ship's layout." He smirked at his word choice, but the women did not react. "You will study them. You will not be caught in a restricted area—and they are clearly marked—or you will forfeit your life. You will remain in your cabins until the fourth bell. I want no distractions with the Seneschal on board. However, once the evening's entertainment is begun, you are free to wander the ship."

The Gardesman turned on his heel and went out, but before the door slid shut, Stella noted he set two of his men to guard it. Before the others began to squabble over the rooms, Stella moved to a door at the right of the foyer entrance. As she approached, the door opened to receive her, and she found herself inside a cocoon of pale green silk and velvet. The room was round and the walls ran up to a small circular window in the ceiling. The window was made to look like glass with a leaded design in green buds. Pale yellow light shone through it, washing down the curved green walls. It was a hidden world, a bubble in which Stella squirmed like a chrysalis striving to escape. She sat down on the edge of the circular bed, glad to be alone.

She chafed at being restricted to quarters. Now that she was on board she wanted action. She smoothed the paper she had picked up with one hand, unfolding it over the bed. It showed the twelve deck levels of the ship with restricted areas marked in red. They were few. All corridors were clearly marked, even little storage areas and maintenance alleyways. She knew at a glance it was an invaluable tool. Outside her door she could hear the babble and squeal of voices as the bickering over quarters began. She got up, set the lock on her door, and returned to the bed. She began to pore over the map spread out in front of her, committing it to memory with the same absorption with which she tackled a new piece of music.

Marc lay curled on his side, his eyes shut against the uninterrupted whiteness of his cell. He was hovering on the far side of sleep, his mind wandering aimlessly in search of answers to questions not yet asked. It was a restful search, without the pressure of consciousness. He reveled in it, knowing at a deeper level he would wake to disquieting problems. The paths of his mind wound and twisted like the forest trails he knew on Adyton. He wandered down them, the refracting light of his thoughts painting them with dappled patterns. Always ahead, elusive as the legendary dynteryx, was a pale gold dream of beauty.

He jerked awake as the door of his cell slammed open.

"Up!" ordered a Gardesman. His dark bulk filled the doorway. Marc swung his legs over the side of the sleeping pallet and sat blinking in the bright light. "Up!" the Gardesman repeated peremptorily. "You have a visitor."

As Marc rose to his feet a peal of laughter floated past the Gardesman's shoulder. Despite the inane inflection, he recognized it, and his heart lifted. The laughter sounded again, and Lar appeared behind the Gardesman's broad shoulders.

"Here you are, minstrel," the Gardesman growled. "Don't stay too long. We may forget you're a guest." The man's smile was not pleasant.

"You jest! To leave me incarcerated with this lowlife would cut off your own entertainment! Where else on the length of this ship are you going to come by a song?"

"The library tapes offer a wider selection than you could know in a dozen lifetimes."

"But," answered Lar in a slightly inebriated voice, "they haven't my charm."

"You overestimate that. When you want out, wave to the monitor. Maybe I'll see you."

With a particularly nasty smirk the Gardesman shoved Lar across the threshold and shut the door. Its resounding crash was a divider solid as death. Lar grinned foolishly, maintaining his pretense of drunkenness. Marc continued to stand where he was, as uncertain as the slave he played. Lar brandished a fistful of white cloth, and a slave's collar of twisted brass wire. From behind his back he produced a pair of sandals which he threw on the sleeping couch. The bundle of cloth he threw at Marc.

"I brought you a change of clothing, slave, so you can dress the part."

Marc, with his back turned to the monitor, raised his eyebrows. Lar let the counterfeit golden slave collar dangle from his fingers. In the cell's brilliant white light it glittered like precious metal. Marc gazed at the collar in fascination.

"A collar to attach your chain to," Lar commented. "The Seneschal can drag you through the streets of Pteron at his heels."

Lar let the collar drop into Marc's outstretched hands. There was an indefinable difference in the cell's atmosphere, a sense of being sealed up, that told Marc the audio monitors had been turned off, but his native caution prompted him to make sure their conversation could not be overheard. He flung the slave collar on the bed with the sandals and the tunic, taking care the complex knot at the center of the collar lay face up. In the heart of the knot was a clear amber jewel. From previous experience, Marc knew it to be one of Inspi's clever communication devices. Altered slightly, it could be set to jam any frequency within a short radius. He cocked an eye at Lar.

Lar's nod was no more than the lowering of an eyelid. He reached for the collar and ran his hand lovingly over the metal, pausing to let his finger trace a circular pattern on the face of the jewel.

"How thoughtful of you," Marc said, indicating the clothing.

Lar grinned, taking care to look a bit tipsy, in case the guard was watching. "Wasn't it? The perfect disguise and no one even questioned my right to give it to you."

"Quit, leave off! I want to know what's happening out there! Here I am, right next to Coryelle, and I can do nothing —not even let her know I'm here."

"She is completely isolated," Lar admitted. "But there may be a way to free all the companions. Tonight there's going to be a party."

"Now you're talking party. I'm going mad and you're anticipating an evening's pleasure."

"Will you calm down?" Lar regarded Marc curiously. In all his experience with his friend, he had never seen him so distracted. "The Commander has unusual tastes in entertainment."

"I don't care about his personal quirks! I want action!" Marc was distinctly annoyed.

"I'm trying to give you action. Ydre is planning to throw a party for the Seneschal. He has a habit of using his prisoners as the evening's entertainment."

"Even Coryelle?"

"I think so."

"Then they'll all be together."

Lar nodded. "It is the best chance we're going to have. Tomorrow Corbin departs, presumably with Coryelle in tow —and perhaps you as well!"

"We will need transportation."

"There is a docking bay on the VIP deck. The banquet hall is one corridor away."

"I need to become familiar with the ship."

"There are detailed schematics taped to the underside of the slave collar. Much better than the general plans we had."

Marc's eyebrows shot up. "You were taking quite a chance."

"This whole mess is a chance."

Marc grinned at him unexpectedly. "By the way, congratulations."

"For what?"

"Being alive. How many others are there?"

"The four ships of our squad—I am not sure of the others. Perhaps twenty people." Lar's eyes took on a darker tinge. "Out of hundreds, that's all we have left?"

"When I left, three craft had made it to the space buoy. Gisarme is alive, and Racque. I sent Stella to the king." Marc caught the quickly veiled relief in Lar's green eyes.

"I knew about Racque." He grinned. "I was there when you arrived. You did give me a turn."

"I know it was harebrained, but it was the only way we could think of to invade the ship. So far it's working. No one questions Racque at all. Blazon is a daunting alter ego."

"I haven't been able to talk to him—for just that reason. Blazon was never known for his dedication to pleasure. He isn't the type to welcome a song. I've been stretching my poor brains to come up with a way to contact him that won't arouse suspicion, but so far there's been no opportunity."

"If what you say is true, you will need to consult him. We must take Ydre and Corbin by complete surprise, cut them off from their Garde, and escape with such speed they are left reeling."

Lar was nodding. "Right now Ydre is feeling as smug as a cat in a nest of field mice. He's overconfident. There will be the usual complement of Gardesmen, but I do not think he'll take extra precautions even for a security prisoner like Coryelle. After all, where would she run?"

"What is his attitude toward a rescue attempt?"

"By now, laughter. There is, however, the matter of his ship's captain, Sphaleros. The man is too competent. He will not allow success to soften his reactions. He may not attend the dinner for Corbin."

"Then his suspicion is the biggest danger we face."

"Once I would have said that."

Marc regarded his friend quizzically. The enigmatic reply was not like Lar. "And now?"

Lar sighed. "Now our biggest danger is betrayal from within."

Marc reacted as if he had been struck. He took a quick step backward. "From within? There are so few of us left . . . who . . . ?"

The unfinished question hung in the air like a sentence. The same question was attacking Lar, but he knew they had no time for it now.

"I have no idea, but so far I've intercepted two messages revealing your disguise. If we don't act quickly, the odds are you and Racque will be found out."

Marc's lips compressed. "You are right. First we must escape the raven's clutches, then we can worry about the traitor in our midst. I will study the plans you've brought me and try to figure a way to make the strike maneuver work for us. You, meanwhile, need to contact Racque and concern yourself with an escape route."

"I will report back before this evening."

"What excuse will you have this time?"

"I shall pretend you stole my alto recorder." Lar's eyes

twinkled. "It's inside the tunic. By the way, it might be wise
to dress as a slave. There are fifty or more of them on board,
excluding house slaves. They are allowed to go about their
business as if they were mindless androids. You would go
unnoticed."

"I hate this."

"It's a fool's errand."

Marc waved Lar's answer aside. "Not that. I hate the enforced idleness, the inactivity, the sense of helplessness."

"You, who were always so controlled, so calm under pressure?"

"I'm still controlled or I'd be clawing the walls. You should
hear the talk about Ydre."

"You mean his ways with women?"

"Yes. The thought of Coryelle in his hands. I want to say
I'd almost rather see her dead, but that is my jealousy speaking. While she lives, there is hope."

"I always wondered about you and Coryelle."

Marc's gesture was an involuntary affirmation.

"She cares for you, you know."

"Of course. But I was her slave, and slaves are cattle."

"All men are born to be slaves to the women they love. I
think you do her an injustice."

Marc shook his head. "It's not possible," he said.

"If it comes to that, you *are* heir to the throne of Dynt."

"Not by blood."

"No," answered Lar mildly, "by virtue."

Marc dismissed Lar's arguments in the warm brown depths
of his eyes. "My head tells me you are wrong," he said, "but
my heart is not so easily controlled. Above all—above my
honor or the crown—I wish to save her. Not even all the
companions, just Coryelle. It frightens me."

"Are you giving in to this rash impulse to ignore the cries
for help from your followers?"

"I cannot."

"Then you have not chosen a selfish path. You are not
likely to. Were Stella in the same position, I could not keep
my sanity."

With his back to the monitor, Marc smiled a sad little smile
as he reached out to grasp Lar's arm. "Thank you, my friend,

for your sense. Locked up here like a slave, I have not always thought clearly. Now I will bend all my energies to the attack. You have given me something to sink my teeth into. And Lar, do your best not to jeopardize your cover. It is invaluable."

"I know. I will not be foolish or rash, but it will be hard to act against my instincts."

"You have always brought me the gift of laughter. That may be the greatest boon to sanity of all. Go now, before the Gardesman becomes suspicious. You have been here too long. And—take care."

Marc deactivated the electronic jammer, and Lar waved to the monitor with both hands, making an idiotic face as he did so. He was still waving when the lock clunked, and the door swooshed open.

"Turn around, minstrel, your audience is over here."

At the Gardesman's dry voice, Lar swung slowly around. "All right," he flung over his shoulder at Marc, "but if you don't dress the part how will anyone know you're a slave? They hang free men."

Lar's speech was just slurred enough to be believable, and the Gardesman was wholly taken in by his deception.

"Come on, come on," he muttered. "I don't have all day."

"Am I interrupting your game of knucklebones?" Lar queried innocently.

The Gardesman growled, shoving Lar out of the cell as roughly as he had pushed him in. Lar waved ineffectively as the door crashed shut behind him.

Marc sank down on his couch and picked up the slave collar. The amber jewel winked at him conspiratorially. He turned it over and detached the twelve microdots from beneath a central plate of metal. He knew the jewel, as well as being a communications device, was capable of magnifying whatever it was held above to three times its normal size. Placed in front of a light source, it was capable of projecting an image. Marc's cell was filled with light. It was part of Ydre's ingenious system of torture to make it almost impossible for his captives to sleep. He knew he would have ample opportunity to study the schematics, for a projection on the back wall of the cell would be invisible to the monitor. Ydre's overconfidence was his tool. His security was lax. So far it

was the only circumstance that favored the companions'
cause.

Ran Corbin's ruthless brilliance did not. Marc owned he
was impressed by the Seneschal. Under his hand Dynt had
become a well-oiled machine not without merit, but in its
single-minded search for efficiency it ostracized the human
heart, much as Corbin had killed his own. To take the machine and turn it into a less efficient but more humane tool, a
tool that fit the hand of every man, was alluring, but it must
wait another day. If he died on the *Ravening*, he would never
have the chance to try.

Marc subdued his concern for Coryelle, his fear of the spy,
and his personal uncertainty. Tenebrae had once taught him to
disregard his emotions if they would not help him. Right now
he needed to commit the design of the *Ravening* to memory
and plot a surprise for Ydre and Corbin. He needed unclut-
tered logic. He slipped the first microdot under the slave collar and held it up to the light. An image of the ship's hold
appeared on the far wall, and he began to memorize every
detail.

CHAPTER 15

The Gardesman snapped to attention, cold sweat popping out
on the back of his neck. Ran Corbin's trim, graceful form did
not move. He waited passively in front of the laser gate which
marked the entrance to *Ravening*'s maximum security section.

"I would like to see the girl Coryelle," he said mildly. His
voice was sheathed, a fine blade in its protective covering.

"At once, Excellency!" answered the Gardesman.

Corbin's posture became taut, and the Gardesman could
feel the cold wind of the ship's air filters on his already sensitive nape. He gulped. "Clearance, Excellency." His voice was

pleading, a far cry from the bold challenge he had been trained to give.

Corbin offered his right hand for inspection by the security computer's watchful eye. His hand was enveloped in a blaze of light and released. The Gardesman remained at attention, trying his best not to meet the Seneschal's eye and yet stare straight ahead. When the computer flashed a blue light on its board, he touched the controls and the laser latticework melted into harmless atmosphere. Corbin walked quietly through the portal without so much as a glance in the Gardesman's direction.

"She is in the fourth cell down on the starboard side of the corridor," he volunteered.

"Thank you," acknowledged Corbin, never turning his head.

"My duty, Excellency," replied the man according to formula. He did not dare accompany the Seneschal, for the computer station was his post, yet he did not like to see him unescorted. He turned back to the computer, and touched the laser field into existence.

Corbin strolled down the corridor with its security scans and multitude of biosensors, secure in the knowledge the information they were recording concerning his vital statistics had long ago been cleared with the central computer. There was not a security outpost in the kingdom he could not enter at will.

He paused in front of Coryelle's cell, and regarded the door as a small child would a gift. Inside the cell was one of the last survivors of Eban Foxxe's family. This, in itself, was reward enough. That his old enemy had not lived to see Coryelle's destruction was cause for regret, but he found satisfaction in the knowledge Foxxe's sins were atoned with the lives of children.

And Coryelle was no innocent. Raised by the woman Corbin loved, she was a mockery to him. Tenebrae once laughed in his face. Now, long after her death, Coryelle's presence was an echo of that laughter. She was the epitome of quality, with the sense of royalty he loved, and later came to hate, in Tenebrae. She, too, was a mortal woman, and she would have feet of clay as well as a princess. For a moment of lust she

might forsake all she knew to be right. His contempt showed
in the darkness of his bottomless eyes.

The girl meant something to Marc. Once he chose to save
her life at the risk of his own. In spite of all Ydre's assur-
ances, Corbin knew he would try again. She was wonderful
bait, yet his infrequently aroused emotions urged her destruction. He knew he would not follow their promptings, but he
was annoyed by them. They had been quiet a long time.

He opened Coreyelle's door to catch her in the act of pacing. At the sound of the door, she paused, looking at the
intruder. With her long gold hair plaited in leather, her high
boots and green tunic, she looked like a woodsman's daughter. Her sturdy figure had nothing in common with Tenebrae's
tall, aloof elegance. Her rounded limbs told of a life of action
totally out of place in the king's court, but in the beauty of her
delicate features he read her heritage. It was echoed in the
patrician hauteur of her expression. She said nothing.

"Please do not let me interrupt your exercise," said Corbin. "I am a firm believer in maintaining one's equipment,
though I am afraid you will have no use for it in the near
future."

"Do come in," returned Coryelle. She was not so polished
as Corbin, and the sarcasm in her voice was marked. She
gestured to her sleeping couch. "Sit down. I am afraid this is
the extent of the hospitality I can offer you, Seneschal, though
you seem to have arranged everything for me."

"It was my pleasure," he responded warmly, accepting her
invitation. Coryelle remained standing.

"I am sure it was."

"Yes, indeed. Your resistance has been an irritating little
tack in my shoe. I am glad to have it removed."

"Do not deceive yourself, sir. The tack has merely changed
position."

Corbin regarded Coryelle silently. He thought to disturb
her, but she seemed perfectly willing to accept his silence.
Her bravery startled him. Many of his officers fidgeted like
children if he held them so.

"I do not believe there is enough left of your resistance to
set up a new base, much less regroup. Face it, my dear, the

coalition fostered by your uncle has crumbled under the touch of the pretender."

Coryelle was nervous, and her temper flared. "You are the only pretender. You pretend to be a man, but you kill innocent women and children with no regard for honor. You, sir, are the imitation—of a human being. Marc is entirely genuine."

Corbin found himself almost smiling at having struck a nerve. "Well, well, well," he said mildly, knowing it would irritate her, "the kitten spits! Honor is a toy for men with nothing better to do. I cannot afford it."

"Well spoken, Seneschal! I am not surprised it is beyond you."

To his amazement, Corbin found he was irritated by her comment. It raised the old issue of paternity. His lack of title still rankled in spite of his complete control of the nominal nobility on Dynt, including the king.

"My abilities surpass anything you can imagine, in ways you cannot fathom. That is not your concern. Your own welfare is."

"You have indicated your preference in the matter. It is clear you are not going to set me free."

"I might."

Coryelle regarded him with scorn. "And the rivers of Dynt might run salt."

His crooked smile, so seldom used, almost lent charm to his face. "I repeat what I said: I might."

Coryelle sighed. "You are now about to explain your terms to me. They will be terms I cannot accept, but the consequences will be so dire I will, in the end, be forced to. It will, however, do me no good. I will still end up in the stewpot."

"I find your comparisons rough, but appropriate." He was enjoying himself.

"I do not care for your opinions. The fact remains that all the discussion in the world will not save me in the end. Why do it?"

Corbin's rusty smile broke through again. "For fun," he replied. "I do not think you can resist learning about me any more than I can resist questioning you. We are caught, you see, by our own curiosity."

Coryelle gave in. An interview with the Seneschal, no matter how dangerous, was preferable to the solitary whiteness of her cell. "Proceed," she said.

"You bow to the inevitable. Your intelligence, young woman, does you credit. As I said, I might be persuaded to let you go."

"And as I said, I have difficulty in believing that."

"I do not lie. I have no need to. I say it again. I would let you go, in return for a simple piece of information."

Coryelle's eyes spoke her question, but her lips remained stubbornly sealed.

"You know how much I want Marc, who calls himself Dynteryx."

"I can guess."

"He is the price of your life."

Coryelle, waiting for this ultimatum, laughed. "You wish me to trade my life for his."

Corbin nodded, his face registering the innocent conviction she would entertain the idea. Coryelle was not seduced by it. "He saved my life once. You wish me to repay him by sacrificing his?"

"He would not wish you to die. Even at the cost of his own life."

Coryelle whirled on him. For a moment he thought she meant to strike him. "You are a viciously clever man, and you are right. But my actions are my own, and I will not give him into your hands."

"I rather expected such an answer."

"Besides, you have neglected something."

Corbin's look was incredulous.

"Even you can make a mistake. You forgot one small detail: I do not know if Marc is alive."

"Of course you don't. You do know what he would do if he were alive, where he would go. For that information I will spare your life."

She shook her head. "If I did what you ask, and you kept your bargain, I would gain nothing. I would lose myself. What is life worth in such circumstances?"

Corbin's eyes flashed briefly in admiration. It was something he did not often reveal. "Under those conditions, life is a torturous purgatory. A greater punishment for your uncle's sins than I could devise in a millennium."

Coryelle's eyes widened as she grasped the devious subtlety of the reward Corbin was offering her. It had a magnitude of evil she could not entirely fathom.

"Check," she said tentatively.

"And mate," Corbin affirmed. "I do, of course, have another option."

"Indeed you are full of surprises."

"Oh, yes. It is possible to have the information I wish forcibly extracted. It is a painful process, involving drugs and a carefully planned program of torture. In the end I will learn all you know of everything. It would be so much easier if you would simply tell me."

"Even in the face of that, I cannot."

"But I will learn it all eventually." Corbin's voice was persuasive, soft.

"But not soon. The process you mention is a time-consuming one. It has even been known to take months. By that time, the information you obtain will be so out of date it will no longer help you. And I assure you, Seneschal, I will fight you with every ounce of strength I possess."

"Your love is stronger than I anticipated."

Coryelle's eyes widened. This man whose life was devoid of warmth detected her emotion as if it were stamped on her face. Perhaps it was. It was the deep center of her life. Perhaps Corbin's cold heart recoiled instinctively from its opposite.

Corbin was staring at her, his black eyes emotionless, flat. She had once seen obsidian jewels, smooth surfaces polished like glass. They reminded her of a pool of nothing, deep and dark as eternity. Corbin's eyes were like that. Pity rose in her throat for a man who had denied himself the pain of living, and the only joy life can bring.

"There is another way." Corbin's soft voice was sinister. He reached for an oblong panel on one of the bare white walls and pressed it. A larger panel slid back to reveal a viewscreen. "This will not work for you," Corbin informed her. "It is activated by my handprint." He pressed the oblong again, and the viewscreen bleeped to life. "Holding cell A-5," he said.

The screen bleeped again, and the cell materialized. It held the men and women of her escape squad. Corbin stood with his hand poised above the control bar.

"These prisoners are of no consequence to me. They can tell me nothing I do not already know. If you do not reveal the probable whereabouts of the pretender, they will die. Now. With one touch of my hand."

The flatness of Corbin's voice told Coryelle he meant what he said. The people in the cell were military statistics to him. He had no use for them.

"But Seneschal, any one of the people in that cell could tell you what you want to know. The rendezvous points were no secret to the resistance."

"You will not convince me that when disaster struck, the trusted few did not flee to a more secret meeting place. Marc would immediately see the danger in following a previously well-known plan."

"I do not presume to speak his thoughts."

"Choose!" demanded Corbin. "The lives of these vermin are in your hands. Their blood will stain them. You will be sullied."

"That is something you cannot do. You will be their death, not I. You run from the responsibility like a squealing pig from the butcher." Coryelle's anger was sparking dangerously. "If you wish to kill, do not try to dodge the blame!"

"Have it your own way," said Corbin, and touched the control bar. There was a thin whine and the airless screams of those already dead. The flash of white fire cleared, and the cell was empty, hushed. Its white walls no longer bore the shadows of the living. Coryelle could almost smell the stench of rotting vegetation this particular form of execution left behind. Nausea swept her soul.

Corbin watched her clinically, noticing her pallor and an involuntary tremor she did not try to hide. "You are right about the amount of time the mind extraction takes," he said. "While I am aboard the *Ravening*, I have neither the time nor the facilities for it. Instead, I will terminate your compatriots every twelve hours until you decide to be more cooperative.

You will watch them die in any number of ways. This was by far the cleanest."

"My uncle thought you were a beast. He was wrong. A beast cares for something. You do not, not even for yourself. You therefore win, because there is no reasoning with you. You cannot comprehend my arguments. They are therefore worthless. I will tell you what you wish to know, and pray that Marc is dead."

"You are a stubborn young woman. It is too bad you could not have come to your senses before your friends died."

Corbin's dry statement was a knife driven into her heart.

"In a direct trajectory from Lazur there is an oblong moon. That moon was our appointed rendezvous."

"Your statement will be confirmed. For the present, you have saved the remainder of your friends."

Coryelle studied Corbin's handsome face, her expression closed.

"You see," he said, "how misguided your love can be. It condemned your friends. Now it is incapable of saving your slave. It is a poor standard on which to base your life."

"It is more painful than I can say, but I would choose no other. You are the murderer, not I. You started with yourself. You care for nothing, not even the kingdom you rule. Seneschal! The title makes me laugh! You are no servant of the state! What do you serve, Ran Corbin? What sinister power drives you?"

Coryelle's words struck sparks. Fire flamed from the depths of Corbin's eyes, fire she thought was dead. It was a violent blast of raw anger, and it staggered her. She had mistaken the darkness of his soul. Beneath the empty ashes there lurked a nest of coals, live coals that leaped into violence with a savagery that was enervating. She realized the man's capacity for passion was enormous. The flames died, and Coryelle distrusted, for a moment, her sensibilities. The black eyes were again empty wells.

"It is not my habit to answer questions from a captive. In your case, I will make an exception. Nothing drives me. I do as I please, and it pleases me to control Dynt. My motivation is none of your business."

"The motives of any ruler are the business of his subjects."

Corbin's laugh was mirthless. "I will attribute that statement to your extreme youth. I had forgotten such naiveté still exists."

"A seneschal is the servant of those he rules. You have enslaved them." Coryelle had forgotten all caution.

"You proclaim your youth by your lack of knowledge. I have no more time for word games. You have cheated death —for now. Be grateful for each moment. You do not know which one will be your last."

Coryelle maintained an angry silence. Her dark blue eyes were flashing with roused spirit, and her chin was set defiantly. Corbin bowed, paying tribute to her beauty and her courage. It was a surprising reminder of his familiarity with the etiquette of court. She received his courtesy with a royal nod. Corbin backed from the room in parody of the courtiers of his youth. At this moment Coryelle reminded him most strongly of Tenebrae. As the door to her cell slammed shut, he had a last view of her standing regally defiant. Preoccupied, he left the security area.

Coryelle, once the door closed, sat down on the sleeping couch, her eyes lost. An uncontrollable fit of shivering engulfed her. Six people she had known and worked with were dead. Corbin had terminated their lives as he would cut a stalk of celery. They were gone. Whatever brave words she threw in Corbin's face, she knew she would always feel their deaths. She stared at her hands, almost expecting to see them stained with blood. It would be easier if they were. Blood on the hands washes off. Blood on the soul is another matter. There would be more. Once Corbin found her information was a ruse, he would avenge himself on her through her colleagues. Her only hope was that by the time the information was disproved, she would be dead.

The spy crumpled a piece of paper, and threw it across the room. There was mockery in the blank piece of paper. His messages were no longer verbal, for his present position prevented such open contact with Corbin's men. Instead they were transmitted in a complex code. The last three messages had not been acknowledged.

He thumbed through the codebook. A change in code might

alter his chances of getting through. He had an uneasy feeling his messages were being intercepted. Though there were no computer taps to be detected from his end, there could be no other explanation for the lack of response. If he changed the code, it would be received by another computer station. The odds of bypassing the break in the chain were estimated at seventy-five percent. He sighed. He was comfortable with the old code and he was loath to change, but he knew he must follow procedure. If he did not, his reward was sure to be withdrawn. He wanted the prize, wanted it more than anything else. For it he was willing to take the most desperate chances. He smoothed the pages of the codebook, and placed it next to the sheet of spotless white paper. He licked the end of his scriber and laboriously began to scribe the symbols the computer would decode into a message.

CHAPTER 16

Coryelle lay on her stomach, her head pillowed in her arms to shut out the ruthless white light of her cell. Tears made a damp patch on the stiff mattress of her bed, but she was silent and still. The surveillance equipment which documented her movements was ignorant of her tears, but under a veil of her shining hair, her eyes swam with them. She was alone. Try as she might, the plain truth of her situation was no longer possible to evade.

She had nothing but the hope of Marc's survival, and that was a dream. The details of her probable fate were vague, but infinite variations of degradation and death clamored at her. As a child Marc had saved her. He gave her years and love. To cheat fate a second time would be a lucky turn of events, but one she could not expect.

Marc would not come. To let those words rise in her mind

caused Coryelle a kind of pain that wrenched the tears from her. It was a blinding, obliterating thought. She swam in fluid agony in the colorless cubic womb. The room closed around her, empty, isolated, and time had no meaning. There was nowhere to turn, nothing to do, and no one to rely upon but herself.

Stella slipped through the door, relieved when it swished shut behind her. She had exchanged the white tunic for a dress of filmy blue-green material that clung to her figure like sea-weed. It was woven with an iridescent thread which caught the light as it moved across her body. It was provocative in the extreme. Her elaborately coifed red wig was adorned with a single green jewel, clear as seawater. She had repainted her face, this time creating a pattern beneath her eyebrows like the delicate veins in a fish's fins. Her mouth was tinted into a coral bow, her cheeks highlighted by coral rouge undercut by silver. The high silver sandals she wore showcased her long legs in their sparkling hose, but they made speed difficult. Nevertheless, she hurried down the corridor.

It cost all her ready cash to bribe two of the girls to seduce the Gardesmen stationed at the door, but if she could find Racque it would be money well spent. Three house slaves were already living in the court, and Stella was quick to scrape an acquaintance with them. One woman had been full of news and the doings of the ship. She was a favorite of Ydre's chef, and there was little that went on aboard *Ravening* she did not know. When she mentioned Blazon's presence, Stella's heart raced. She questioned the woman about him, and the house slave laughed in Stella's face.

"You don't think you'll get near that iceberg, do you?"

"My specialty," responded Stella, "is thawing ice."

The woman shuddered. "Who would want to. The man's a cold-blooded killer. He's slaughtered hundreds from all I'm told. To have him would be like sharing a bed with death itself."

Privately Stella wondered how the woman regarded Ydre and his officers, who had probably killed thousands in their careers, but she replied, "I find it exciting. Are you going to tell me where he's quartered or not?"

"What is it to me? I'll tell you. He's on the VIP deck, but at the opposite end of the ship from the Seneschal's quarters. Room one-fifteen."

Stella smirked at her. "For someone who has no interest in the matter, you certainly know where he is."

"I admit to some curiosity, but that's all it is. That one scares me."

"Wish me luck."

The woman shook her head. "You'll need more than that."

But luck, thought Stella as she tripped down the long hallway, was what she did need. She knew no one would give her a second glance except the two Gardesmen who were supposed to be watching the new arrivals, or the officer of the Garde who had escorted them to their quarters. It was a big ship. If she could get clear of the slave quarters, she would not be stopped.

She paused in front of the lift tube, tapping her foot impatiently as she waited for it to reach her level. She watched its slow descent with mounting annoyance, hoping her money would keep the Gardesmen occupied for more than a few minutes.

Racque lay back on the yielding solidity of his bed and stared at the ceiling. It had been many years since he felt such luxury. The floating foam cushions in the mattress molded themselves to the contours of his body, and muscles he had not thought were sore relaxed gratefully. He sighed, reveling in the moment of physical indulgence, even if he could not escape the desperate plight of his friends. So far he had been almost totally hamstrung in his attempts to reach Lar without arousing suspicion. Soon suspicion would make no difference. He would have to chance breaking the musician's cover before tonight's show. Surely Lar, in his capacity as minstrel, would be asked to attend. Racque knew it would be an opportunity to free the companions, particularly since they were to be gathered in one place, and under looser security than he would have to face in Ydre's detention center.

He stretched, thinking of Marc alone in the bleak whiteness of his cell. He knew his prince was enduring torture more acute than anything Ydre could devise, for he was waiting in ignorance—in ignorance even of Coryelle's continued existence. Racque ached to tell him she was still alive and there was a chance to save her, but his notoriety worked against him. If he presumed to check on his prisoner, he would be insulting Ydre's security and offending the Commander's delicate feelings. He had no wish to antagonize the man while he still needed him. He was forced to save a visit until it was absolutely necessary. In the meantime Marc would tear at himself over Coryelle.

Racque smiled, wondering how aware Marc was of his feelings for Coryelle. He had long ago discovered the depth of feeling between the two. Coryelle was easy to read. Her eyes, in unguarded moments, roamed toward Marc like a homing pigeon. Marc's feelings had been more deeply buried. Had the ex-slave misgivings about aspiring to the hand of his former mistress, despite the fact his tenderness for her was clear in every word and gesture? Or was there simply the blindness of familiarity, of the knowledge of Coryelle as a child? Racque did not know. It was not a subject he could broach, close as he had become to Marc. There were depths of privacy in the man he dared not plumb. He had a feeling Coryelle would have to storm the citadel if she wanted him. . . .

His thoughts were abruptly interrupted by a knock on his door. He was on his feet and across the floor in a few swift strides, fully alert. He placed himself to one side as he opened the door. His years as a bounty hunter made such reflexes automatic. When the open door revealed a seductive vision in green and silver, he was dumbfounded.

"Well, don't just stand there!"

"Stella!"

"Of course Stella. Who did you think it was?"

"How did you get here?"

"On a ship," she answered reasonably, as one would address a small child.

Racque waved a hand, erasing his question. "You were supposed to be on Dynt, with the king."

"I was."

"Then why . . . ?"

Stella's dark eyes were bleak with pain.

"Lar," Racque said quietly.

"I don't even know whether he's alive."

"He's alive. On top of that, he's managed to maintain his cover. No one seems to know of his participation in the resistance."

Stella reached out to Racque for support, her fingers tangling in the blue cloth of his shirt. Racque could feel them trembling.

"Headstrong Stella," he said softly. "Still, I would have done the same. You do love him, don't you?"

"I had not realized how much until I thought he was dead."

"It is deathly dangerous for you to be here."

"I had to come."

"I can see that." In spite of the danger, his eyes twinkled mischievously. "I don't think Lar is going to approve of your new profession."

"I couldn't think of any other way. It gives me the freedom of the ship."

"It may come in handy, but have you thought what will happen if one of Ydre's gentle officers decides he wants you for the evening?"

"I've tried not to . . ."

Footsteps sounded down the long corridor, and Stella cast a wild glance over her shoulder. The dark figure striding down the hall sent her into Racque's arms. "Kiss me," she said.

Racque obliged, enjoying Stella's beauty and sensuality even in pretense. His enjoyment was short-lived. Stella was ripped from his arms, her cry of protest ineffective against the man's anger. Racque had a brief glimpse of her flung back against the opposite wall, her eyes frightened, her face ashen under the flamboyant paint.

The man struck him like a ton of rock and he went down, vainly trying to twist out from under his heavier opponent. His hands found the man's shoulders, and he heard the grunt of surprised pain as he touched a pressure point and the grip on his left side slackened. Racque heaved to the left, his free arm braced against his opponent's chest. The man's arm was at his throat, and he was finding it hard to breathe.

As his vision blurred he heard Stella's staccato footsteps as she ran across the hall, and the soft swish as the metal door of his cabin closed. He could feel the other man rocking under

Stella's onslaught, but he knew her efforts would be ineffectual. He strained upward with his free hand, but the man leaned away from it, pinning him tighter.

"Lar! Stop that! Stop it!" Stella's voice was sharp, commanding. Racque felt the arm at his throat ease. "Lares Harken, if you do not release him this minute I will never speak to you again! Let go!"

Stella's determined words seemed to be penetrating Lar's rage, for he rolled slowly off his astonished opponent, breathing hard. Racque braced himself on his elbows, shaking his head. Stella slid down beside Lar, supporting his shoulders.

"You idiot! You might have killed him! Whatever possessed you?"

Lar was staring glumly at Stella. Her protective embrace undercut his anger. He was dumb.

Racque heaved himself to a sitting position and achieved a smile. "Lar, you bonehead. Stella comes halfway across a galaxy, disguises herself as a house slave—with all the risks that entails—all because of you."

"Then why . . . ?"

Stella was still emitting sparks. "Because," she answered sarcastically, "I needed to talk to him, and some oaf was coming down the corridor. I made him kiss me!"

"Not that I wasn't enjoying it," returned Racque with some of his old insouciance, "but the price was a bit high."

Lar's anger crumpled. "Racque, I'm sorry. I don't know what came over me. I might have killed you!"

"You were well on your way." The mocking light in Racque's eyes was oddly comforting. "Do you realize what that would have done to my reputation? 'Famed Bounty Hunter Killed By Minstrel.' I would have been the laughingstock of Dynt. You must promise me you will not make another attempt."

The hand Lar extended was shaky. The enormity of his actions was a shock. Racque grasped it warmly, his slim, elegant fingers surprisingly strong.

"I . . . promise," answered Lar.

Stella dissolved into tears. Both men looked at her in astonishment, then at each other. There was camaraderie in the look they exchanged. Misunderstandings they might have, but there was no way to comprehend a woman.

"It's all right, Stella. Don't cry." Racque's voice was soft.

"Don't, Stella," entreated Lar. "I know I'm a bonehead. Without you I would have murdered a dear friend. It's all right now."

"I . . . know. That's . . . why . . . I'm crying," she managed, her words interspersed by sobs and hiccups.

Racque tried another approach. "Crying makes your nose turn red," he commented. "An interesting shade of crimson. Perhaps you could duplicate it for a costume."

Sparks flashed in Stella's watery dark eyes at the jibe. Racque smiled at her as she realized what he was doing. "All right," she sniffled, "I came here to talk, and I'm going to talk."

Lar chuckled. He loved Stella when her asperity overcame a difficult situation. "So did I," he replied. He and Racque exchanged another look. "If we're going to do it, it has to be tonight."

Racque nodded.

"Do what?" Stella sounded irritated.

Racque took a deep breath. "Free the companions," he said.

"We can do it?"

"We're going to try," answered Lar.

"The chances are about a thousand to one, but it doesn't make any difference. That's why it's so dangerous for you to be here."

"It may be dangerous," answered Stella, "but it's also going to be helpful. I can move about the ship at will. No one will question me." She lifted her chin and regarded both men with haughty determination. "I intend to help."

"I would not presume to stop you," answered Racque.

"The party tonight is the key."

Racque nodded. "All the prisoners will be assembled— even Coryelle, I think. No one will be expecting anything. It is too long after the attack on Lazur. They are lulled into carelessness. We must be swift and completely organized."

"We will need transport in case of success," mused Lar. "There is a small docking bay on the VIP deck. Corbin's ship is there, as well as escape craft for Ydre and his officers in case of emergency."

"We need to commandeer one and put the rest out of action."

"That won't stop the four squadrons of *Ravening*'s fighters from following," said Stella.

"No, but if we can isolate the officers—most of whom will be at the gathering—we can slow down their pursuit. Not one of those fighter pilots will leave the docks without the express command of his superior."

"Sphaleros." Lar's voice was heavy.

"He's the captain, isn't he?" asked Stella.

"Yes." Lar's brow furrowed. "Racque, if we can't isolate him, we don't have much of a chance. He's a cracking good officer. He'd get us before we cleared the ship."

"Then we're going to have to cut off communications to the VIP deck."

"That can be done."

Both men looked in surprise at Stella.

"I haven't been wasting my time," she smirked. "House slaves are given plans of the ship. We are not supposed to have minds or technological expertise, and are therefore not considered dangerous. The VIP deck has its own communications link, but it's channeled into the main power system. If we can disengage that connection, we can isolate them. It will even shut down the in-ship transport system."

"How?" questioned Racque.

"One laser blast will do it. The linkup is just inside the hangar door."

"Stella, you're a treasure."

"I know," she answered modestly.

"What about weapons?" asked Lar. "I can't carry anything but a dress knife, and a house slave is forbidden weapons."

"They aren't my style. I've always found going unarmed much more intimidating, but we're going to need them now."

"There is the armory..."

"No."

Lar's eyebrows rose in surprise.

"Lar, we're going to do our best to maintain your cover. If

it works and you stay on board the *Ravening*, you can bring us the best intelligence we will have had in some time."

"And what about the spy?"

"Spy?" Racque and Stella exclaimed in unison.

"I forgot. A spy. He knows about Racque and Marc. I've intercepted at least five messages. I'm afraid he's going to try another contact and I won't be able to intercept it."

"You're sure none of the messages got through?"

"No. That's the rub. They could know and be lying in wait for you, just biding their time and enjoying themselves. But I don't think so."

"All we can do is proceed as if they don't know. If we get out of this . . ." Racque let his words trail off.

"Yes." Lar responded to his unfinished statement with that single chilling comment.

Racque was silent, considering the coming coup. "Lar, both you and I will be at Ydre's party. That leaves Stella a free agent, to take care of any unexpected details."

Stella smirked again. "He'd like to tell me it's too dangerous, but he knows better," she said.

The look in Lar's eyes confirmed Stella's words, but he replied, "We'll have Marc, too."

"I wish there were some way to plan this better." Racque's words fell into the silence like stones thrown down an empty well. Stella reached up and kissed him.

"Good luck," she said.

Racque's mocking blue eyes became bleak. "If we fail," he said, "I hope we're all dead. Especially Coryelle."

Lar's strong fingers closed on his arm like a vise. "Sometimes where there's no hope some twist of fate gives an impossible chance."

Racque returned Lar's gesture, his affection for the musician rising like a warm tide. "Take care," he said.

As the door closed behind them, Lar took Stella in his arms.

"Lar! Someone might come."

"Don't care if they do."

"But what would they think? Lar!"

"They would think," he said sweetly, "that the musician has managed to catch the most beautiful house slave on the ship."

Her eyes grew soft as he bent over her, and the kiss he gave her was fierce, passionate, and possessive. She sank into the safety of his arms.

"Oh, Lar, I thought you were dead. There was no word— only of Coryelle."

"If it had not been for Coryelle, I might be dead. She thought of the ruse that convinced the Gardesmen of my innocence."

Stella snuggled close to him, the solid warmth of his body and the strong beating of his heart a reality more important to her than anything else.

"When I thought I had to live on the memory of your arms around me, I did not want to go on. Whatever happens now, I will always have this."

Lar looked down at her flaming red wig with its artistically gauche adornment, and thought how ironically characteristic of Stella it was. He knew underneath it there was a halo of glossy dark hair, just as underneath her bristling, confident exterior lurked a shy, vulnerable girl. He tightened his arms around her, as if that would keep all the forces of evil at bay.

Stella lifted her face. Even the dramatic paint could not hide her feelings. For once she was not wearing the hard mask with which she protected herself. "Lar, I never thought I would love like this. When I am in your arms, I am not afraid."

"I wish I could protect you, but I cannot hold back death."

"We will face it this evening."

Lar ran the backs of his fingers across her cheek. "Whatever happens, remember that I love you," he murmured.

The light in Stella's eyes burned deep and warm.

CHAPTER 17

Lar's eyes snapped green fire. "Let me in there!" he demanded.

The Gardesman in charge of security did not flinch. "I must have either the password or a priority one security clearance with the computer," he answered.

"I was here two hours ago! I had clearance then and I want it now!"

"You came with a Gardesman's authorization. I cannot allow anyone inside the security barrier without specific clearance."

"Listen to me, you knucklehead! That...that...slave stole my recorder! I want it back."

The Gardesman was dumbfounded. "Your what?"

"Recorder. Alto recorder," explained Lar patiently.

"I cannot allow you inside."

"Very well, then you go and find it."

"I have no time to waste on itinerant minstrels who cannot keep track of their own possessions."

"That recorder is not, as you put it, a 'possession.' It is a tool. I need it. I need it for the Commander's entertainment. I would not like to deny him."

There was a sliver of hesitation in the Gardesman's expression.

"Look, I understand your position, but try to understand mine. If the Commander does not get the music he asked for this evening, he will be angry. I will be forced to explain to him his elite security Gardesman allowed a prisoner to steal it from me and then denied me access to the same prisoner to recover it. I would hate to have to do that."

"I act according to my orders."

"Are your orders more important than the Commander's desires?"

The Gardesman said nothing. He was plainly at a loss.

"If you were to allow me to search for my instrument, I would not have to mention the incident. No one need ever know. The Commander will be happy with his hunting song, and I will be happy to have pleased him. Surely if I had security clearance a mere two hours ago, I am a safe risk now."

"I must check the screens," the Gardesman said.

He turned away from the laser field and his elbow brushed the switch that controlled it. Lar watched the net melt out of sight as the Gardesman surveyed the computer screens. He hurried to Marc's cell, trying not to let his eagerness show. As he reached the door, it slid open, revealing a startled but not surprised Marc. Lar stepped inside, and the door slammed shut. He listened for the distinctive hum of the intercom system and did not detect it. Marc reached for the jamming device, but Lar waved it aside.

"Don't dare," he murmured, "we'll have to take our chances." He raised his voice. "Where is it, slave?"

"Where is what?" asked Marc as he rolled a square of cloth into a tight cylinder.

"My recorder!" shouted Lar, advancing threateningly.

"This?" faltered Marc, holding out the instrument so the Gardesman could see it before Lar's advancing form blocked it from sight.

"That's it. Sniveling thief." Lar was making conversation while Marc unscrewed the wooden flute and slipped the roll of material inside it. He knew it contained plans for the evening. With his back to the monitor, Lar had the luxury of a smile of anticipation. Marc looked up and met his eyes. Lar was caught by the dancing yellow lights in his prince's eyes, lights of recklessness and daring he had not seen before. He knew suddenly that Marc was supremely dangerous, possessed of a power he did not entirely understand. He might even be a match for Ran Corbin. Much as he cared for Marc, this idea was a new one. It gave Lar an illogical glimmer of hope. "My prince," he murmured.

Under the cover of Lar's broad shoulders blocking the monitor, Marc's smile flashed out like quicksilver. He gripped Lar's hand, but said nothing.

"Hand it over!" said Lar loudly, and Marc meekly passed him the recorder. It was again an innocent antique flute. Using the gesture, Lar whispered, "We have help we did not expect. Stella is here in the disguise of a house slave. She can move freely throughout the ship."

"That accounts for the light in your eyes," said Marc softly. "Take care of her."

Lar grimaced.

"I know she makes it hard. Luck to us all," said Marc as he gripped Lar once more before cringing away from him. Lar helped him along with a shove.

"That will teach you to steal from an honest man!" he said, and turned on his heel. The door opened as he reached it, and his suspicions of surveillance were confirmed. He strode from the cell with his precious instrument clasped in his hand, muttering darkly. The Gardesman ignored him, but the laser screen vanished as Lar approached it. He forced himself to move naturally, though every nerve tingled to be away. Once beyond the laser field, he turned to the Gardesman.

"You run a tight section, Gardesman," he said. There was the barest touch of mockery in his voice.

The man did not answer him, and something about the set of his mouth told Lar he had not made a friend.

The recorder was burning his fingers, the information it contained the fragile key to life for all of them. He found his quarters and sealed himself inside them. He found the security monitor, then pushed his harp across the table so the decorative silver roses on the frame sparkled in the light. He casually adjusted its position until light flashed off a rounded rose petal, sending its blinding glare straight at the monitor. One of the *Ravening*'s hundreds of eyes was closed.

Lar set the recorder on the table in front of the harp. Now he had the opportunity he was loath to touch it. A siren was singing in his heart. It had a soft voice, low and breathy, sending out a sweet lure. It sang of the madness of an attempt to snatch prisoners not only off a fully armed battle cruiser, but from directly under Corbin's nose. It was a futile action, capable only of failure. They would all go to their deaths. But, the voice murmured, there was an alternative for him. He and Stella might steal away. No one would miss a house slave and a minstrel, at least not enough to pursue them. They would be free. They would have each other. The sweetness of the voice made Lar's stomach turn. Stella's face spoke the words, but he knew the voice was not hers. The temptation to yield to it was aching. He was being offered paradise, the chance to escape to a life with the woman he loved. The voice persisted, but he closed his mind against it. He knew he could not live with the consequences of betrayal. If he tried to save Stella by it, he would lose her. Abruptly he reached for the recorder.

He twisted it open and extracted the material. Spreading it out under the light, he began to decipher Marc's plans for escape. As he mastered the details, he realized it could work. In theory it was possible, but theory so often fell apart in practice. He folded the message for Racque. They must all know every step by heart or the dance would not succeed. He slipped the message inside his shirt and stared glumly at the strings of his harp. The siren voice had faded, but the harp stood there in the slowly dimming simulated daylight, awaiting the touch of his hand to dissolve into melody. He ran his fingers across the strings and a rush of sound followed them like the wind in the trees.

Coryelle was still crying. The tears that made wet trails down her cheeks were unsupported by sobs. She did not care that she was the representative of the resistance forces and must act with strength and dignity. She used her strength and dignity to answer Corbin, but they were depleted. Her body ached with the longing to be held as she had been as a child. The feel of Marc's arms, warm and strong and secure, haunted her. She could feel the broad solidity of his chest and the gentleness with which he held her, but memories were not enough. She needed him now, needed the wholesome strength that was like being enfolded in the arms of the world.

She hugged the thought of him to her heart, reveling in a remembered embrace. It was a protective device of the moment, all that stood between her and madness. She could no longer deal with the sterilized bell jar atmosphere of the cell.

As her memories assumed color and form, Coryelle's tears slowed and finally ceased. She turned over on the bed, rubbing her burning eyes with the back of one hand and trying not to sniffle. In imagination she wrapped herself in Marc's arms, and for the present she could cope with what lay ahead. She did not know how long she could survive, but she blessed the strength of affection that could offset the inhumanity of her surroundings. She closed her eyes and held on to it with every bit of strength she possessed.

The *Ravening* was quieter than usual, her crew relaxed. The ship's officers were invited to the Seneschal's dinner, and except for a skeleton crew, they all felt the necessity to accept. Even Captain Sphaleros, who loathed social occasions in general and Ydre's bizarre dinners in particular, made it a point to attend. With the officers concerned over the creases in their dress uniforms, *Ravening* was left in the hands of her crew.

The main communications center was short-staffed, manned by a crew of two. They were experienced men who had a thorough knowledge of the mechanics of the different coding systems and methods of communication, but they had never attained rank in the Garde. They were competent technicians, but they had no wish for the responsibilities of command. Both were looking forward to a quiet night of chitter-chatter between the ships of the squadron.

The eldest of the men, Huntergreen, pushed back from his console and narrowed his eyes at the blinking lights on the computer panel.

"What'd you give, Cirra, for a cold mug of black Modos beer?"

Cirra made a face. "Not much. Too rank for my taste."

"You have no taste."

Cirra chuckled. "You know that stuff curdles my stomach. We should be grateful for a quiet night, with no brass hanging over our shoulders."

Huntergreen sighed. "You're right. I guess I'm never satisfied."

"So I've noticed."

The computer emitted a warning bleep that startled both
men, then returned to its everyday electronic sounds.

"What was that?" Cirra was staring blankly at the now quiescent computer.

Huntergreen leaned forward, watching the patterns of the
lights. They flashed in their normal mathematical progres-
sions, the familiarity of their responses puzzling after the surprised little cry.

"I think," said Huntergreen, "that when the linkup has to
adjust to a set of codes not commonly in use, that's how it
tells you."

"You mean we've got a coded message in there now?"

Huntergreen nodded. "Probably high priority, too. Anyone
else would use one of the simpler codes. This is probably for
the Commander."

Cirra groaned. "I am not going to volunteer to interrupt the
Commander at his pleasures."

"Can't say as I blame you. Myself, I can't see any reason to
bother him unless it's a code blue message from the Seneschal's office."

"That's policy, isn't it? We can get out of it that way? I
never pay any attention. The officers usually handle that."

"That'll teach us to be so lazy . . . where's the manual?"

Cirra stretched an arm to a storage shelf and dug out a slim
volume. He riffled pages worn ragged by frequent handling.

"Here it is." Cirra placed his finger next to the passage and
handed the book to Huntergreen.

"Looks like you're right. We can get out of it."

A red light flashed above a slot marked "hard copy."

"Here it comes now. A sealed message, just like those
others that go directly to Ydre." Cirra's voice was doubtful.
"Maybe we should ignore the book and deliver this one."

Huntergreen held the sealed white square of paper in his
hand. "It doesn't say anything about being a code blue message. Let it wait."

"We do have policy to back us up." Cirra was trying to
convince himself. "Policy is all Ydre cares about."

Huntergreen placed the message in a box with other com-
muniqués and promptly forgot about it. Cirra eyed the box,
but turned away from it to replace the manual on its shelf. He

knew that to substitute personal impressions for rules led down only one path. It was a road he did not like to contemplate.

Marc was pacing his cell. His tension was rising to the breaking point. The clock in his head counted the hours since Lar's visit. He knew Ydre's dinner was about to start. In his soundproofed cell he could not hear the other prisoners being escorted to the banquet hall, but he could picture it in his mind. He expected to be among them.

His footsteps became savage, quite unlike the cringing Drusillus'. Perhaps the isolation disturbed his time sense, and it was really no more than late afternoon. Perhaps he miscalculated. This attempt at reason failed miserably, for Coryelle intervened. She sang in his blood, and he was beginning to feel he could destroy the cell door with one blow. It was an unstable anger he was feeling, based on the impotence of his position. He knew it would betray him, but he no longer wished to control it. Time was slipping inexorably away.

"All the gods of Dynt!"

The sweet ejaculation jerked Marc's head around. He would have known Stella's voice anywhere, but dropping into the silence of his cell, it was a surprise. He searched for its source.

"For pity's sake, help me!"

"How? Where are you, Stella?"

"Where would I be but at the door?"

The dainty, coral-tipped ends of her fingers were barely visible at a crack in the door. Marc worked his fingers into the opening and his bunched muscles drove all his strength toward his hands. The door creaked and screamed, but it moved, slowly at first, then with a rush that almost knocked Stella off her feet. She stumbled back, and Marc leaped from the cell to catch her. She flexed her fingers.

"I should have thought of that when I drugged the guards," she said.

Marc slipped his arm around Stella's waist and pulled her close. "Thank you," he said. "In one more moment I would have gone mad."

She smiled at him and followed his long strides down the

hallway. The empty cells confirmed the accuracy of his calculations. At the laser field the two Gardesmen on duty lay sprawled on the floor. Marc dragged them to the inside of the laser gate.

"How did you manage it?" he asked.

Stella twinkled. "There are advantages to my assumed profession. I drugged them. With lip rouge."

Stella made a small moue with her coral-tinted lips, and Marc actually chuckled. His spirits were high now he was free. "Help me with them. We don't want any unexpected interruptions."

"What are you going to do with them?" returned Stella, gathering up the Gardesmen's weapons.

"I think a sojourn in their own prison will keep them quiet. What do you think?"

"Particularly if we were to use your cell."

"Stella, you're a devious woman."

"Thank you."

Marc got a shoulder under the first Gardesman and hoisted him. When he reached the cell door, he dropped the man unceremoniously on the floor and returned for his compatriot. Stella deposited their weapons outside the laser gate and followed Marc as he dragged the second Gardesman down the hall. He heaved the man's unconscious body through the door, unconcerned when it landed on top of the other man.

Stella pulled a long, curling green feather from her hair and let it fall on the Gardesman's chest.

"Are you sure you want to sign your work?" asked Marc.

"Why not? I'm doomed if we're caught. They can both identify me."

Marc slipped his arm around her again. "You should not have come."

"So I've been told. Where would you be if I hadn't?"

"In my cell. But you still should not have come."

Stella looked up at Marc.

"I know," he said. "You had to, just as I did." He pulled her close once more. "Where do we stand?"

"The party has started. Coryelle is there, but Corbin did not want to risk you. Why, no one knows."

"Then we begin. Aside from this, all is going as planned?"

"Yes."

"I'm glad you changed to the slave's clothes Lar brought you. It is not uncommon on this ship for a house slave to be accompanied, particularly if she is the property of one of the senior officers."

Marc looked ruefully down at the white tunic. He had not worn white since he discarded his slave's clothes so many years ago. The brown leggins with their laced sandals felt familiar, even comfortable. He fingered the twisted metal slave's collar. "It seems," he murmured, "I cannot escape."

"What?"

"Nothing. The idle rambling of pride. Now for transport."

They stepped beyond the defunct laser gate, and Marc activated it.

"That laser field has been off for too long."

"It couldn't be helped. We'll have to hope it's overlooked."

"If anyone checks, they'll know something's wrong."

"Which means we should get going."

Stella nodded shortly. Marc dropped two paces behind her and they proceeded down the corridor, Stella walking with the slowly provocative swing that was characteristic of her. She made a convincing house slave and she knew it. It was a fate she narrowly escaped on Modos. Only her disguise of filth and her violent temperament had saved her. She had a sudden flash of understanding for Marc's murmured words. He had been a slave and now he wore a slave's garb once more. He was likely to die in it. He was prince of Dynt, heir to the throne, endorsed by the king himself—something she railed at herself for not thinking to tell him—and he was likely to end his life as a slave.

Marc, behind the subservience of his posture and the slightly lazy pace he was setting himself, was concerned with the next phase of his plan. His mind surged forward. It was like following a set of footprints across a swamp, and knowing if you kept to them exactly you would be safe. He knew he could place no stock in the idea, but nevertheless it was a spur. It made the impossible easier to attempt. He grasped the idea, channeling it toward the goal he had come to realize was his destiny: the pursuit of freedom.

CHAPTER 18

The clink of fine glassware raised in toast made a musical accent to the opulence of the scene. Marcel Ydre did not do things by halves. He honored the Seneschal with a formal banquet, his selected house slaves serving guests, with his own personal valet as wine steward.

Ydre's officers were enjoying themselves, indulging in food and drink and lascivious jesting far beyond the bounds of good taste. Ydre led the revels, and though he had already emptied one bottle of the potent vintage he owned, he was not drunk. Coryelle, seated between the Commander and Ran Corbin, noted this. She was brilliantly alert.

Her crying jag had left her exhausted. She had fallen into a deep, feverish sleep, to be roughly awakened by a Gardesman who threw her a handful of clothing. Too weary for asperity, she complied with his command to make herself presentable. Now she found herself between a dragon and his lord, and the softly flowing dress she wore, pale blue as the far horizon and dusted with a rimy hoarfrost of sparkles, was no protection.

Ydre was ignoring her, but she could feel Corbin's eyes, cold as the bottom of the sea. The glasses raised in toast honored him. He lifted his glass in an inconspicuous courtly gesture toward Coryelle. She lifted her chin.

"My compliments," he said.

"Thank you," she replied coldly.

Corbin smiled his frosty smile. "I have great respect, you know, for a worthy enemy."

"As do I." She turned the full intensity of her velvety blue eyes on him, and decided she had nothing to lose. She would push. Freedom from the confinement of her cell was exhilarating, and she was unafraid of the consequences. "You find me worthy?"

Corbin's smile twisted. "You are not afraid of me. That is a rare quality, one I admire even though I do not encourage it in my followers."

"That is understandable."

"I was also pleasantly surprised to find you intelligent and articulate."

Coryelle graced him with a haughty look, and Corbin's lips twitched. He raised his wineglass and sipped the golden liquor.

"Your uncle," he answered, "was not a man of particularly quick wit or great intellectual attainments. He was handsome and he had a charisma which drew men to him. It was certainly not virtue."

"My uncle's affairs were his own."

"Indeed they were."

"Yet you persist in punishing his whole family for his choices."

"Is that what you think?"

"That is what I see."

"I will admit I have enjoyed the destruction of your family. They were symbols of all the forces of Dynt that would have thrown my talent and intelligence away."

"And you tortured and killed them for that? I am sitting next to you, and I simply cannot understand such evil. It is incomprehensible."

Corbin's short laugh was drowned in the general clamor, but it was rare enough to elicit a look of surprise from Ydre. "Perhaps that is why I succeed. I am incomprehensible. Still, there are other reasons for the destruction of your family."

"I should be interested in knowing them."

"Since you will be in no position to extrapolate on the information, I will indulge you. I allowed your uncle to live for many years, even though I knew he was capable of mustering forces against me, while I had your father killed. Did you ever wonder why?"

Coryelle's eyes opened wide. "I did not think to question."

"That was a mistake on your part. Your family was in a key position on Dynt. Your uncle Eban did succeed in stopping the destruction of the outer colonies, but he also did me a favor. He consolidated the forces of the opposition. I destroyed many of them in that encounter, and I gave them a reputation to avoid. Wherever the resistance goes, death, in the form of my fighters, will follow. What forces were left after his death were unwelcome on the larger colonies, the very colonies they had fought to save." He chuckled softly.

"I find no humor in pain."

"And I find a great deal of humor in irony. At any rate, your uncle brought the forces of the resistance out in the open where it was much easier for me to destroy them."

"You let him live for that purpose."

"Yes."

"And my father? He never held a weapon."

"He held the greatest weapon of all: his tongue. He spent twenty years hammering away at the senate, doing his level best to procure slave rights. In part, he succeeded. Because of him it is no longer illegal for a slave to read and write. He was slowly building a faction in favor of abolishing slavery."

"That has been talked of forever."

"So it has. But your father had a chance of succeeding. He was respected and admired. He would have pushed for the power of the people. The senate was beginning to get ideas, to ask for a voice in the major decisions of government instead of acting as an advisory council. Your gentle, mild-mannered father, Coryelle Foxxe, was a veritable hotbed of insurrection, more dangerous to me than twelve resistance leaders."

"So you trumped up that story and killed him."

"On the contrary. I didn't have to manufacture that story. He actually did run an underground escape route for slaves. It was a convenient charge to level against him, and one that would stand up to scrutiny."

"You killed children." Coryelle's voice was low, but it vibrated with the cold strength of a rapier.

"It was regrettable, but I could not afford to have one of them stirring up trouble. See the annoyance you have caused me. If the Garde had been more thorough, I would have been spared the search for you."

"I have never before met a man with no heart. If your heart were evil, I could hate you, but there is nothing to hate."

"A heart is an inconvenient instrument. More often than not, it betrays you. I have discarded it."

He took another sip of the wine, and Coryelle absently watched the transparent gold of the liquid as he raised his glass to the light. She was bewildered. Corbin could not even be called an enemy. He murdered children, he destroyed her father and uncle, and sent her on a path of flight that was not yet ended, but there was such emptiness in the man. He existed, but did not live. Even in the face of the blood of millions, she could not hate him.

"What drives you, Ran Corbin?"

"You expect me to answer that? And flaunt my deepest secrets? My enemies would enjoy that."

"It was worth a try."

"Now it is my turn."

"What could you possibly wish to know about me?"

"Your relationship with Marc Dynteryx, for one thing."

"You did not call him the pretender."

"There does not seem to be a need for pretense between us."

"You admit his claim?"

Coryelle was surprised. She was lucky Corbin's answer prompted such a reaction, for the shock in her eyes had nothing to do with the legitimacy of Marc's claim to the throne. Across the room she glimpsed a tall figure in blue. Racque was seating himself in an out-of-the-way corner. Her brother's presence shot a surge of adrenaline into her system. Something was afoot.

"Unofficially, yes. I am aware of the details of Tenebrae's life. I know she signed those adoption papers because I know every twist and curl of her handwriting. As far as his abilities go, that remains to be seen."

"Marc has no need to pretend anything." Coryelle's attention was split. She forced herself to attend to Corbin's reply.

"You care for him, then."

"He is the center of my life."

"That is the way of history. The young are incapable of learning from the mistakes of their elders. If you make another person the center of your life, that center will fail you and leave you with nothing."

"He will not fail me."

"And if he dies?"

Coryelle's face was closed.

"He is a mortal man, remember that. If, by some crook of fate you should chance to survive and live out your lives, he will hurt you, disappoint you, fail you—again and again. It is better to stand upon solid ground."

"As you do?"

"Yes. I have learned to live with facts."

"Not all of them. Pain there may be, but there is also love. You deny that."

"Only because it is a cheat." Corbin's voice retained its even, cultured accent, but it seemed heavy. There was something in his statement that struck Coryelle as central to understanding his character.

"Have you no rejoinder for me?" Corbin asked, prodding her silence.

Coryelle shook her head. "I can only wonder," she answered, "why you chose to speak to me so freely."

"You will be in no position to repeat what I have said—and our conversation amuses me."

"You do not often discuss your reasons," Coryelle guessed.

"There is no one who can be entirely trusted, therefore it is better to keep my opinions to myself."

"Are you not afraid your officers will overhear your answers?"

"No." His eyes were amused, and amusement lent undeniable charm to his handsome face. Coryelle glimpsed a hint of the beauty Gisarme described. She studied his face in more detail, putting aside her previous notions of the man's ruthless viciousness. There were no marks of it. It was as if an implacable hand wiped his features, stripping them of all emotion and reaction. The silver that frosted his dark hair told of the passage of years, but his face bore no imprint of tears or laughter. It was not an evil face she saw, but an inhuman one.

There was a rush of strings behind her, and she started, so intense had been her concentration. She barely escaped crying out Lar's name. Corbin's amusement even touched the bottomless depths in his eyes.

"From him, at least, you have nothing to fear," he said, indicating the minstrel.

"I am at the lady's service," said Lar smoothly. "Is there some melody that would please her?"

"Lady?" inquired Corbin.

"I would trust the jongleur's judgment," Coryelle returned, oddly touched by Corbin's question. She knew he would kill her with no hesitation, yet she was beginning to see he was no simple military monster. He was a complex individual, a man of such a wide range of ability and knowledge that it would take a titan to combat him. There was no chink in his armor, no feeling to play on. He was a man who had turned his back on his race.

Lar's hand swept across the harp strings, and the selection he picked sent a chill across her shoulder blades. It was a hunting ballad she had always loved, one Marc had sung to her as a child. It had to do with the pursuit of a stag, which, against insurmountable odds and with the hounds at his heels, gets away. The sense of encompassing danger blossomed and grew, tingling in her veins until she could not see how Corbin could be oblivious to it.

Stella peeked over Marc's shoulder, the strength of her heavy perfume an enveloping aura. His heightened senses made him conscious of her presence, of the touch of her small hands on the arching muscles of his shoulders.

"The big one is Corbin's ship," she whispered. "I got it out of one of the security guards."

"The rest?"

"Ydre's personal fighter and its escort. I got the impression they were emergency escape craft."

Marc surveyed the docking bay in silence. On its central disc stood a black bird of death, its upswept tail proclaiming its kinship with the Seneschal's forces. Tow lines still hung from her nose and landing struts, relics of her journey from the main hangar. Her name, painted neatly beside the hatchway, was *Ravensong*. It was appropriate to the savage curves of her fuselage. She was spare and lean, battleworthy, without frivolous adornment. Every line screamed power.

"Did you happen to find out how many she'll carry?"

"She was made for a crew of six, but she can be flown by one man. Corbin often pilots her alone, except for a security detail. The hold can accommodate sixteen or twenty adults."

"Good. We'll take her, but we'll need to put the other fighters out of action. Ydre should have posted three men on patrol here, making irregular rounds. We don't have time to wait for them and pick them off one by one. I need a diversion."

"I suppose that means me."

"Stella, you're spectacular enough to divert twenty men. This should be nothing." There was a chuckle in Marc's voice.

"Wish me luck."

"Just make sure you disrupt one of those electronic eyes." Marc indicated the unblinking transparent discs set at intervals along the wall. "That will bring them out."

Stella tripped furtively onto the landing area, looking apprehensively over her shoulder. The high heels of her sandals made a surprisingly loud noise, like the measured clicking of a dancer's castanets. Marc slipped behind a maintenance cart, keeping Stella in view. She was moving across the landing pad in short bursts, taking care to appear lost. It was hard to parallel her movements and still keep alert for Gardesmen.

"Halt!"

Marc, hidden though he was, involuntarily froze. He saw Stella stop in her tracks, whirl and look wildly around for the source of the voice.

"Stay where you are or be lost!"

Stella did not move. "Please," she ventured, "I am already lost!"

With her wide, dark eyes she was convincing in the role. Marc sank on one knee, prepared to move with lightning speed once Stella's captors appeared. As two Gardesmen swaggered across the landing pad, his muscles tensed. One of the men trained a spotlight on Stella, blinding her. She raised a hand to shield her eyes.

"Some saboteur," he scoffed. "It's just one of the Commander's new house slaves." He turned to Stella. "Didn't you know this was a restricted area?"

Stella peeked from behind her fingers, and the man lowered the light.

"I was afraid it was, but I couldn't remember the map, and I was lost. I'm trying to get back to my room."

The eyes she turned on the Gardesmen were appealing in their painted setting. With the practice of an accomplished entertainer, she leaned imperceptibly forward so the shadows would accentuate the curves of her bosom. Marc, his eyes on the two Gardesmen and his senses alert for the one he had not seen, knew she was drawing the men to her, consolidating his target. The temptation to deal with them as they stood was strong, but a misstep would destroy all chance for escape. He dared not.

Instead, he skirted the landing pad, moving like a breath on the wind. The stark shadows of the ships and maintenance equipment were his refuge as he circled the enclosure, heading for the auxiliary flight control room. He could hear Stella's voice, low and musical, as it pleaded her innocence. She was adroit at the kind of double-talk that would keep the Gardesmen at bay and yet fascinated, giving him time to locate and dispatch the third man.

The space between the wall and the last ship, a three-man shuttle used for major repairs on the exterior hull of a vessel, was empty. The transparent panel that revealed the interior of flight control showed him the indolent form of a young lieutenant, his feet propped comfortably against a computer console, a half-smile on his face as he watched Stella. Marc sent a quick glance toward her, hoping she would remain the center of attention.

As if on cue, she stepped forward a pace, directly into a pool of light. At home in the spotlight, she paused for dramatic effect, her weight on one leg to make the folds of her dress swirl provocatively around her hips. The lieutenant's smile broadened, and Marc knew his best chance had come.

He dropped low, slithering across the open area, certain the lieutenant would look down and he would be discovered, or one of the men Stella held would turn and see him. His luck held, and he gained the wall of the landing area undetected. He made his way under the window, then rose to flatten himself against the wall. The shuttle cut off his view of Stella and protected him from the two Gardesmen's eyes. He moved in front of the door, nerves charged for action. He took one step forward, and the automatic door opened. He was through it and on the man before the lieutenant's surprise registered. There was a muffled exclamation as the man sagged under him. Marc took a deep breath and got to his feet.

The plans of the *Ravening* disclosed all storage areas, and Marc knew there was a storage compartment at the rear of the auxiliary control room. With a powerful wrench he dragged the unconscious man from his chair and hauled him to the rear of the room. The cabinet was barely wide enough to accommodate him. Marc folded the man into the closet and shut the door, then slipped from the room as quietly as he had entered it.

Stella was still in the spotlight, engaging the Gardesmen in conversation, though from the cast of their gestures it was evident they intended more. When he heard the nervous tremor in Stella's coquettish giggle he knew time was running out. With the lieutenant in safekeeping there was no need for stealth. He launched himself at the two Gardesmen in a long running jump. He landed on the balls of his feet, balanced like a cat, with both hands flying. The first man crumpled from a blow to the side that cracked his ribs as the second man turned on Marc.

As Marc slammed a fist into his adversary's stomach, and then delivered a stunning two-handed blow to the back of the neck, he saw the other man reach for Stella with his good arm. It was an ill-conceived move. Stella whirled, evaded him, and kicked him brutally. The man staggered, and she landed another kick on the opposite shin.

Marc stepped over the prone figure of his opponent and grasped Stella's attacker by the shoulders, forcing him to the ground in one swift, hard shove. The man did not expect such a simple move. Marc touched a pressure point, and the man slumped, unconscious. Marc rose from the prostrate form, breathing hard.

"You took your own sweet time," said Stella, finding herself in his arms. He gave her a quick hug.

"You," he said, "were magnificent."

"Well."

"Let's get these two out of sight."

Marc and Stella dragged the men into the control room, binding them with lightweight cable. The bonds were stiff and none too humane, but they were available. Marc's eyes were light as he looked up at Stella. His smile flashed.

"Now for the ships."

He pried open a panel on the nearest vessel and removed the converter block, a two-inch-square complex of circuitry that boosted the energy ratio of the fuel Corbin's ships burned. The device made it possible for a single pound of fuel to power a cruiser for a month. Without it, the engines would turn over but not catch. There was simply not enough power to kick them over. He threw the converter into the nearest disposal unit.

Stella, watching him, nodded curtly. Between them they disabled all of the ships on the VIP pad in less than ten minutes—all but Corbin's *Ravensong*.

Marc's smile as he regarded *Ravensong* was impish, rife with unholy mischief. "It will be a pleasure to use the Seneschal's ship against him." The low tones of Marc's voice were full of the enjoyment this unexpected twist gave him.

"If we expect to use her, we'd better free the landing hatch, and set it on automatic. And slip those towlines."

"I leave it in your hands," Marc answered. "I'll tend to the communications link."

As Stella went toward flight control, Marc retraced his steps to the door of the flight pad. According to the diagrams, directly to the left of the door, behind a protective metal wall, lay a major communications circuit. If he could disengage it, he could isolate the entire deck. He looked for a tool to pry the metal covering away, but none would fit under the thin skin. He rubbed his fingers together, closing his eyes in concentration. He channeled all the power at his command into his fingertips and placed them inside the edges of the panel. His hands slid over the panel, sensitive, searching. All at once he paused, then jabbed sharply. The panel popped, lifting at the edges so that he was able to insert a cable tool under the edge and lift it. The tearing sound of the metal being ripped from its welds seemed to fill the world, but he had no choice but to continue. Once he exposed the circuits he picked up a welding torch and seared them to a mass of melting rubble.

"All set."

Stella's voice startled him. He had not heard her approach over the roar of the torch, and it rattled him. He could not afford to be surprised. He replaced the torch, giving no sign of his feelings.

"Stella, this is going to be the worst for you. I need you here." He shook his head as she started to protest. "I know you have no patience with inaction, but I need you. We all need you. Someone has to stay with the ship. It's a dangerous position. If anyone comes . . ."

"I'll just have to take care of it."

Marc squeezed her hand. "Lar will be all right. If all goes as planned, he'll meet us in a week's time."

"I know."

Stella's voice was small. Marc pulled her forward and kissed her on the forehead.

"The things we do for love," he said, and was gone.

CHAPTER 19

Cirra eyed the white square with distaste. "I wish this thing didn't make me so nervous," he said, picking up the crisply folded paper.

"Look, we've been through this before." Huntergreen's voice was patient, conciliatory. "We have policy on our side. Let it wait 'til the next watch."

"We could take it to Sphaleros, let him decide."

"Didn't you hear? Sphaleros went to the party."

Cirra expressed his surprise in a wry face. "That lets him out, then."

"And keeps us on the hook. I know it's a touchy situation.

We have standing orders to deliver those messages directly into the Commander's hands, but you remember what happened to the last man who interrupted one of his socials."

"I heard about it." Cirra looked at the neatly sealed message and sighed. "I still don't like it. I never thought I'd wish there was some of that unnecessary brass around, but when it comes to a decision like this, I want no part of it."

"Me either. If we stick to the rules we might be wrong, but the worst we'll probably get is demoted. Toss that thing back in the basket and quit stewing about it."

Cirra sent the message deftly through the air with a flick of the wrist that retained the form of a champion stone skipper. "I give it up," he said.

"What, Gardesman, do you propose to give up?"

Both Huntergreen and Cirra stiffened to attention at the nasal voice of their immediate supervisor. Lieutenant Naedre wandered into the communications center with his hands clasped behind his back. He was a small man. Both of the Gardesmen towered over him, but it was evident they lived in his shadow. The unctuous fluidity of his irritating voice controlled them. He walked around the stiffly posed Cirra as if he were studying a particularly baffling piece of sculpture.

"I repeat my question, gentlemen. What do you propose to give up?"

"Nothing, sir. I mean, we have a problem, sir. We needed your advice."

"And why was I not informed? You are wallowing in a wealth of equipment expressly designed for communication."

"We were told you were not on duty, sir." Huntergreen's voice was flat, stoic.

"Gardesmen," Naedre's tone was warm, "you have served me for more than a year. You know I am always on duty."

"Yes, sir."

"Now what is the problem you are incapable of solving?"

Cirra picked up the message, and handed it to his superior. Naedre turned it over once.

"From the Commander's spy. Why was it not delivered to him?"

"We hesitated to disturb the Commander," stated Huntergreen. "Had we realized the lieutenant was available, we should have asked his advice."

Circumstances forced Huntergreen to grovel, but he did not enjoy it. Naedre was a small but deadly viper who had a knack for placing his enemies in the way of the Commander's displeasure.

"I am surrounded by idiots," murmured Naedre.

"Regulations . . . ," began Cirra.

The lieutenant rubbed his forefinger across the bridge of his nose, his expression pained. "You are not responsible for interpreting regulations. That is the prerogative of an officer. How many times do I have to tell you to seek out the nearest ranking officer and put your problems to him?"

"We are pleased to be doing that," ventured Huntergreen.

Naedre shook his head, marveling at the ingenuous stupidity of his staff. It would do no good to argue with them. They were both dumb as rock and twice as thick. "I shall deliver this to the Commander in person. Do not concern yourselves further."

The two Gardesmen missed Naedre's sarcasm. They watched him depart with considerable relief, waiting until the door shut behind him to relax their rigid postures.

Naedre, on the other hand, remained tense with annoyance. His short stride was a soft staccato on the deck. Unlike the clods he commanded, he knew the message must be delivered. Ydre would not be pleased, but the message could be handed over without causing undue havoc to the festivities. So intent was he on ways and means of accomplishing this while retaining both his head and his stripes, he did not notice the maintenance beast.

It was a mechanical buffer which spent its days and nights wending its dutiful way through the ship, buffing and polishing the myriad surfaces to glossy perfection. The beast covered all surfaces of the ship about once each month, leaving shining cleanliness in its wake. At present it was industriously scrubbing the corridor's dark metal floor. It worked its purposeful way toward Naedre, emitting a soft whir. The floor behind it shone like a mirror.

Naedre, intent on his thoughts, did not see the beast until he was almost on top of it. He shifted awkwardly to one foot to

avoid it, and the beast made a short rush forward to elude
him, running under the raised foot. The heel of Naedre's boot
caught the contrivance and sent it spinning, but the results for
Naedre were disastrous. He lost his balance completely and
crashed forward. His feet slid on the slick floor and he presented a wild spectacle of waving arms and thrashing legs as
he strove to maintain his balance. Dignity was cast to the four
winds in a futile attempt to remain upright. It would have
been easier if he simply surrendered to the inevitable and allowed himself to fall.

When he did go down, it was with a crash that resounded
down the hall, but since the rooms were soundproof, no one
heard his spectacular mishap. The force of the fall jolted his
neck, snapping it like a kite string in a brisk wind. His head
struck the floor with a crack, and he lolled to a stop, unconscious. The envelope was jarred from his hand. It skittered
across the floor and lodged in an air duct, a neat white square
against the black grill.

The beast retraced its progress, picking up its chores where
it left off, oblivious to the prone figure in the middle of the
deserted hall. It chugged forward, buffing industriously, softly
chirping to itself over its work.

The atmosphere was thick with overindulgence. Coryelle's
eyes burned and she yearned to escape Marcel Ydre's stifling
presence. Unlike his guest, Ydre was enjoying himself. Sated
with a gourmet meal fit for the king of Dynt, he was now
indulging his penchant for perverse entertainment. Ten men
and two women, Coryelle's comrades in arms, were perform-
ing a complex and erotic folk dance for his pleasure. It was
demeaning, showing Ydre's total lack of respect for his prisoners. Coryelle found it so offensive her stomach recoiled,
shifting uneasily.

"Your choice of entertainment reveals you, Commander,"
she said acidly. Conversation with Corbin had made her bold.

Ydre, well under the influence of vintage wine, grew ex-
pansive, his snake's eyes alight with satisfaction. "I take infinite pains to please my guests." The snake's eyes glittered,
taking pleasure in her revulsion. "I will say your friends are
quick studies—all except the two we lost. Unfortunate, but

they were dreadfully stodgy in cooperating with my plans for the evening."

So. This was what was left of the resistance forces. Twelve people. Coryelle shuddered, angry at herself as she realized Ydre enjoyed her reaction. She looked across the room for Lar, hoping some fleeting expression would give her strength.

Lar was playing his harp in dutiful accompaniment to the dancers. His fingers flew with their customary agility, but his eyes were hooded. His expression was exceptionally bland. Coryelle knew he hated what he was doing as much as she hated watching it, knowing it was for her discomfiture that her friends were being humiliated. Ydre chuckled at a humorous twist in the dance, and the sound struck her ears as an obscenity. She could feel her revulsion catching fire, blazing into anger, and she sent an iron band of control across her soul. She would not allow Ydre to force her actions. Were she to turn on him like a fighting cat, it would be the climax of the evening for him, a source of pleasure his jaded sensibilities craved. It would change nothing, and it would further endanger her friends. She stole a furtive glance at Racque, and caught the flash of blue fire in his icy eyes. It checked her anger as effectively as if she had been slapped.

For a moment her own emotions had seduced her from the facts. Something was going on, something she must wait for, trusting her companions. She looked again at the dancers, forcing herself to study their faces and put the shame of their actions aside. What she saw gave her a lift of pride.

The dancers, too, saw Lar and Racque. They were waiting, without question, for events to break. Their performance was a ruse. She could see expectation in their carefully flat eyes. They were playing along. She could do no less. At the next rude gesture she allowed herself to flinch, and was rewarded by a glitter of laughter in Ydre's eyes.

Corbin, on her opposite side, observed Coryelle with quiet admiration. He respected courage and he respected dignity. Her flinch surprised him. He examined her face, noticing the pain that drew her cheeks flat with tension. She was little more than a child, and Ydre's methods of torture were exquisite. She had reason to flinch, and yet he was surprised.

"I see you do not care for our host's entertainment," Corbin observed mildly.

Coryelle's lips compressed to a tight line. "Why do you allow this perversion?"

Corbin took a sip of wine and rolled it on his tongue, savoring it. Dinner had come and gone, and still he had not drunk a full glass. "I make no judgments on my officers' morals," he answered at last. "I require one thing from them: absolutely efficient application of my orders. What they wish to do on their own time is not my concern."

"Not even when it is unnecessarily cruel?"

"This is not something I would do myself. I haven't the patience, for one thing. These are his prisoners. Ydre is what he is. And what he is to me is an officer whose work has given satisfaction."

Coryelle looked Corbin straight in the face for the first time. She allowed the fathomless blue depths of her eyes to lock with the emptiness of his. "And yet death at your hands would be clean."

"I am essentially neat. I dislike mess and disorder."

"You deny even that slight indication of humanity."

"The panther kills quickly, and a snake strikes clean. Yet you call it humanity."

Coryelle's eyes never left his. "As Seneschal of Dynt you are empowered to grant me a favor."

"I have the power, but seldom the desire."

"Nevertheless, I am going to ask one."

"You are a rebel without a country and not entitled to any privilege."

"I am a citizen of Dynt, and I serve her always, or I would not be your antagonist."

Corbin did not dispute her statement. "It is a pity," he said, "that fate makes enemies of those whose motives are most similar."

"I ask that I meet death at your hands, not be awarded to a beast like Ydre."

"You plead for mercy where there is none to give."

"Still, I ask it. A simple thing. It will not bother you, and it would be a grace to me."

"Such an action on my part might cause dissension between myself and a valued commander. Ydre expects to have you for his own, to use and then destroy as he has so many others."

"In the face of this I ask. For the man you once were, I ask."

Anger flashed from the unplumbed depths of his eyes, anger so palpable it seared her like flame. "What can you know of the man I was, or the man I am for that matter? You are nothing more than an ignorant child."

The words were low, but they snapped with passion. She had stung him. She risked doing it again.

"For Tenebrae, I ask."

"You ask for mercy in the name of the woman who showed me none?"

The words crackled around her, and she was afraid she had gone too far. She could not detach her gaze from the man's eyes. Usually flat, they were ripped by an anguish he was trying to subdue. It was a short battle, but one that tried his will. His voice resumed its quiet, courteous tone.

"I will consider your plea, not for your reasons, but for mine. You have touched me as no blade has touched me in years. You have pressed the attack, and made me misjudge myself. I think you are most truly my prisoner. It is likely you will die under my command. More, I will not give."

"More I would not dare to ask."

Coryelle sensed in Corbin's anger the end of the banquet. The atmosphere of lascivious frivolity was marred, for the Seneschal was no longer the courteous guest gracing the occasion with his presence. He retreated into himself, brooding in terrible silence. Slowly the power of his personality pervaded the room, and men spoke in low tones or not at all. The subdued voices and manners made Lar's music a demanding irritant instead of pleasant background.

Finally even Ydre, deep in the clutches of wine, recognized the change. His gaze swept the room brokenly, meeting Sphaleros' alert eyes and following them to Ran Corbin. Ydre raised his wineglass, and the room hushed but for the zinging strains of Lar's harp.

"I toast the Seneschal!" Ydre's voice was slurred but coherent. Bloody droplets of red wine sloshed from his goblet as he raised it to Corbin.

"The Seneschal!" responded the company as one man.

Ydre drained his glass and his men followed his example. Corbin remained withdrawn, oblivious to the tribute.

"His Excellency is fatigued," said Sphaleros smoothly. "We should not detain him for our own pleasure."

"Quite right, Sphaleros. A good evening, Excellency."

"Commander." Corbin was preoccupied as he acknowledged Ydre's pleasantries.

Ydre swayed to his feet, supported by two house slaves. Sphaleros snorted with disgust at the sight, but Lar's eyes lit like candles at an unholy altar. Coryelle saw all of this, and the surcharge of excitement she felt from Lar rose within her. Whatever was going to happen, would happen soon. She searched the room for Racque and found him near the door, in the vanguard of those escaping Ydre's gathering. All at once Corbin was awake and brushing past her. She saw him stop Racque with a look. The raking insouciance of her brother's expression chilled Coryelle.

"Blazon."

The cold clarity of the name cut like a chisel-stroke into Racque's heart. "Excellency."

"I have questioned the slave you brought me. Are you sure of his identity?"

"Quite sure, Excellency."

A surge of pure joy swept Racque. Over Corbin's shoulder he saw the prisoners being marshaled. The junior officers were leaving, but a detachment of Gardesmen formed the prisoners into ranks, and were preparing to march them back to security. The ranks were headed by ten armed Gardesmen, followed by Coryelle. She was flanked by two Gardesmen, and behind her came the other prisoners two abreast. They were followed by Sphaleros and another detachment of armed Gardesmen. It was perfect.

Corbin was regarding the cool blue eyes of his bounty hunter with doubt. "He does not ring true."

"I assure you, Excellency, I have full knowledge of his background. He was born a slave."

"You have missed something with this one, Blazon. Check further."

Racque inclined his head, acquiescing to Corbin's opinion and following him out the door. From the corner of his eye he saw Lar move to the door's control panel.

Lar, from his position near the door, watched the exodus with the gentle smile of a tipsy jongleur. He carried a full glass of wine. As the prisoners started through the door he swayed precariously, rocking on the balls of his feet. When the last of the resistance prisoners cleared the opening, he stumbled, falling hard against the door lock. The doors crashed shut, causing Sphaleros to jump back.

"Don't touch that!" shouted the captain as Lar lurched drunkenly for the controls. He was too late.

Lar's free hand struck the lower button, a button the ignorant could assume released the door, when in fact it activated a time security lock. For good measure he managed to spill wine down the panel. Circuits blanked out in a shower of sparks.

Sphaleros leaped for the in-ship communications panel. It was dead.

CHAPTER 20

Corbin whirled. There was a breath of stunned silence before either Gardesmen or prisoners reacted to the thud of the sealed doors, then the Gardesmen had their hands full. The prisoners fanned out. So quick was the onslaught that the Gardesmen did not have time to make full use of their weapons. One man got off a laser blast that ricocheted wildly off the shielded walls of the antechamber.

"Cease fire!" Corbin's voice cracked like a whip, and the man lowered his weapon. Ydre moved to the communications panel near the door with surprising swiftness for a man who had been staggering drunk seconds before. He slammed his hand against the activator button, but there was no opening signal. He turned back to Corbin, surrounded by the battle, and yelled over it.

"We're cut off!"

Corbin nodded and addressed himself to the conflict. Coryelle was the only prisoner still in custody. Her escort had closed in on her like a vise, forcing her back against the wall. No false heroics prodded the two Gardesmen into aiding their comrades. Their duty was to safeguard Corbin's prisoner. Coryelle, for her part, was in no position to defend herself.

Racque materialized before her. He ignored her captors.

"So you finally got here?" queried Coryelle coolly.

"I am sorry to be so long," he replied.

"You should be."

The crustiness of Coryelle's words was negated by the leaping joy in her eyes. With blinding speed Racque lashed out at one of her guards. A sickening crunch of breaking bones was followed by the man's cry of pain, and the release of his hold on Coryelle. Partially freed, Coryelle spun in the other man's grasp, driving her foot down in a painful blow to the inside of the ankle. The man rocked on his feet, but grabbed for her other arm, trying to pin her against him.

It was useless. Coryelle was quicksilver. The man could not hold her, and all the while he grasped at empty air she was delivering short, sharp blows with her feet. Finally the man broke his stance and lunged, trying to regain his balance. It was the opening she sought, and she put all her strength into a scissoring kick that knocked the man's feet out from under him.

He fell heavily, but retained his grip on one of her arms, and with a cry of frustration Coryelle went down. If he pinned her to the ground her chances for escape were halved, and she writhed in his grip, seeking a pressure point. She was able to paralyze his free arm, but the other remained an iron manacle. He was so strong he could hold her at arm's length while she wrestled.

She glimpsed the flash of worn blue leather boots, and knew Racque was looking for an opening. She put a fresh surge of effort into maintaining her position. Her captor saw Racque too, and slung his legs sideways in an effort to knock him off his feet. Racque lightly evaded the powerful but clumsy move, and his hand moved like lightning to the Gardesman's wrist. The man yelped as his hand fell limp. Coryelle was free. She rolled to her feet and jumped out of the Gardesman's way. She need not have worried.

Racque dropped the Gardesman's nerveless hand. While he was still stunned by his own helplessness, Racque's fingers closed on a pressure point. The man collapsed, unconscious and groaning.

"Not so fast, pigeon."

The oily voice directly behind her made Coryelle start. Ydre's hands clamped like steel on her shoulders as Racque leaped to face him. Ydre placed Coryelle as a shield before him, and laughed at Racque over her head.

"You are full of surprises, Blazon."

Racque said nothing, but his heart sank as Ydre moved one hand and a dagger sparkled into existence. It was like the commander to have a spring knife strapped to his arm. He tickled Coryelle's neck under the left ear with it.

"There is no escape, at least not for her." When Racque said nothing, his grip on Coryelle tightened, causing her to sink in pain. "What is she to you, Blazon?"

Ydre's voice was light, mocking, in control. All vestiges of overindulgence were gone. He was careless and deadly. Racque's eyes were for Coryelle, and Ydre saw it. He crushed her shoulder again, making her writhe, and smiled at the pain in Racque's eyes.

Coryelle was using the occasion to good advantage. As she squirmed in pain, whimpering, she raised a foot. Racque saw her move, and a zinging shock of anticipation shot through him. She came down hard on the Commander's toes.

Racque leaped for the man's knife as Coryelle ducked and twisted out of his hands. Racque wasted no time on scientific attack, but landed a powerful blow to the Commander's stomach. Ydre doubled up like a broken toy, and Racque stepped back.

"Did you think," he said conversationally, "that I would let my sister die?" He had the satisfaction of seeing the shocked surprise in Ydre's eyes before he closed them with a right cross to the chin. He reached for Coryelle's hand.

The battle still raged unchecked. The prisoners were slightly outnumbered, but they were holding their own. One man was down, his neck broken, and Racque recognized Corbin's work. He squeezed Coryelle's hand.

"I don't want to lose you," he said.

"You won't."

Coryelle flashed her smile, so like his own in its flare of light, and let him go. She delivered a chopping stroke to the broad muscles of a Gardesman's lower back and was rewarded by his grunt of surprise. Racque found himself engaged, and the battle was on.

Corbin had worked himself to the edge of the conflict. He saw Ydre go down under Racque's assault. If he was surprised, he gave no indication of it. If anything, he rather enjoyed the idea of testing Blazon in combat. Worthy opponents were hard to find, and he knew Blazon was capable of surprising him. He had no fear for his own safety.

"Corbin."

Corbin actually started at the sound of his own name spoken in cultured tones. It came from the corridor he thought empty, but this was not the cause of his reaction. The voice sounded on his soul as the voice of fate. He held himself erect, controlled, and deliberately turned to face it.

"The slave Drusillus."

"No."

The soft answer sent a thrill of excitement flying down his veins. The man who stood before him, dressed in a white slave's tunic and wearing a twisted slave's collar, was no slave. The clear hazel eyes regarded him with an open intensity which penetrated the black depths of his own. Like a man sleepwalking, Corbin drew his short dress sword and held it before him in his two hands.

"Once," he said, "I would have discarded this in deference to your lack of weapon. Now I am not so foolish. There is only one purpose before me. To kill you."

"And it does not matter how."

Corbin's sardonic smile barely touched his lips. "It is a case of the end justifying the means. You are an offense to the security of Dynt."

"I know."

From his poised, quiescent attitude Corbin launched into violent action with unbelievable speed. Marc had only encountered such reflexes in Gisarme, and he could not repress his admiration for the man's sheer physical prowess. The sword flashed in his hands like thought, so quick the eye could not follow it, but Marc had no need of his eyes. Instinct guided his actions with unerring accuracy. His body and the singing weapon danced. He whirled and dodged, landing occasional blows, with a sense of increasing power. A flash of gratitude for hours of enforced practice heightened his sensitivity another notch. He knew he was playing for time, keeping Corbin's attention while the battle worked itself out. As he evaded the dazzling swordpoint his mind catalogued the individual conflicts raging beyond him.

The companions were holding on. The number of their opponents had dwindled until it matched theirs. The Gardesmen fought with trained skill and ruthlessness, but the resistance fought with the desperation of a trapped animal. It made the daring of the Gardesmen pale by contrast.

Corbin's eyes never left Marc's elusive white figure, though his sword sought it in vain, slithering determinedly toward its mark to find empty air. At Marc's first move, Corbin realized he was dealing with a kind of disciplined opponent he had not encountered in years. The boy fought with the composed skill of *auctorite,* and the mastery of his movements testified to the years of discipline behind him. Corbin's joy in his opponent grew with the testing. He had no doubt he would win in the end, for the boy's youth and strength were no match for his whipcord muscle backed by years of experience, but he reveled in the ability Marc showed.

"There is no chance for escape," he said calmly, adding the wiles of a psychological battle to the physical one.

"There are always chances," Marc returned. "You may be surprised."

"That," answered Corbin, "would be a pleasure, but one I do not expect. The last surprise I had was Eban Foxxe."

"And I worked with Eban Foxxe."

Corbin's sardonic smile twitched his lips as his sword arm stabbed straight for Marc's heart—and found nothing. He dropped and whirled as a blow from Marc missed him by a cat's whisker.

"I do compliment you, however, on your skill. Not a man on Dynt could have maintained his position with me this long."

Marc smiled. "You may pay your compliments to Gisarme Dynteryx."

"I suspected that." Corbin's sword slashed. Marc doubled up and rolled, rising to his feet in one fluid, balanced movement. Corbin whirled on one foot, and lunged. This time the sword brushed Marc's tunic, slicing a piece of fabric as if it were cheese. "I have been called the best swordsman on Dynt, but I would not want to match blades with him."

"He is not a man who makes much show of anything. He is aware of your abilities, but there is no lack of confidence in his regard."

Marc jumped and Corbin's blade flashed in a glittering arc beneath him.

"You are a satisfaction to me," remarked Corbin. "I will regret your death."

"You find it a necessity."

"You are a disruptive element."

"Disruption means change. Sometimes change is for the better."

Corbin ducked and rolled as Marc's feet lashed toward his chest. He was up and attacking as his adversary turned. "I am not impressed by violent change."

"And change by degrees?"

"It has the virtue of being tested by time."

"Yet you destroyed Coryelle's father, who spent his life bringing change to the laws of slavery by slow degrees."

"His legal methods were a shield for the covert freeing of slaves."

Marc drove forward in a two-handed slashing assault that sent Corbin back a few paces. Corbin rocked, balanced, and countered with an arabesque in steel. The sword moved so quickly it seemed made of light.

"You were afraid of a slave rebellion!"

"Such a man inspires confidence. He was a more dangerous leader than his brother. As I said, Eban surprised me. I didn't think he had it in him to plan such a brilliant coup."

Marc's mind was tuned to the entire combat while his instincts were engaged with Corbin. The prisoners were holding their own. Hope touched him with its inflammatory fingers. He saw Racque get the best of his opponent, and begin to fight his way to Marc with Coryelle close behind him. The other prisoners strove to follow, forcing their opponents back. Racque delivered a brutal blow to a Gardesman, and the man crumpled under it. Marc concentrated on keeping Corbin's back to the spectacle, though he had no illusions about the Seneschal's knowledge of the turn of events.

Corbin gave no evidence of distress. He continued to fight with the single-minded determination for which he was famed. It became clear to Marc Corbin considered his death to be the one important factor. He did not care if the resistance forces escaped, even if Coryelle escaped, if he could secure Marc's head in exchange.

"Run!" called Marc across Corbin's sword. He saw Racque lean back and say something to Coryelle as he stepped over a Gardesman's inert form. Coryelle nodded and answered him. Racque dodged combatants until he was even with Marc and Corbin. He faced the conflict.

"Go!" he shouted, and Coryelle slipped by him and fled down the corridor. One by one the other prisoners fought their way toward Racque. When he saw an opening his signal sent his comrades to freedom, and he stepped into their place. Within minutes the bodies of three Gardesmen lay at his feet, unconscious or dead.

Marc redoubled his efforts, fighting desperately to contact his adversary. He managed to land a few body blows, but they rang off Corbin's torso like a slap on armor. Corbin sliced and parried, but his blade met the unresisting folds of cloth or empty air. Two more Gardesmen fell to Racque, and Marc saw one of the companions dispatch another. "Your men are ill-trained," he taunted.

"They are well enough trained, but they lack dedication."

"Ignominious. Felled by unarmed rabble."

Again Corbin's sardonic smile pulled at his mouth. "Perhaps it will inspire them. Hatred is a powerful motivation."

"One you know well." Marc's answer was not a question.

"Intimately," replied Corbin.

"You don't expect to lose, do you?"

"Never in the end. The odds are with me."

Yet in Corbin's heart there was a glimmering of doubt. He had used every clever trick, every ounce of speed and strength he possessed, yet his adversary stood before him, unharmed. There was nothing remarkable about Marc's compact, well-proportioned body, yet the ease and lightning quickness of his responses overshadowed anyone he had faced. Though he did not show it, Marc's blows found their mark, bruising two of his ribs. There was a channeled power in those blows that astonished him. They were an indication of the strength of the mind which drove them.

The ancient practice of *auctorite* was cherished by the royal family. It was a slow, demanding method of combat. Never popular, it had fallen into the domain of legend with the general availability of more blatant weapons, but Corbin understood its uncanny effectiveness. He was close enough to the royal house to know its virtues, and even frail, unathletic Pavis had been able to disarm his best-trained Gardesman. Though he had never seen it done, he suspected a man with the proper training could even elude wide-angle blaster fire.

The realization of Marc's methods sent a chilling vein of anger through the fire in his blood. He had never been offered that training, but this changeling had been handed it all. Knowledge had been spread before him in a feast. Corbin's attack took on a personal note.

Marc was quick to see the spark of anger in Corbin's black eyes. He did not know the reason, but Corbin was no longer fighting with his characteristic deadly calm. There was a recklessness in his movements that might break his defensive shield.

"You are going to lose this battle." Marc's voice was soft. It taunted Corbin.

"I shall not lose the war. You have no place to go. The kingdom you would rule is in my hands. I have already won."

"All you have is a collection of maps, a plotted geography.

Men's hearts are all that is worth ruling, and they must come to you freely."

Marc's forearm met Corbin's, forcing the Seneschal's short sword up. Their arms clashed and held like crossed weapons. Marc probed deep into Corbin's eyes, using this moment to discover all he could of his soul. He found a fire of anger lost in the dark. He had a fleeting impression of power frustrated. Corbin was far beyond simple unhappiness. He was desolate.

"You are a fool." Corbin's voice grated between his clenched teeth.

"I never denied that," Marc managed. The effort of keeping Corbin's sword arm raised made the sweat pop out on his forehead. He fended off a horizontal punch that almost threw him off balance.

"You risk everything for a woman and a handful of rabble."

"They are everything."

"Bah. They will drag you down, clutching at your knees for support."

Corbin struck again, and Marc met the blow. They were deadlocked.

"I would rather fail than succeed at the price you have paid."

"What can you know of my price?" Corbin snarled between clenched teeth.

"I can read it in your eyes. You denied your heart. You are dead."

"I am in power."

"Even physical death can be no worse than the living death you have chosen. It is not for me."

"Then feel pain!" Corbin rasped. "Feel anxiety and anguish! They are all you will ever know! I can teach you their exquisite torture."

Marc rocked at the adrenaline-backed strength in Corbin's arm as he bore down on him with crushing force. Beside him Racque grappled with the last of the Gardesmen. Suddenly the man went down, kicked flat by Racque's left foot. Before he could recover, Racque was on him, his arm jammed against the man's neck, choking him. Marc was aware of the precise instant when the man ceased to struggle. He saw Racque launch himself at Corbin, his hand slashing toward

Corbin's neck in a chopping blow. He felt Corbin's awareness of danger come too late. The blow connected with such force it staggered Marc before he felt Corbin crumple. As Corbin went down, Marc reached for his sword.

There was a hiss like the breath of a dragon as it wakes, and Marc's hand froze inches from the weapon. "Gas," he said.

Racque raised his head, listening. "The automatic security system! We've exceeded the time allowance. Jamming those doors must have triggered it."

"Go!" said Marc, "before we're sleeping at Corbin's feet!"

Side by side they ran for the door. The dragon's breath was close behind as they stumbled into the corridor, choking on its sickly odor. They gulped clean air as the door clanged shut.

"Close," panted Racque.

Marc's eyes danced. "Not close enough," he said.

Racque answered him with a wicked grin, and they raced down the corridor.

CHAPTER 21

"Took you long enough!" The doors to the VIP hangar crashed shut behind Marc and Racque, underlining the note of relief in Stella's cryptic comment.

"Everyone aboard?" queried Marc as he slipped a blaster from a fallen Gardesman's holster.

"Almost."

Marc raised the weapon and aimed it at the door controls. A single shot burned the circuits and turned the door into a thick slab of metal impervious to all but the most powerful cutting torch.

"What do you mean, almost?" said Racque suspiciously.

"Coryelle is making sure we get a start," answered Stella.

"From the center of the squadron?" Racque was incredulous.

"If we can block all communications from the *Ravening*, we'll surprise the other vessels with Corbin's ship. It will not be questioned," said Marc, his eyes sweeping the deck, checking off the incapacitated ships and men.

"That's what Coryelle is doing. No one ever gives me a chance to explain," muttered Stella. Her words were crotchety, but the tone was not. "Lar?"

"Still with Sphaleros and the rear guard in the banquet chamber. He'll come after us as soon as he can."

"It was a stroke of luck Sphaleros was with the company. He's more dangerous than Ydre in battle, though not so reckless."

"Yes, and another stroke of luck we didn't break Lar's cover. There's no reason to think he won't be safe on the *Ravening*."

Coryelle emerged from the auxiliary control center and ran toward them. The light in Marc's eyes welcomed her.

"I crossed the circuits," she said. "If it works, when the main communications center tries to contact any of the other vessels, the connection will be rerouted to auxiliary control and killed there. The hangar doors are set on automatic. We can go."

The look Marc sent her was fleeting, but it lent wings to her feet as they fled toward *Ravensong*. The ship's gangplank was lifting as she reached it. She found Cowell, a quiet, reliable man in his early forties, in the copilot's seat. The ship's engines were humming, vibrating through the hull in arousing movement. *Ravensong* was ruffling her feathers preparatory to flight.

As Marc slipped into the pilot's seat, he smiled at the man. "You're always ready for me, Cowell."

"She is yours."

Marc's hands slid over the unfamiliar controls with the surety of a virtuoso at a strange instrument. Gone were the days when inexperience sent him crashing ignominiously to earth. He could handle this ship by feel as expertly as if he had flown her for years. He knew Racque was a better pilot than all of them combined, but he was given to recklessness, and the departure of *Ravensong* must be as natural as her arrival, and as precise. His meeting with Corbin had taught him much about the man. He knew the Seneschal would fly the ship himself and do so with a precision that pushed her to the limits but was never uncontrolled. He would have to try to emulate that style.

Marc gave the boosters a push and the ship lifted from the landing pad. He was aware of another factor as well. This entire operation, the resistance as a whole, was his responsibility. If his desperately conceived plot failed, he did not want it to be at another's hands. He sent the ship forward, and the hangar door parted for him. As it began to open, he accelerated, hoping he was judging speed correctly. He knew Corbin would exit at the maximum speed for safety. *Ravensong* whistled through the lock with inches to spare and sailed out into open space. The other ships in the squadron noticed their comrade, but did not question its flight. She was no prey, to be harried, but their unquestioned master. She flew swiftly through them, her destination sure—and her own business. They kept their counsel.

Corbin felt the dull ache spreading from his neck down his back. It sent pounding waves through his head. His eyes were leaden. The temptation to fight returning consciousness, to return to unknowing oblivion, crossed fleetingly through the pain. He rejected it. He forced his eyes open, blinking against the soft lights, and stared at the ceiling. He demanded his breathing slow, become regular. Gradually his eyes focused, and pinpricks of color faded from his sight. He blinked once, hard, and rolled to one side.

The movement pulled an involuntary groan from him. He held himself on one arm, hating the tremor this effort caused. Too slowly his arm steadied, became firm. He raised a hand to his head and ran it gently through his crisp, dark hair. His pallor matched the silver hair at his temples. He was haggard, but he felt his strength begin to return and he waited for it—not patiently, but because he knew no other alternative. Presently he raised his other hand and spoke into the computer link on his wrist.

"Corbin."

The voice-activated link fluttered to life. "*Ravening*. Communications." There was a series of cheeps as the link confirmed contact. "This is *Ravening*. Identify."

"Corbin."

"Yes, Excellency." The reply was immediate and obsequious.

"The prisoners have escaped. They had access to the VIP hangar deck."

"*Ravensong* cleared the hangar door some time ago."

Anger washed over Corbin, placing pain in abeyance. His voice was cold. "Pursue her. When you find her, blast her out of existence. Get a crew up here to free the doors."

"At once, Excellency."

Corbin cleared the link and sagged. He pushed himself against the wall and relaxed, closing his eyes. Once freed, he would need his strength.

Sphaleros, on the other hand, was most active. He was cursing. Quietly, in a steady stream of profanity, he berated himself. The murmuring monologue accompanied his attack on the cover of the door controls. He removed a digital panel. Sticky with drying wine, it was totally useless. He tossed it into a chair.

Lar had removed himself to the rear of the company, to observe and escape notice. He continued to play the innocent drunk, but his green eyes missed nothing. He noted the time required to pry the panel loose, and exulted over each passing second. As Sphaleros picked up a napkin and began to wipe out the interior of the control housing, he smiled. It had not been a waste of good wine. When Sphaleros tried to jump the circuits with a table knife, he had a moment of alarm, but in spite of the captain's ministrations everything was still too wet to function. Sphaleros threw the knife down and stalked off, knowing time was the only cure. He stomped up and down, wearing out his frustration in physical activity. Lar was close enough to pick up the comments Sphaleros' men were so studiously ignoring. No one lifted a hand to help or hinder the captain, they simply remained quiet and kept out of his way. Lar found this significant. He reeled in his chair and listened shamelessly.

"Idiot! Fool! Stupid, slow-witted son of Dynt! You should have foreseen the attempt! You should have known!"

Sphaleros' railing at himself was not something Lar expected. The man was normally controlled, but it was obvious he was no cold-hearted machine. He kept himself under a tight rein. He had evolved methods of dealing with a volatile nature.

"Known, but how could you have known? You had no word. Where was the Commander's precious spy? No word at all from him! That should have told me!"

Lar's fingers burned as he thought of the messages he had intercepted.

"If I ever get my hands on that useless hunk of meat I will wrap that slave collar around his neck and twist it tight."

Slave collar. The informant was a slave? A frown puckered Lar's brow. There were many ex-slaves in the resistance—seven of those rescued had once been slaves. Marc himself had been a slave. The spy must be someone close to the handful of people at the top, or he would not have been privy to the information he was dispensing. A slow suspicion dawned in Lar's heart, a suspicion he did not want to face.

The *Ravening*'s fighters broke from their hangar like mettlesome chargers eager for a race. They split into squads of six and swooped off on divergent courses, following a prearranged search procedure that seldom failed, breaking up the area into sections and methodically searching each one. The last plotted course of *Ravensong* placed her in the first sextant, but she could easily have doubled back or veered off. She could have headed straight for the nearest shipping lanes, hoping to exchange transport, but Lieutenant Nowt did not think so.

Sniffing along at the head of his fighter squad, he was drawn forward by a bloodthirsty attraction to his quarry. For the fifteen years of his service in the Garde, he had pursued the rebels, sought them out of their dreary hidey holes and sordid refuges. He could feel the presence of the pretender prince, feel the heat of his blood through all the vast, cold reaches of space.

Besides, in the heart of this sector was the abandoned space

station that served as a waypost to Lazur. It was a useful
rendezvous and trap he had often used. It was a perfect place
for the pretender to take refuge. It might even be possible to
hide a ship the size of *Ravensong* within its corral, but not
from him. He knew every nook and cranny of the station,
every place a man or ship might hide. The pretender could not
escape. If he took refuge there, it would be his last stand.

Corbin, through clenched teeth, ordered the pretender's
death. His own ship was to be blown apart, no section left
intact, no survivors possible. Nowt smiled in anticipation. He
enjoyed destruction. He liked the beauty of the explosion, the
delicate colors in which a ship died, like the legendary dol-
phin that flushed the colors of the rainbow at its death. Each
ship was different, a surprise. *Ravensong* was a large vessel as
fighters went. She would probably furnish multiple explosions. The thought quickened his blood.

The methodical monotony of the search procedures galled
him. Cruising back and forth, checking and counterchecking,
manacled his instincts. He yearned to make straight for the
station, but discipline held him in check. Whatever his own
desires, he set them aside in favor of his life. Corbin brooked
no breach in his regulations.

"Vessel dead ahead," announced his right wing. Darq had a
facility for the sensors that had saved his life more than once.

Now he had it—a familiar blip on the sensor screen. He
knew the configuration before the computer checked it out.
Ravensong. They were approaching rapidly, but *Ravensong*
was dead in space. She floated outside the station entrance.

"What do the scanners tell you?" Nowt asked his copilot.

"I can't read anything. The shields are up."

"Gray wing. Hold position. Defense one." He thought out
loud, in a murmured undertone. "If the shields are up, she
must be carrying crew. You can't debark through shielding. If
she's not moving, she's either crippled or waiting for us.
Which?"

"Procedure says . . ." began the copilot.

"Don't quote the manual to me!" snarled Nowt. "I helped
write the book while you were still in the nursery. Just figure
out a trajectory for an implosion charge." He switched on the

communications link. "This is Nowt of the Garde's gray wing. You are surrounded. There is no escape. Surrender or die." A buzz of static blasted Nowt's ears, and he pulled the receiver off with a curse. "I repeat, you are surrounded. This is your last chance to escape destruction. Acknowledge."

The static came again, and he was prepared for it, but this time it was followed by a voice.

"This is Marc Dynteryx. We will surrender *Ravensong* on one condition."

"You are in no position to make conditions," returned Nowt. He was elated. To return with both Marc and *Ravensong* would boost his career.

"You will free my companions. I will go with you willingly. With my death the rebellion will be crushed."

"We will consider."

Nowt pushed in the communications link to close the line and activated the coded frequency he used to communicate with his men.

"You are to go to defense three," he said. "Plot your implosion charges carefully. We don't know what tricks he is planning. I want to get him on the first run." He switched back to the normal frequency. "Your terms are acceptable."

"Then let me send my companions to safety."

"Negative. You must surrender to me. I will make arrangements to free your companions."

"Forgive me, Lieutenant, if I do not trust you. My companions go free or you will never see me."

"I remind you that impasse means extinction."

"Bluster away, Lieutenant. I know you would like to save the Seneschal's ship. I cannot blame you. She is a beauty. However, we must find an alternative satisfying to both of us."

"I am open to suggestions." Nowt's voice was icy.

"I have one. You trust me. You have nothing to lose. I have everything. Let me send my friends into the space station. I will remain on board *Ravensong*. When they are safe, I will drop her shields and you may board her."

"We will try it."

"What do you think?" asked Racque.

Marc leaned back in his chair and smiled. "He will not be

able to resist violence. He cannot be sure of getting us any other way. Besides, he won't disobey Corbin's express orders. You remember the edict that came through. He is supposed to destroy *Ravensong* and everyone on board her."

"I agree with you. Isn't it lucky we aren't on her?"

Marc nodded, twinkling. He looked around the old space station's main communication complex and grinned. They had channeled *Ravensong*'s communications system through it. The ship had been docked to camouflage the link. To the approaching craft it seemed the messages were coming directly from *Ravensong*.

"This is Lieutenant Nowt. You may disembark your friends. I warn you, we shall monitor your shuttle. If you try to escape with them, we will destroy you."

"Acknowledged, Lieutenant. They will depart immediately."

The *Ravensong*'s lower hatch parted, and she gave birth to a circular escape shuttle. The little vessel dropped a hundred kilometers and began to move slowly toward the station.

"Sensor scan," barked Nowt.

"I can't, sir. It's shielded too."

Nowt's voice rose in a grim laugh. "Then he'll get what he deserves. Open fire."

The first fighter in the wing shot forward, turned belly-up and sent a blazing red implosion charge toward *Ravensong*. The others followed in quick succession. Only the last ship was able to see its danger and angle off. The charges rocked Corbin's ship, punching holes in the shielding, but they caused a reaction as well. Once they met the hull of the ship, they were repulsed, shot back along their previous trajectory at twice the speed. Two fighters were destroyed before Nowt knew what was happening. Even then, it was too late for him to escape the consequences of his own fire. His ship went up in a cloud of blue smoke and sparks worthy of a man who loved explosions, a fitting epitaph.

The remaining two ships frantically altered their courses, climbing out of the way of their own weapons. One made it, the implosion charge sliding harmlessly beneath its wings to explode in space. The other flew a wild zigzag, with the charge gaining at every turn. Whether the pilot panicked or not, the last Gardesman could not tell. He only saw the results. The ship never made a sharp enough deviation in course to escape the charge. The bomb exploded on its tail, sending the fighter in a whirling dive that ended in another explosion. Shaken, the last fighter regarded *Ravensong*. His companions failed to destroy her. It was therefore his duty to make the attempt again, but he had no wish to die. He hovered in space, watching *Ravensong* in deadly fascination. The ship's shields were destroyed. Jagged streaks of power sputtered around her tail section. It was the sign of a failing engine, and a failed engine meant failed life support. No one aboard her could possibly survive, or would not for long. He watched blue lightning crackling angrily over the tail, and waited.

"Do you think she'll blow?"

"Let's wait."

Neither pilot nor copilot desired suicide. They watched as the power surges grew in violence. The ship rocked, and one of the Gardesmen expelled the breath he had been holding.

"She's going."

"Lucky for us."

"What'll we report?"

"What do you think?"

"She's destroyed. Doesn't seem to matter how."

"No."

They watched a series of explosions travel the length of the ship, finally reaching the command console. When that blew in a shower of red sparks, the pilot turned away. The Seneschal would be awaiting a report. He punched in the home frequency.

Corbin turned away from the communications panel in disgust. His ship was destroyed, but not before it had brought down five of his fighters. He made the surviving pilot repeat all he could remember of the conversation between the pretender and Lieutenant Nowt. It was not encouraging.

Corbin could recognize a stall when he saw it, and Marc had launched a beautiful one, completely throwing the Gardesmen off the scent. Corbin had not one doubt Marc survived the *Ravensong*. The entire maneuver reeked of a trap, yet he knew the futility of following a cold trail. Immediate search of the space station was an impossible task for two men. No, *Ravensong*'s destruction was an efficient mask for escape.

Corbin turned to face Sphaleros, who hovered over the search. The cold emanating from the Seneschal was penetrating. It froze the spirit. Sphaleros felt it sinking into his bones as he stiffened to attention.

"I have reconsidered." As always, when most dangerous, Corbin's voice was soft as velvet. "I do not want the pretender killed. He is to be captured alive. Now that we have his description it should not be so difficult. See to it."

"Yes, Excellency."

Corbin was aware of Sphaleros' activity as he turned and stalked from the room. He knew his orders were in capable hands, but he feared his temper was not. He sought his quarters where he could fight down the anger raging within his heart. As the doors closed after him, one of the technicians spoke.

"Lor!" he muttered. "Did ya see his eyes? Black flames feedin' on his innards!"

"You play a dangerous game, my friend. If you are not careful, it will cost you your life."

"I sent messages." The spy's voice was emotionless.

"So you sent a message. It was too late, even if an unfortunate accident had not prevented its delivery." Sphaleros' tone was hard. He had determined to deal with the spy in person to make sure he was aware of the consequences of failure. He was in no mood to listen to explanations.

"No. I sent messages."

"Forgive me if I don't believe you," retorted Sphaleros.

There was silence at the spy's end of the conversation.

"I will tell you this," continued Sphaleros. "There is no room in this business for cowards or cheats. You are lucky Commander Ydre does not know of this. His reactions are more severe than mine. I, on the other hand, will grant you this one mistake, but if you fail again, all the wide reaches of space will not be enough room to hide. I will hunt you down and flay you like a side of meat. I will make it a personal matter. Do you understand me?"

There was a long and sullen silence. It irritated Sphaleros, yet he put up with it. He knew if he pushed the man he would lose him.

"I sent messages," the man replied finally. His surliness rasped on Sphaleros' nerves like sandpaper.

"Have it your own way. Only remember one thing: if you fail me again, you are dead."

Sphaleros closed the communication abruptly. The spy looked down at the quiescent communications link in his hand. He had given them Marc. He had given them Lar and Racque and Coryelle. He handed them the resistance, and they allowed all of it to slip through their fingers right under the Seneschal's nose. Now they were blaming their own mistakes on him. He was so angry his hand shook.

He dropped the communications link as if it might bite and rubbed his hands together in an automatic cleansing action. He had come within sight of the reward he coveted to lose it through another's bungling. Anger steamed in his blood, yet he knew he would continue to work for Ydre and Sphaleros. He could not help himself. The reward they dangled in front of him was too attractive. He could not resist the elusive hope of freedom.

CHAPTER 22

Marc stood on a hill overlooking an open plain. The wind ruffled his hair and sent his cloak billowing behind him. After the artificial atmosphere of ship and space buoy, the pungent air of Kingsfalden was unutterably sweet. He closed his eyes and breathed it deeply, grateful for this abandoned planetoid.

Kingsfalden was originally a summer home and hunting lodge for the royal family, high-ranking officers, and officials. Pavis' seclusion and Corbin's lust for power made short shrift of recreation, and Kingsfalden was abandoned, though it was still protected by a high-priority security screen Inspi had not been able to bridge.

"This system is an antiquated piece of junk!" he had stormed.

"Is that why you can't break it?" Racque inquired mildly.

Inspi's black glower would have silenced another man, but it did not inhibit Racque.

"It's got some kind of idiotic key I can't identify."

"A key?"

"Some sort of musical progression."

"That minstrel is never around when you need him."

"Let's hear it," said Marc.

"What?"

"Let's hear the melody."

"It's hardly that," said Inspi dryly, but he put the computer link on audio.

A glissando of notes played on some woodwind rippled into the freighter's cabin. It was repeated at thirty-second intervals. Inspi allowed it to run through several times and was about to silence the code when Marc's hand shot out and stopped him.

"Wait," he said.

Fido was barking. More accurately, the little android that had attached itself to Marc was making noises. It flew over Marc's shoulder, emitting its own series of sounds. They were birdlike chirps compared to the haunting notes the security system was sending out, but as Marc listened, he realized they were in harmony with the original glissando.

"The security system is down!"

Racque's exclamation took Inspi's eyes off the metal watchdog and redirected them to the computer panel. He muttered under his breath as he acknowledged Fido's efficacy. Marc chuckled as he recalled the calculating look Inspi turned on Fido. He knew his computer genius wanted to take the android apart.

So they invaded Kingsfalden, a pathetic remnant of men and women. Their safety here was tenuous, secure as long as no one realized the planetoid was inhabited. They were dangerously close to Dynt, but for the moment Marc did not care.

It was the alternative that presented itself, and its audacity was some safeguard, if not for the spy. Lar managed to get away from Ydre at the first space station, and he sent the disquieting news that the spy was both male and a slave. Given the peculiar circumstances of his knowledge, there was one distinct possibility, a possibility that twisted Marc's heart. He waited for the spy to reveal himself.

Marc knew he would try to transmit the new location of the resistance to his superiors. It was a matter of waiting him out and being there when he tried to make contact. The confrontation was something he shrank from. He pushed his problems away and allowed his spirit to spread on the wind, becoming one with the clear air, the ocean of rolling green grass, and the solid earth under his feet. It was good to escape the restricted life of a star pilot and revel in a more natural environment. The wind ran through his hair like caressing fingers, and he thought of Coryelle.

He had barely seen her since the rescue. There was no time, and now when there was time, he found himself running from a private meeting. The danger of her abduction forced him to put into words feelings that frightened him. He had been willing to sacrifice everything to save her. He had not realized how much a part of him she was. She had been an arresting child he loved without thinking about it. Now she was a woman who enchanted him unknowing. He could feel her flawless, silky skin slide under the fingers of his mind. It was intoxication he did not wish to escape.

Stella tripped down a long side corridor leading to the king's study. The hallway was lined with windows opening onto the palace's manicured green park. Sunlight streamed through the leaded panes, making extravagant geometric patterns on the smooth stone floor. Her ears rang with birdsong, for Pavis' collection of wild songbirds was housed on the other side of the hall and ran the length of it. A miniature jungle of tropical foliage sheltered over two hundred birds. So well had Pavis designed his aviary that the birds lived much as they would in the wild. Their chattered comments as they haggled over food were punctuated now and then by a clear

burst of notes, songs sung for the joy of it. It was rejuvenation
for Stella's senses after the sterile metal world of space.

On her return to Pteron, Stella found a message from the
king. It requested her presence at the earliest opportunity, and
it was written in such a spidery, shaky hand that she dreaded
what she would find. Pavis was failing in earnest. At every
visit she noticed a change. It was painful to watch him grow
weaker. She longed to reach out and hold him back from
death.

So preoccupied was she, Stella almost bumped into Chevie,
who was softly closing the doors to Pavis' study. The elderly
slave bowed out of her way, but Stella reached out impulsively: "Please wait."

Chevie raised her beautiful eyes inquiringly. The sheer re-
gality of her presence was startling. Without saying one word
she dominated Stella. In a flash of intuition, Stella realized
she was looking at the queen of Dynt, official or not.

"At your service, Mistress."

"I wish . . ."

"So do I, but wishes will not keep him back. He has held
Dynt for many years. To some he was a weak king who abandoned his people. He was not. He was a broken man who put
himself back together for Dynt. Now he has but one desire.
He will secure the throne even on his deathbed."

Chevie was speaking to work out her own thoughts. Her
eyes grew frightened as she realized what she had said to a
complete stranger. Stella put a hand on her arm again.

"Do not worry, Chevie. That is my concern, too. I will not
stay long."

"Thank you, Mistress. Indeed, he tires easily, but I think
your visit will rest him more than sleep. He has been waiting
for you."

Stella pushed open the door to the king's study, dreading
what she would find.

"Stella! Come here and let me rest my eyes on your beauty.
You give an old man more pleasure than is good for him."

Stella laughed and advanced. Pavis was reclining in a
lounge chair, his spectacles in his hands and a manuscript
spread across his knees. He shuffled the papers into a pile, his

stiff fingers making heavy work of a light task. Stella knew better than to offer assistance.

"Come here and sit down."

She obeyed him, trying not to see how the rings slid on the wasted flesh of his hands.

"I need to know the news. All I get are disquieting rumors. The boy escaped?"

"Yes. But the resistance is almost broken."

"Then there is still a chance. As long as the boy lives, there is still a chance." Pavis drew a deep breath of relief, and his eyes were bright.

"He is only one man."

"No. He is a symbol, a rallying point. He may draw all of Dynt to him." Pavis' eyes twinkled back at Stella. "I have not struggled to go on living so he might give up!"

"He will never give up, even if he is the only one left, but there is heartbreak in it. From thousands the resistance dwindled to hundreds. Now it is a handful. They died because they followed him."

"They would have died eventually, whether they followed him or not. They served some cause. It is more than I have done for most of my life. I am therefore aware of its virtue."

"That may be some comfort to him, but I doubt it."

"The crown is a heavy burden. When it comes to his hand he will be more aware of its weight because of its cost. It is an unpleasant fact, but it will make him a better king."

Stella's eyes darkened. "I am glad I do not have to carry such a load. Other people's lives . . . it is too heavy a price."

"That is why so few wish to lift it, and even fewer are worthy of it. Tell me, Stella, what are the boy's motives?" There was an undercurrent of urgency in Pavis' voice, a desire for reassurance.

"To tell the truth, I do not know. Yet I can tell you I trust him."

"That is your woman's heart speaking," Pavis said indulgently.

His tone made Stella's hackles rise. She found his occasional patronizing comments difficult to tolerate. There were times she had to remind herself he was both an old man and a king.

"I do not believe so," she answered slowly. "It may be my woman's intuition. He does not seem to care for power or wealth, and yet he loves the life he has chosen, with all its hardships. I think he is suited to it."

"Temperamentally born to be king?"

"I know it sounds silly, but I really believe it. Sometimes I think he is not aware of his own charisma, at other times, I wonder. He has a way of twisting an onerous duty into a personal favor. I cannot speak for anyone else, but I can say I follow him now for the love of the man."

"Stella, you are a fickle jade. I always thought that young rogue, Lares Harken, was for you."

"He is. Yet there is that about Marc any woman must love and any man must follow. He is an elusive siren song of possibilities."

"It is not easy to be a symbol. I know. I am supposed to be a symbol of Dynt. At least, by the time he ascends the throne, he will have had practice."

"I think he will need your help if he is to succeed."

"He will get it." Pavis indicated the manuscript in his lap. "This is one way. It has taken me over a year to prepare this manuscript."

"What is it?"

"It is an annotated history of Dynt as compiled by the ruling family." Pavis swept his arm toward two shelves lined with bound manuscripts. "There is the original. However, until Marc has access to my study, the annotated version will do. It contains a great many observations not available anywhere else. It may help him in determining his course of action."

Pavis lifted the neatly stacked sheets of paper, and Stella took them out of his trembling hands.

"You will take it with you when you go, disguised as a musical score."

"Of course."

"There will be others things as well. When you come again, I will have them ready for you. You must be prepared to take them away in the utmost secrecy."

"Whatever you wish, my lord."

"Thank you, Stella. You are a humbling experience."

"Me?"

Pavis nodded solemnly. "You are young and you have little
to gain by risking your life. You serve other people. I have
only now attained such wisdom."

"You, my king, are a scholar and a gentleman. I will never
attain either distinction, the first because of laziness, and the
second because of an unavoidable physical problem."

Pavis chuckled, and she chuckled back. Her rich, throaty
laughter was a counterpoint to his amusement. She was happy
to give him pleasure. He was as Chevie had said, almost
transparent.

"Stella, if you have a problem, it is not physical." Pavis
held up his hand. "No. Don't drop your eyes and blush and
look modest. It will not work with me. You are entirely aware
of your beauty, and you use it like any true performer. I remind you not to dispute my judgment. I am both your king
and a respected connoisseur of beauty."

She dropped a courtesy, but her cheeks still flamed. "Thank
you, sir."

Pavis regarded her with a smile in his eyes. "You and Chevie. You are the only ones who still treat me like a human
being instead of a piece of glass. You rest me. I am glad of
your presence."

"But you would be even gladder if I would sing." Mischief
danced in Stella's dark eyes. Pavis' innocent expression reminded Stella of a little boy caught with a forbidden sweet,
and she laughed again. "I am happy to sing for you, lord. Do
you have a preference?"

"None. I leave the selection in your hands."

Stella perched on the edge of his desk and thought, then
her full contralto took up the melody of a half-forgotten
ballad.

"Oak leaf, wilted-leaf, flat pine, harrow.
Many make the forest grow,
On valley, plain, and barrow.

Flaming fire, curling blight, rushing flood
Threaten all that grows,
Cutting off the green life's blood.

The clever woodsman makes the difference,
Keeps the forest green
Growing tall and straight and dense.

Oak leaf, wilted-leaf, flat pine, harrow.
Many make the forest grow,
On valley, plain, and barrow."

The notes of the song died away. Pavis spoke softly, his voice scarcely disturbing the silence. "The king is like that woodsman," he said. "Other people live their lives. His life is safeguarding theirs."

CHAPTER 23

"Attack squad, close ranks."

The order drew the coterie of fighters together like fingers closing into a fist, the five ships in a tight formation. Their combined firepower was capable of destroying half a planet. It was to be aimed at one small stationary target.

"Target coming up on the sensor scans. Plot your trajectories."

The Gardesmen's computer screens disclosed the structural readout of an automated fuel dump. Its power source was located at the base of the station. The fighters would concentrate their fire there. They moved in like a pack of wolves.

A freighter was docked on the far side of the station. Its cables were connected to one of the pumps, and it was supposedly taking on fuel. In reality it was transporting slaves. Its computers picked up the approaching fighters as the Gardesmen were targeting the station. The ship's copilot whirled in his chair.

"Captain! It's the Garde. Closing fast."

The captain hauled an old man through the hatch with a none-too-gentle wrench. "Drop the cables!" he ordered, and reached out the door to help a woman and her two small children climb aboard. A tall youth followed them. "Hurry!" he said, and a middle-aged woman ran up the ramp, pushing two more children ahead of her. The captain caught the children as they tumbled through the door and the woman followed. "Hatch!" he yelled, and leaped for the controls.

The hatch closed with agonizing slowness, and the captain fought down his rising adrenaline. "Do they know we're here?"

"I don't think so. They're targeting the station."

"A prearranged target?"

"That's what it looks like."

"They've broken the whole system."

The copilot nodded grimly. "Hatch sealed!" he said.

"Let's go."

The captain rammed the ship into full reverse. The vessel shot back, taking the fuel outlet with it. Fuel erupted into space in flat globules. The captain knew it would not be a hazard. When the Garde's volley struck, it would be caught in the explosion and dissipate harmlessly. The space station grew smaller on the viewscreen, but not fast enough. The captain feared he would not entirely escape the Garde's attack.

"They've fired," his copilot reported.

"And struck," added the captain as a mass of blue flame enveloped the station's power block. The ship's engines were grinding in full reverse, but they still had not put enough distance between themselves and the station. As they watched, the flame licked around the station's inverted cone. There was a dull boom and the structure dissipated.

"Position of the Gardesmen?"

"They sheered off before the blast. They're headed home."

"Sure of themselves," muttered the pilot grimly. "Hang on!" he yelled to his passengers. Debris from the station's disintegration grazed the shields, then a ripple of spatial distortion struck. "Cut the engines."

As the engines whirled to a halt, the ship surged forward, caught in the explosion's backlash. It spun, drawn back to its former position. The captain let it spin, then he pushed her slowly forward. When she straightened out he sent her across space like a skittering coney bound for its hole. The station's destruction was a major catastrophe, for it was a reliable link in the slaves' escape route. The captain did not relish reporting its loss.

The Gardesmen were unaware of the freighter's escape. They fired on their target, and tallied it in the computer log. Their shift was almost complete. Their compact wedge spread out and they turned for home.

"Ydre reports the three wayposts have been destroyed." Lathric's voice contained no emotion.

"Good. Casualties?"

"Only the space station was inhabited. Perhaps thirty."

"The price of treachery is high." Corbin's voice was cold, justified.

"That spy is proving valuable."

"To us he is valuable, but he is a danger as well. A man who will betray his own has nothing to live by. In the end we will have to kill him," answered Corbin. "I speak from experience."

"I know."

"Use those three wayposts to plot a probable course for the escape route. Once you have the route, check it against vessels that make regular stops in the area. Give me a list of the likeliest candidates. We will take their ships, send them into slavery in the mines of Antos, and sweep space clean along the route. I shall expect some information in two hours."

"You shall have it, sir."

Corbin put his hand on Lathric's shoulder in a rare gesture of affection. As always, he was surprised by the strength of Lathric's unimpressive frame, and a little uneasy at the man's uncanny efficiency. It was not natural to be free from error, yet he had never caught Lathric in a mistake.

Lathric, for his part, neither flinched nor relaxed under Corbin's hand. He remained his own cool and efficient self, unperturbed by his superior.

"See to it, Lathric."

"I shall, sir."

Lathric was already studying a computer scan of the wayposts as Corbin disappeared into his office. The computer plotted three possible courses for the slave route and presented the alternatives to Lathric. He began to correlate them with flight plans filed over the last five years.

Marc reread the message with a sinking heart. Thirty more people had died in the name of freedom. He grappled with the news, wringing the implications from its heart. Ran Corbin knew of the slaveway. It was most probable he gained his intelligence through the spy. It was necessary to expose the man and stop him, equally necessary to evacuate every outpost along the slaveway before Corbin could destroy them. He crumpled the paper in his hands.

"Well?" Racque's sardonic question drew a flash of anger from Marc's honey-colored eyes. It stained the gold dark.

"Mobilize anything that can fly, all the fuel they can carry. We're going to clean out the system before Corbin can. Get Inspi to wrack that computer's brains for temporary quarters for the refugees. He'll send it in code as soon as he gets it. Contact the freighter captains, and tell them what's going on. Assign them to the larger wayposts, the ones that can house more than ten people. We'll take care of the rest. We'll be in the air in half an hour. And Racque . . ."

Racque stopped in mid-turn, his blue cape flowing around him.

"Make sure you let everyone know."

Racque's half-smile was both sad and bitter. "I will make sure everyone on Kingsfalden knows," he promised.

"Everyone will be needed. Two to a ship."

Racque nodded and departed. Marc took the crumpled piece of paper and spread it on the table before him. He read it numbly this time, not taking in its meaning, but seeing the intricate pattern made by the crushed paper and the printed message. He allowed the disaster to fade to an abstraction. It would be easier to deal with, and he had no time for self-recrimination if the refugees were to be saved.

The hunting lodge where he and his followers set up headquarters was a rambling, tumble-down structure capable of housing two hundred. Their few numbers were lost in it. Marc had the common room to himself. He awaited Racque's return in silence. The early morning was cool, even in the heart of summer, so there was a fire burning. The flames sent dancing, mesmerizing lights over the hearth, and Marc let his eyes rest on the continual subtle changes as the flames flickered over their food. It was a restful moment, one he needed before the desperate action ahead.

Presently Racque returned, and Marc motioned him to a seat. The sounds of quick footsteps told of the evacuation of the lodge as the resistance went to succor its own. Marc waited.

Silence descended on the old building, the deep silence of desertion. The sound of the flames in the grate murmuring over their meal was loud in his ears. He saw Racque's head lift at the sound of cautious footsteps. He extended a hand at Racque's move to rise, stopping him before his chair could scrape the floor. The surreptitious footsteps became louder, then halted. The man had stopped, probably in front of the door to a storage pantry that served the common room. The corridor was dim and neither Marc nor Racque had a clear view of it from where they were seated, but the skreak of a metal key inserted in a lock was easily audible. The lock turned, and the heavy, old-fashioned tumblers fell into place. They could hear the key withdrawn and the soft squeak of the hinges as the door was opened.

Marc rose silently and glided into the hallway, Racque trailing him like a shadow. The door to the pantry was open and a shaft of light spilled into the hall. They could hear the low hum of a power unit and the chirping noises of a computer link. Marc motioned Racque to remain in the background as he stepped forward into the doorway. What he saw made his heart sink.

"So it was you, Suzerain," he said softly.

Suzerain jumped as if he had been shot. He turned to face Marc, the red light from his computer staining him with a bloody glow. His broad shoulders drooped. The big hands, powerful enough to snap a man's neck, but in Marc's experience lifted only in the service of others, hung open, impotent. There was anger on the man's face, and anguish. The fear in his eyes was not that of a hunted animal, but of a man who has betrayed himself. Marc's heart ached for him, in spite of the lives he had cost.

"Why?" he questioned. The gentleness of his voice seemed to inflame Suzerain.

"Why not? You with your courtesy and understanding! You cheat. You lie. You make a man feel human and then use him. Slave? You a slave? There be no knowledge of it."

The anger boiling out of Suzerain was a deep-seated, festering wound. Marc's forehead puckered as he tried to sort out the man's reply. He could feel the resentment Suzerain was aiming at him, but surely a personal vendetta would not extend to innocent bystanders. Marc searched his memories for any slight or evil done to the man.

"But Suzerain, to betray your comrades just to destroy me . . ."

"Comrades? Companions? They be that for you. They be my masters, all of them, but you be the biggest cheat. Everything, all this death, in the name of freedom! You treat me like a man, then leave me to rot. Worse than being treated as the slave I am."

Suzerain was shaking with anger, and his deep voice had a hysterical edge. Marc sifted his words, seeking the key to his rage. Though it was centered on him, Marc could feel a deeper current, and he dove for it.

"Suzerain, what did they offer you? What price was so dear you would sacrifice your friends?"

"There be no friends. I know where I stand. They offered me the only thing that matters."

Suzerain's voice had dropped to a surly growl. He was getting control of himself. Marc could see him calculating the chances for escape, and his heart sank. He had no wish to fight Suzerain. He was afraid the man was so violent he would be forced to injure him badly.

"And what is that?" Marc's voice was scarcely above a whisper.

"Freedom!" returned Suzerain savagely. "Freedom from the slave chain."

Marc's eyes widened in surprise, and his answer was so genuine and immediate it stopped Suzerain in his tracks. "I never realized you were a slave, though you wore the white tunic for Foxxe. I thought you were his retainer, loyal to him."

"Retainer! I were dirt under his feet, a slave conquered and bent to his will. Long ago, in my own country, I were king. Slavers destroyed all I held dear and roped me down. I were beat and starved to submission." He emitted a bitter laugh. "It be easy to break a man who has nothing left to live for."

"Suzerain, there are no slaves here. Only free men. You have been free since Foxxe's death."

"I belong to the children. It is law."

"It is not my law. Have Coryelle or Racque ever treated you with disrespect? Answer me!" Marc's words cut through Suzerain's confusion. He shook his head slowly, like a bewildered lion.

"No."

He continued to shake his head, as if the motion would clear his thoughts. Marc allowed him time, though moments were precious. Finally Suzerain raised his head and looked directly into Marc's eyes.

"I hated you," he said, "because you made me remember I were a man. It hurt. When Foxxe died and I were still a slave, the servant everyone took for granted, I knew your fine words were a cheat, and I hated you even more. Hate were a poison in my blood."

"Hate is like that."

"I were wrong." The pain in Suzerain's eyes was almost unbearable. "I were wrong, and the innocent be dead." He dropped on one knee before Marc in an archaic gesture of fealty and bowed his head. In body and in spirit this battered warrior was offering himself as a sacrifice. "My life be yours. End it in honor."

The words were as old as Dynt, so long forgotten they were made new. Marc reached out and placed a gentle hand on Suzerain's shoulder. "If your life is mine, I will set it a harder task than death. You will never be able to wash the blood from your hands. Its stain reaches the soul. I know. I cannot wash it away either. It is a burden we must carry. Right now I need your help to save men and women along the slaveway. Corbin has discovered three of the wayposts. From those he will deduce others."

"There be no reason to trust me, but I will follow you through death."

"There is a ship waiting for you."

The look of dumb worship Suzerain turned on Marc was painful, but Marc knew he had asked for it. He smiled. "Never kneel to me again, Suzerain. A free man can stand before anyone."

The worship in Suzerain's eyes changed to wonder. Marc turned away from him, trusting the man to follow. He did not think Suzerain was acting, but in any case there was nothing to be done but allow the man to prove himself. He turned his whole attention to the coming evacuation.

Suzerain watched his departure. He was shocked by Marc's trust, and by his total dismissal of the past. Suzerain's thoughts were sometimes slow, but they arrived at just conclusions. The big man's shoulders straightened. His whole posture changed. He would never kneel to Marc again, but he would act as a king who owes his loyalty to a higher power, and gives it gladly. There was a flash in his eyes as he followed Marc's footsteps, and his tread was that of a war leader, yet there was no pride. He accepted his assignment from Racque with the deference due to a trusted companion.

Marc, intent on last-minute plans, still noticed Suzerain's manner. He liked the fact that Suzerain did not grovel or ask forgiveness. This was a man who would accept the consequences of his own actions and live with them. He offered his life to Marc. He would accept whatever use Marc chose for it.

"I see you found the spy." Gisarme's dry voice was solely for Marc's ear.

"I found him. There will be no more to fear from that quarter."

"So I see."

There was a warmth in Gisarme's voice Marc had seldom heard and even more rarely deserved. He turned to face his teacher. Gisarme's eyes were smiling.

"What pleases you?" Marc asked, really curious.

"My own intelligence and good judgment." Gisarme's smile extended to the rest of his face. "To be a warrior and a military leader and a king—these things are of no great consequence. But to take a man's twisted thoughts and pull them straight, to soothe the bruises on his battered heart—most of all to make him accept your help—this is something worthwhile."

Marc reached involuntarily for Gisarme's shoulder. He needed support. "I do not know what to say," he managed, his eyes touched by golden lights.

"There is nothing to say. I will say I am proud to have had a hand in your education."

"If there is anything in me of value, it comes through your training—even more through your example. Most men are not so lucky."

"Most men would not have benefited by instruction. To teach you was merely to remind you of something you already knew."

Laughter made the golden lights dance. "Aren't you afraid I'll become insufferable?" Marc asked.

"You would have no chance." Gisarme chuckled. "Your companions would not stand for it. I am thinking particularly of Stella's acid tongue."

"It also occurred to me."

"To horse." Racque's voice cut into the conversation. It was light with anticipation of danger. Gisarme reached out and grasped Marc's arm.

"Come on, boy. We've a match to play."

"Let's hope for the luck of Dynt."

"With the dynteryx along, we already have it," replied Racque. He motioned to the flying horse engraved on Marc's ring, but the play on words included Marc himself in the compliment.

The ships that rose into the atmosphere of Kingsfalden on their errand of mercy were a pitiful, straggling wing barely deserving of the name. The men and women who piloted them did not care for appearances. They were concerned with a necessary action, an action which could not be evaded. That they were throwing a handful of soft snow in the face of a wood bear did not deter them.

The ships cleared atmosphere without an attempt to cloak their presence. They took the chance of detection in stride. Precious fuel would be needed later. They flew in a loose phalanx until both Kingsfalden and its neighboring Dynt were out of sight, then they peeled off, one by one, heading for their evacuation targets and praying they were not being followed. To lead the Garde to more slave stops was an alternative they did not dare to contemplate. The ships were swallowed by the expanse of space, connected only by the tenuous threads of their coded communications links.

CHAPTER 24

"My lord, I cannot."

Stella's voice broke with emotion. She knelt before the king, her head bowed to hide the tears rising in her eyes.

"Stella, you must. It is the one thing I ask of you."

Pavis' words, soft and steady, fell like lead weights on her heart. She knew the truth of them, but rebelled against them as she fought Pavis' impending death. The king extended his hand once again, the square, flat links of the gold chain he held winking in the lamplight.

"Stella, hold out your hands."

It was a command she obeyed dumbly, extending her cupped hands toward the king. He allowed the chain to fall into them. Its musical clink broke the silence of the shadowed room. Stella stared at the pile of gold in her hands as if wishing would make it go away.

"You cannot hold back the inevitable," said Pavis softly.

"That does not mean I don't want to," she responded.

"The chain of office goes to the king. If you do not take it, it will be lost, for Ran Corbin does not intend to crown another king."

Stella raised questioning dark eyes to the old man's. Pavis nodded.

"For some time I have been sure he desired more than a regency. He wants total power over Dynt. He is not satisfied

with military control. He wishes to guide the heart and soul
of Dynt as well. He is not foolish enough to set himself up
as king. He will choose another route. He will do his best
to kill Marc, calling him a pretender. Failing that, he will
discredit him, erasing all record of his claim to the throne.
He cannot erase this." Pavis gestured to the chain. "With
the chain in his hands, Marc will command the hearts of the
people, and Ran Corbin will find it hard to tear him down.
And there is more."

"More? I don't recall ever seeing you with more than the
chain to proclaim your title."

Pavis smiled. "You forget how I hated my estate. Under the
bed you will find a box. Pull it out."

Stella deposited the chain on Pavis' reading stand and knelt
by the king's bed. As she fished under it, she tried to think not
of Pavis' physical weakness, but his request. She rebelled at
his death, and she knew her reaction made his task harder.
The box was farther under the bed than she had supposed, and
she had to stretch for it. When she did touch its mellow
leather surface, she found it much lighter than she expected.
She dragged the box out and dusted it off.

"Give it to me." Pavis spoke with the authority he so seldom used, but which no one ever disobeyed. Stella placed the
box next to him on the bed. Pavis caressed the dark leather.
"This, too, you will take to Marc. It is the last of the royal
treasures. He already wears the royal signet. With the chain
and this, he will hold all the emblems of authority."

Pavis lifted the lid and reached into the box, his hands
trembling with emotion as well as fatigue. He lifted the crown
of Dynt and held it in his two hands. It was a thin circlet of
gold, perhaps half an inch wide, gradually rising to a peak
three times that height. It bore no jewel, but it was engraved
with a ramping herd of flying horses, their wings lifted to the
air. It was simple and beautiful, somehow appropriate to
Marc's dark head. In her mind's eye she saw him wearing it,
and it was no weighty burden, but a fitting accent to the
power that was his own.

"What do you see?" Pavis nudged her intuition.

"I see Marc, wearing that crown."

"I, too, have seen that vision. It becomes him."

"More than I knew."

Pavis' frail fingers closed over Stella's hands. They were dry and warm. Stella's hand trembled as she accepted the fact she would not see him again.

"You must understand the importance of the trust I give you. Between the crown and the chain, you hold Dynt. They are symbols of leadership so deeply engrained in the nation's heart it does not even realize their power, but I do. So does Ran Corbin. Marc may wield these like a sword against him. I believe I have caught Corbin off balance for once. He does not think me capable of this. Moreover, he does not know my commitment to Marc. He will discover that when I die."

Stella ran a reverent finger around the metal circlet. "To take these from you is like killing you, saying you are no longer king."

"Stella, the trappings of office do not make a king. That lesson was a long time in coming to me, but I finally learned it. With or without the symbols, Marc will be the leader he was born and trained to be. With or without them I will hold the throne until I die. Take them to him as the useful tools they are."

Stella picked up the crown. It was heavier than it looked.

"I am a goose."

"Emotions are unpredictable things. Who would have thought at my advanced age I would discover a beautiful young girl I could love as the daughter denied me? Do not apologize for your feelings." Pavis ran his fingers down Stella's cheek. "You care for me, and that is the most precious thing of all. In my whole life, Stella, but three women have loved me: my sister, my slave, and you."

Stella could no longer stop the tears. They welled up and spilled slowly down her cheeks. "I have no words."

"You need none. Your tears speak for you."

Stella swallowed, willing her voice to obedience. "I will do as you ask, my lord," she managed.

"I never doubted it, Stella. Dynt will live or die by Marc's hand. He needs all the help I can give him to save it."

Stella nodded.

"In these last years, Stella, I have lived for Dynt. Now I

will die for it. You have given me the ease of knowing my
work will be continued. Along with these tokens, I ask you to
give Marc one other thing. Give him my love. My heart is old
and brittle, but sometimes it astonishes me. I find he has become dear to me as he was to Tenebrae." Pavis' eyes were
shadowed with fatigue, but he smiled whimsically. "This may
be his biggest talent, to make people love him. It may be the
source of his power—who knows?"

Impulsively Stella reached for the king's hands and kissed
them. "Long live the king," she said.

Pavis' hands closed on hers in farewell.

Marc approached the Pebbles at an oblique angle and swept
over the top of the asteroid belt, looking for Peter I. One of
the resistance's more ambitious projects, it was a space station
disguised as an asteroid. It had been Inspi's pet, and as the
man's genius with computers was immeasurably valuable to
survival, no one questioned him when he announced his in-
tention of constructing the station.

There were scoffers, but Inspi grandly ignored them and
proceeded to revamp a scrapped space bubble. The once
smooth hull of the antiquated structure was textured to resemble the rocks among which it would be hidden. Inspi stripped
the interior and rebuilt it to house twenty people in more comfort than most free-floating space stations could offer. It was
entirely computerized, requiring power boosts once every five
years.

When the station was complete, Foxxe authorized its place-
ment in the outer rim of the Pebbles. Its installation required a
full week of carefully timed approaches, until Peter I could be
inserted into the complex network of the asteroid belt. Inspi
had been cocky about the station's success, but even he
heaved a sigh of relief when it was safely in place, its dis-
tance-activated shields fending off approaching chunks of
rock when they ventured too close for safety. These same
shields required Marc's careful approach. He had to sneak up
on Peter, coming close enough to feed the computers the
override code that would allow him to dock, but not so close
he would be bounced away. It took a clever and daring pilot to
land on Peter. One miscalculation could send a man and ship

to oblivion, smashed by an actual asteroid. The danger did not make Peter a popular stopover, but it was a safe one, most often used for refugees of high standing. A senator had taken refuge there, as had one of Corbin's officers.

The pockmarked surfaces of the asteroids slid past his viewscreen, but Marc paid them no mind. He was intent on his computer screen. It searched through the asteroids, discarding them one after the other. Finally it zeroed in on a distant body and bumped its sensor scan to extreme magnification. Within seconds the computer reproduced the interior in a three-dimensional linear graphic. The virulent green lines showed a circular station beneath its camouflaging rock, with living quarters, life support stations, and power source. Letter by letter, the computer spelled out the word "confirmed."

Marc punched the identification code and relaxed. He was no longer in danger of being thrown into the Pebbles' interior. He concentrated on missing the obstacles directly in his path. He dodged a chunk of rock a kilometer in length and headed for the open space around the station. Smaller asteroids struck the ship. The sound of them sliding off her shields was like gravel flying from the wheels of a fast-moving cart. Larger pieces of rock battered the shields as he tacked toward the space station. Once he was rocked by the impact. The ship swayed, threatening to break free of his control, but he coaxed her back. As he neared Peter a rectangular slit appeared in what seemed a solid mass of rock as the magnetic fingers of a tether were thrown around the ship. He cut power and allowed the vessel to be pulled toward the station.

He felt a stab of panic as the walls closed in around him. There were no approach lights in the landing chute. It engulfed ships in darkness and silence. Marc felt, rather than saw, the ship hover motionless, then settle to a landing pad. The space doors slowly closed, blocking out the starfield. They met with an old-fashioned metallic clang that was oddly reassuring.

Safe in the station's hold, lights were no longer a risk. They bloomed around him, flooding the ship. Marc's eyes, accustomed to partial darkness, rebelled, and he squinted against it, at the same time activating the hatch. By the time it was lowered, he could see. Six men and women were gathered at the foot of his gangplank, their upturned faces like flowers on a single stem.

"I am Marc Dynteryx," he informed them. "We must leave immediately."

An older man stepped forward. His thinning hair did little to mask the shine of his cranium, but his eyes had the calculating quickness of an astute mind. "We were instructed to wait for a freighter captain."

"I know, but your plans must change. Ran Corbin has discovered the slave stops and will destroy them. We must be gone."

"What assurance have we this is not a trick?"

"Corbin has no need of tricks. He would either kill you and destroy the station, or take you into custody by force. I can do neither. I am one man. You must make your choice now, or none of us will survive."

"You say you are the prince . . ."

"Does it make any difference who I am if I can get you to safety?"

"I just wanted to know why you would say that. Did you think to overwhelm us?"

"I said it because it is the truth."

"He wears the dynteryx, Evan."

Marc sought out the source of the comment, a stout matron with a child clinging to either hand. One of the children pointed to Marc.

"It's him! Look, look there!"

Marc, puzzled, glanced over his shoulder for the cause of the disturbance and was annoyed to see the android Fido. Fido's single red eye blinked, and he emitted a pointed electronic beep. Marc had no idea what it meant.

"The familiar." Evan's tone was reverent. He bowed his head. "Forgive my doubt," he said. "There is little in this world that is as it is represented. We will come immediately."

Marc had no time for explanations. He waved them into the vessel. "Come then. We must hurry." He sent Fido to a far corner of the ship's hold, but its sensor unit remained aimed in Marc's direction.

Marc hurried his charges onto the ship, impatient with the clumsiness of the adults and the inattention of the children, though he was solicitous and courteous. He saw no sign of Corbin's forces, but the hairs on the back of his neck were erect. He knew the Seneschal was bearing down on his targets. He locked his passengers into their seats as a precaution against their panic at the rough ride he meant to give them, pleading the turbulence caused by the asteroid belt as his excuse.

Once they were safely secured, he set takeoff coordinates and felt the ship rise to his touch. He headed down the docking tunnel at half throttle, a dangerous speed in the confined space. Peter I's space doors opened with agonizing slowness as Marc blasted toward them. He was glad his passengers could not see the narrow opening he planned to slide through.

As he neared the space doors, he checked his sensors for approaching spacecraft, and was not happy to see a wedge of fighters ahead of him, flying a parallel course. Their direction suggested their target was the next slave stop in line from Peter, and Marc prayed Racque had managed to clean out the solar power station and destroy the life support bubble hidden beneath the huge solar collectors.

As he cleared Peter he sent the ship straight up and over the station, avoiding the Pebbles' smaller members in a seasick tacking course. There were some close brushes before he escaped the asteroid field and headed for the emergency rendezvous. One last task and Peter would be secure.

Marc fed Inspi's private security block into his computer and coded a tie-in with Peter's main computer network. He pressed the activator and watched as a list of Peter's systems appeared. The word "void" followed each system as it was erased, canceling Peter's power except for deflectors. It was a dead hulk, indistinguishable from the asteroids that were its neighbors.

Marc set a course and went to check on his passengers. They were as he had left them, but Evan's complexion was pale, his expression strained. Marc had seen enough space sickness in his life to know the signs. He repressed a smile.

"I'm sorry for the rough ride," he said, "but the Pebbles are no pleasure cruise, and we were in a hurry. Corbin's fighters were kilometers away."

There was an exclamation of dismay from the two women

in the party. "Did they see us? Will they destroy the station?" asked the elder.

"To your first question, no, they did not see us. Their minds and their sensors were on the next waypost, a solar power station more easily accessible than your asteroid. As a matter of fact, I do not believe they realized there was a stopover in the Pebbles, but it was just as well you are gone. Eventually they would have plotted trajectories and destroyed everything along them. That, I believe, answers your second question."

"Where are you taking us?" asked Evan.

"To a harbor where you will be safe until you can be relocated."

A strident beep rang through the ship.

"What was that?" Evan was panicking. Marc had no time for his nerves.

"Another rescue ship. Excuse me." Marc turned back to his cockpit. His sensor screen showed a single vessel pursued by five of Corbin's finest. As the ship came into visual range, he realized it was Gisarme.

"Marc! Run!"

"Too late, Gisarme! The fighters have seen me."

"Come on, then! We are the foxes playing the hounds for fools."

"I'll follow your lead, but I've passengers aboard."

"It can't be helped. I transferred my lot to Racque, then acted as a diversion while he got them away. I thought you'd be gone already, or I'd never have come this way."

Marc sent his ship after Gisarme's smaller craft, praying he could keep up with it. He had more power, but he also had more drag.

"We had a bit of discussion or I'd have been away sooner."

There was an unintelligible mutter from Gisarme. "Hug my belly. I'll shield you all I can."

"Forget the shield," responded Marc. "Let's fly these hounds into a bramble patch."

"What did you have in mind?"

"I was thinking of a dimensional warp."

"I suppose you didn't intend to get caught in it yourself,"

said Gisarme, slamming his ship into a half roll and smiling as Marc followed him like a shadow.

"Actually not."

"I suppose it's worth a try. Hit your throttle and drag them into our wake. They'll have to be at least twenty kilometers behind us to get caught in the backlash of a jump."

"That's closer than I thought."

"They won't expect a space jump near the Pebbles. If we can put them between the asteroid belt and our jump we may be able to rattle their engines. If we succeed, they'll be so busy compensating for distortion we should be halfway to the rendezvous before they can level off."

The two ships turned toward the asteroid belt, drawing Corbin's fighters with them. Their course was a long, loose arc that was conducive to speed. The honed wedge of fighters closed on their quarry, nipping the little freighters' tails impudently. As they came into range, Marc and Gisarme began to sweep outward into open space. The fighters closed in, an exhibition wedge.

"They'll pay for showing off," said Gisarme. When the distortion hit, the fighters would be hard put to it to keep from crashing into each other. "Get ready."

The fighters made the last two degrees of their turn, placing them directly between the Pebbles and the two ships.

"Now!"

Gisarme's order coincided with the movement of Marc's finger as he pushed his ship into overdrive. The vessel jumped in a jerky tesseract, arriving at a point five thousand kilometers distant in a breath. "It worked!" he said.

"Of course it worked. A bit rough, but definitely effective."

Marc's computer told him their pursuers were rocking frantically in spare, their superb training and reflexes the only reason for their survival. Wings cut past each other with a breath to spare, wildly waving tails threatened the bellies of their cohorts, and cumbersome hulls presented suicidal obstacles to their neighbors. By the time they compensated for the distortion, Marc and Gisarme could hardly distinguish their movements. Soon they were entirely beyond sensor range, safe in the hospitable reaches of empty space.

CHAPTER 25

". . . destroyed everything along a two-hundred-kilometer projected course, except for the Pebbles and the Blackland Vortex."

Corbin listened to the report with polite seriousness. It was impossible to guess he was cataloging the deaths of innocent people and the destruction of millions of dyntares' worth of equipment.

"Thank you, Fafnir. I trust all the verified targets were contacted."

"Of course, Excellency." Fafnir's voice lacked the clinical quality of his master's. There was enjoyment in it. "We found no resistance, though we did encounter one or two unauthorized freighters."

"And?" Corbin was immediately curious.

"We fired upon them."

The Seneschal was not satisfied. "What identification did they give you? Did you destroy them?"

Fafnir hesitated before replying. Corbin saw him weighing words and discarding those that did not suit him.

"There was no time for identification. We were able to eliminate one of the vessels. We gave chase to the rest, but they eluded us."

"Eluded you? A freighter eluded a fighter of Dynt? That is not possible."

Fafnir struggled for words. "They seemed to be equipped with some sort of power booster and almost unlimited fuel . . ."

"Rescue! I'll wager most of the runaways were lifted off those stations before you arrived." Corbin's thoughts turned inward and Fafnir, at the other end of the visual communica-

220

tions link, quailed at the partial failure of his mission. Suddenly Corbin snapped out of his abstraction. "No matter. The network is destroyed. That is most important." His eyes shone cruelly. "The pretender has so few followers left, I grant him a handful of escaped slaves. They have found a worthy leader."

Fafnir discovered he was holding his breath. He let it out. "Do you wish a return sweep of the area, Excellency?" he asked.

"No. We have wasted enough time on stragglers. Return to Dynt. Upon arrival, you will make a full report about those freighters to the dock officer—everything you can remember. We cannot allow ourselves to be bested by rabble. But next time, Admiral, I suggest you be more careful. Circumstances favor you this time. You may not be so lucky if you do not adhere to the complete spirit of your orders. As incentive, there will be no spoil." Corbin saw the effect of his rebuke in the Admiral's carefully blank features.

"Certainly, Excellency. We shall return at once."

Corbin gave Fafnir a long look before he ended the interview. Fafnir met his eyes, but with a veiled expression the Seneschal noted. Corbin knew his potential for violence, but the man's fear of him held it in check. As he terminated the transmission, Lathric's voice came over his shoulder.

"The computer reports are in on Fafnir's mission."

"I will look at them later. Right now I have a job for you."

Lathric did not reply, but awaited the assignment.

"Did you hear Fafnir's comments on the freighters they sighted?"

"No, but the computer projects they were at least three times faster than our fighters. All we have that can compete with them is a stripped-down scout."

"I want a special fighter squad. Five ships. Use everything at your disposal to increase their efficiency. Use Fafnir's report, the computer, and some sage experience. Find the best shipwrights on the planet."

"Might I add a computer expert to that list?" Lathric's question was low and deferential. Corbin looked at him quickly.

"Why?"

"I think the speed of those ships may be due in part to a more sophisticated computer system than we possess."

"Well, well, well. I had almost forgotten Inspi. That was a mistake." His sardonic smile wrenched the corners of his mouth. "You, Lathric, shall have Fafnir's spoil."

"Thank you, Excellency."

"Take whatever crew you need. I want a unit capable of keeping up with any invention Inspi can throw at us."

"Of course, Excellency."

Corbin's mind slid away from his assistant. He knew his orders were in capable hands. With the elaborate underground railway gone, the rabble could not rally to Marc's cause. His pathetic clutch of followers would not be augmented. Corbin smiled at the disintegration of Marc's forces. Soon he would have no place to turn. He would give up or run. In either case, Dynt was safely under its master's hand.

Corbin savored the fruition of his labors. He held Dynt. Marc was reduced to a wisp of wind, the refrain of a song, a voice in the wilderness. The pretender was no longer capable of damage. His ability to rally others to his side now existed in a vacuum, and his personal charm was useless. Marc's face rose in his mind's eye. He acknowledged and dismissed its beauty, but he could not evade the boy's eyes. The fire in their depths was suffused with a captivating light and variable color that continually altered their expression. They spoke more clearly than words. He tried in vain not to listen.

All his life he had fought for control of himself, for the subjugation of emotion to his goals. He allowed his emotions freedom when they would serve his purpose. Not for a second had he reacted. In Marc's eyes he read a man who accepted his own unpredictable behavior, a man who chose his own course, yet felt no need to repress feeling. Corbin knew the boy's vulnerability would be his downfall. He would not outlast youth.

Corbin held in his hand an accomplished fact. He had broken the pretender's support. Marc would never be king because he would never be able to claim the throne. Corbin had plans for the throne. It would remain empty, its vacant arms a reminder of a lost leader. The image would act strongly on the people's imagination. The Seneschal would run the government as a sacred trust for the absent ruler. Long ago he began to manipulate the populace into demanding the senate award him the crown. Corbin smiled to himself, a smile of such evil anticipation even Lathric shrank from it.

When the royal family that spurned him was deposed he would hold the office he deserved by every law of talent, ability, and intelligence. Never again would a drunken lout of a nobleman question his right to rule because of his birth. Never again would any man dare lift a finger of reproach against his most wicked decrees. He would be subject solely to his own whim. Like Pavis, he would eventually succumb to the grasping hands of death, but unlike the aged king, he would maintain lines of command until the end, and he would safeguard the prospects of his heirs after him. No longer would the king be a figurehead ruler, but an absolute monarch.

The thought of Pavis intruded upon Corbin's daydreams. The old man was a crumbling piece of parchment. He would not last much longer, tough though he proved to be. He had not seen the king since the previous winter, though Lathric handed him daily reports on the old man's condition and activities.

"Lathric, you last reported the king had failed markedly. What were the projections of his physicians?"

Lathric responded smoothly, apparently unruffled by the random question. "The physicians say he has no more than a week. He could die any time."

Corbin's back was to him, so Lathric could detect no expression, but he thought the Seneschal's posture changed. There was a touch of sorrow in the man's stance.

"There is an emptiness in the loss of an enemy," he murmured to himself. "He was never afraid of me."

Lathric, knowing his seneschal, let the words slide by as if he had not heard them.

"Free the afternoon, Lathric. I am going to see the king."

"As you wish, Excellency."

Corbin's exit had, as always, the stalking grace of a lion. Lathric watched his departure with speculative eyes. Of late he noticed a tendency toward introspection not before apparent in Corbin. The years crouched at his heels. Corbin was remembering, and the memories sometimes cracked his calm exterior. Lathric left the thought for later and returned to his work.

Corbin was deep in one of the moods Lathric noticed. He was thinking of his youth, of the reserved, slightly shy but openhanded young man Pavis had been. Colorless compared to his sister, he was lost in the glittering society of the old king's court. Corbin remembered the awe with which he regarded Pavis, heir to the throne, the brilliant scholar ten years his senior. In the privacy of his own thoughts he knew he liked Pavis, liked him even now. It was ironic he was one of the few people who knew what a difficult mistress the crown had been for Pavis. Yet if he liked the king, he did not respect him. Pavis was gentle and weak. He hid from conflict and responsibility. For this Corbin despised him.

Corbin sent his aerfoil toward the palace. He was unaware of the paths clearing before him as the streamlined black bullet tore through the city. He was paying little attention to his course. His mind ran before him, luring him toward an encounter with himself. He was aware of the gates that opened before him, programmed to the approach code of his craft, but the big open park surrounding the palace called him. In its well-cared-for perfection it was an embodiment of the king, yet its great natural beauty was something he had not noticed in years.

He set the aerfoil down under the outspread arms of an elderly tree, feeling an odd sense of homecoming which had nothing to do with his imminent plans. The idealistic dreamer he had been lurked in the background of the royal court. He ignored the presence.

As he made his way past the elite corps of Gardesmen who protected the king, he was met with the unquestioned deference a slave gives to his master. In this place, with the king still living, he found it made him uncomfortable. It was a squeamishness he tossed away.

At the entrance to Pavis' quarters the Gardesmen on either side of the door stepped back and raised their swords, clashing the metal points in an honorary archway for the heir to power. He stepped beneath the portal and into Pavis' world.

The king's rooms were free of military taint. The regiment surrounding him came no farther than the door to his study.

Beyond the door was the sunshine-filled sanctum of a scholar. Taste and wealth were apparent in its furnishings, a love of beauty in their arrangement.

Pavis lay on a cushioned chaise, and the sunlight washing over him seemed to filter through his fragile frame. His profile was edged in golden light. For a moment Corbin thought he was too late. Pavis raised a hand, drawing his visitor closer. Corbin approached with his clipped, military step ringing on the stone floor. His strength and good health were an affront against the king's wasted frame. Pavis' eyes halted him, still clear and vital despite his frailty.

"This is unexpected." The king's voice was steady but so soft Corbin had to lean close to catch his words.

"For me, too. I had not thought to come."

"Then why?" The king's curiosity was genuine.

Corbin's dark, empty eyes sought the monarch. "I wished to look upon the last of the royal house."

A chuckle rose in Pavis' throat and almost choked him. It took him several breaths to regain control. "You forget the boy."

"I forget nothing. His organization is broken."

"He escaped you."

"This time. He cannot win."

The king regarded his seneschal with the compassion of a man who understands the blackness in his own soul. Except for the silver over his temples, the years had left Corbin untouched. Pavis found this more pathetic than the most ravaged countenance. Corbin took no part in the business of living.

"I think he surprised you," said Pavis. "I think you were not prepared. I think you came face to face with something you had buried in the depths of your being. I think you saw a shadow of yourself, and you were afraid."

"I did not ask for a psychological profile." Corbin's voice was harsh.

"I am dying, Ran. I say what I wish. My life, sheltered as it has been, has also contained bitter experience. We are not unalike, you and I. We both turned our backs on our feelings because they were too painful for us to deal with. I tell you now it was a mistake, a mistake that led to more pain than I could possibly have caused otherwise."

"What can you know of pain? You, who have wrapped yourself in a cocoon apart from the world. What can you know of the cold, the hungry, the helpless?"

"More than you, who manipulate and plunder with no regard for the common welfare."

Corbin surveyed the old man with a countenance of stone. His eyes held the merest hint of irony. "For a lifelong scholar, your ignorance is appalling. Perhaps your studies should have placed the human animal in a more prominent position."

"The human animal, as you call him, was always of primary importance to me. I know what I am saying." Pavis' words were labored. It was becoming difficult for him to speak.

Corbin watched him passively. "Not this time," he said softly. "Your arrogance, Pavis, was always your downfall. Presume to understand me?" The irony spread to Corbin's lips as he smiled thinly. "You could not. Neither age nor experience can plumb the depths of my soul."

"What then?" breathed Pavis.

Corbin's smile stretched, twisting the corners of his mouth. "Perhaps passion. It is not a part of your vocabulary."

Pavis turned his head, looking Corbin full in the face. "You are right. I do not understand what tore Tenebrae or you. It was a madness I do not comprehend."

"In that you are lucky. Your pain has been milder because of it." Corbin swept the conversation aside with one hand. "All of this is of no consequence. The past does not interest me. It is the future that is of paramount importance."

Pavis smiled wanly. "On that we agree."

"You must know with your passing the government will be openly in my hands. There is no real reason not to acknowledge it publicly before you go."

"Again you forget the prince."

"And again I tell you he will never rule. The game is over. The consequences are clear. He is dead."

"So sure of yourself." Pavis moved his head in imperceptible negation. "So sure of your calculations and projections. You twit me with passion, Ran, but I tell you you have forgotten the human heart."

"I have forgotten nothing. No paltry affection will defeat

me. Do you really think love will draw followers to his side, when they see the hopelessness of his situation? Those he holds most dear will desert him in the end, convinced of the madness of his obsession."

Pavis' smile was an effort and as slight as the shake of his head. "We shall see. All you say may be true, but I have spent my time wisely, and I have studied the boy who will follow me. It is the quality of his heart you must fear, Ran. It may destroy you." The words were labored, the king's breathing shallow.

A bitter laugh broke from the Seneschal, and Pavis knew he placed no credence in his words. In his last moments it gave him some pleasure to know Corbin was deceived in Marc, and underestimated him.

"No more of your protests." Corbin waved a hand in a short, angry gesture. "You might as well authorize an endorsement for me. You know I can manufacture one."

"Not fast enough."

"I will waste no time on courtesy. You may die alone. I shall take what I want."

Corbin rose from his seat and went to the far wall. The heavy wood paneling was carved in an intricate geometric pattern interspersed with stylized roses. He counted down from the ceiling and pressed the center of one of the carved flowers. Silently a panel slid back to reveal a dark and empty opening. Corbin turned slowly to face the failing monarch.

"The crown and the chain of office."

"Beyond your reach."

Corbin stalked toward the chaise, his anger surging from his toes up through his shoulders and into his hands. He stood above Pavis, aching to strangle the old man whose eyes were alive with laughter against him.

"You lose, Ran."

Corbin's fingers twitched. His voice was icy. "There will be duplicates."

The king's eyes still laughed, and Corbin caught himself in an involuntary movement toward him.

"Know this, old man," he said haughtily, "none of your machinations will make the slightest difference. I will rule.

The rebel slave will not. Nothing you can do will change that."

Pavis' eyes still smiled. "Checkmate," he whispered.

Corbin's cold anger ate into his soul. He stared down at Pavis, his passion masked by control. As he watched, the laughter died out of Pavis' eyes, and they changed to expressionless orbs set in a marble face. He watched until he was sure the king was dead, until there was no hint of breath or surge of pulse. When Pavis' frail frame assumed the heaviness of death, he turned on his heel and departed.

As the door closed on Corbin, Chevie appeared from behind a set of curtains and dropped to her knees by the king's lifeless hand. She grasped it and raised it to her lips, the tears coursing down her cheeks.

"O my lord," she mourned, "my sorrow is stained. I should be drowning your memory in tears of anguish, but that bloodless beast intervenes. I hate him! To have robbed me of your last moments, of the small comfort I could give. For that I sorrow."

Her silver head bent over her liege's hand. The same light that had touched the king bathed her in a golden glow. It faded as she turned away from the insignificant mortal remains of the man she had loved to the tangible presence of loving memory.

CHAPTER 26

The Seneschal of Dynt walked down the tree-lined avenue to the palace. Dappled sunshine rippled over his bowed head. He had not expected to witness Pavis' death, or be disturbed by it.

The king's passing was a relief, a last bridge to fall before Dynt was secure in his hands, yet Pavis' words ruffled his feelings like a rough handstroke. For the first time in years he felt deep apprehension. He had controlled Pavis' life. Every moment, every breath was monitored. He knew all there was to know about the king, yet a trapped, infirm old man outwitted him. He shook his head in disbelief, the sunlight gleaming on crisp waves of silver hair over his temples.

It did not matter the power of Dynt was securely in his hands, it did not matter the crown and chain of office could be duplicated, and it did not matter Marc was as good as dead. Pavis had managed to outmaneuver him. The foundations of his confidence rocked. He was so sure of the man, so sure of his reactions, and he had been wrong. His judgment was at fault. He could not believe it.

Pavis' tactics were an effective security check. Corbin's thoughts went into high gear as he reviewed his recent actions. In the end he turned on himself. He was smug, so confident of his knowledge he ceased to acquire more. One fact stood unchallenged before him: he had been warned, and that was Pavis' mistake. The old king might have rumpled Corbin's feelings, but his words roused the Seneschal from the dangerous clutches of self-satisfaction and threw him into headlong flight. He would not be caught again.

He thought of Pavis lying in peaceful state, and bitterness caught at his throat. The man had lived a life of self-indulgent ease, only at the last thinking of a greater good than his own pleasure. Everyone thought him a gentle, kind man, but Corbin knew better. Pavis escaped the stern necessities of command. In his ivory tower existence he had no cause to raise his voice, no need for a trained body to survive. He had not had to prove his quality over and over again. He never shed blood. Corbin looked at his hands. They were good hands, strong and well shaped, with the sinewy strength that comes from handling a blade. They were hands that had done things. He thought of Pavis' delicate, knotted fingers, and hated the dead man.

The anger of a lifetime surged in a floodtide through his soul. Corbin knew Pavis would be remembered as "good king Pavis," and the mournful dirges sung at his funeral would permeate the land, yet what had Pavis done for Dynt? In all the years of his life, what had he accomplished? And one day

when the Seneschal of Dynt went to his knees with a death
wound delivered by some backstabbing weasel, there would
be no tears for him. There would be murmuring rumor, but
there would be no songs. Yet he had transformed the kingdom
into a prosperous economy. Injustice rode the flood of his
anger.

And how, he wondered, had this come to pass? An un-
thinking reverence for the royal family was the key. It made
the royal household a wonderful political tool, but it did little
for the feelings of those who would deal with them. In his
life, Corbin could trace the lines of disaster directly to the
Dynteryx, to the ostrich that had been Pavis, and the proud
lady Tenebrae who had killed one man in him and given birth
to another.

The anger of his thoughts was no less intense concerning
her, but it flamed into color, blood red passion, and royal
purple glory. After all these years, long after her death, the
thought of her had the power to rouse him. Her name alone
tore banked coals from his wounded heart. His anger boiled
up, obliterating the name with a cleansing sheet of white fire.
Cool gray control followed on its heels as he shut down his
emotions.

He was surprised again. He thought Tenebrae robbed him,
but he was wrong. She gave him anger, and anger had been
his strength. It prompted his rise to power, and it helped him
to maintain his position. Now it recalled him to duty.

He opened the door of his aerofoil with the spare motion so
characteristic of him. As he slid behind the controls, he activated the communications link in a direct channel to his headquarters.

"Raven black." It was Lathric's voice, delivering the security identification Corbin had instituted.

"Raven blue," Corbin answered, and waited for the security
screen's static to dissipate. "Scramble," he ordered as the line
cleared. Lathric's impassive face appeared, and Corbin
blessed the man's calm. It salved the smarting sting passion
dealt him.

"The system is scrambled," responded Lathric.

"Good. The news I have is high priority. The king is dead."
If he had expected an obvious display of feeling from his

aide, Corbin was disappointed, yet something did shadow Lathric's eyes. Not sorrow or regret, Corbin concluded, but the merest flicker of foreboding. The coming days would be a delicate time for diplomacy. Lathric knew how much of it would fall on him.

"The standard arrangements have been in readiness for some time."

"They will be no problem. I leave such details in your hands. Once the announcements and services are prepared, bring them to me for authorization."

Lathric nodded. "What of the boy, sir? He's sure to start tongues wagging."

"You are right, Lathric. That is why my appointment as regent must be announced immediately. You will have to take care of the documentation. The old fool was stubborn to the last. He kept babbling about Marc."

Corbin could see Lathric's fingers flying as he set up the computer banks for Corbin's falsified appointment. As Corbin watched, Lathric's calm exterior dissolved into the panic of a first-year recruit, but he did not let his emotions rule his responses. His fingers moved with speed and precision in an attempt to correct whatever difficulty he had encountered.

"Well?" snapped Corbin.

For the first time in his memory, Lathric ignored him. His fingers were still flying, and all his concentration was given to his computer screen. It was a tribute to Lathric Corbin waited for him to handle the situation without prodding him for information. At length Lathric dropped his hands, defeated by an accomplished fact. He raised his eyes to the Seneschal, eyes as flat and dead as Corbin's own.

"The news of Pavis' death triggered a prearranged reaction in the main computer. I don't know how he did it, but the confirmation of the king's demise resulted in a message being sent out simultaneously to every computer terminal on Dynt and beyond."

It was plain Lathric did not wish to continue, but Corbin commanded him. "The message."

"The message, in the king's own voice, announces the appointment of Marc Dynteryx as his sole heir, and awards his legitimate claim to the throne of Dynt and all the accoutre-

ments thereof. The message ends with the king's hand signing
the document into law and affixing the royal seal below his
signature."

Corbin slammed his hand against the aerfoil's steering gear,
almost sending the little vehicle into a nearby tree. He righted
it automatically.

"By the blood of the flying horse," he said through
clenched teeth. The words were low and too controlled.

A shiver ran up Lathric's spine. He had programmed the
king's death into the computer, therefore he was to blame for
Pavis' triumph. He knew the end had come. The color
blanched from his face.

"You could not stop it?"

"No, sir. The transmission was instantaneous, almost as if
the information were waiting in each of those terminals, ready
to be called up."

"Is such a thing possible?"

"Theoretically." Lathric knew he was speaking too quickly,
but he could not help himself. "In fact it would take tremen-
dous organization and time."

Corbin's eyes narrowed to black slits. "O, Pavis had time."
The sarcastic tone of the Seneschal's words eased Lathric's
fear. "We've been projecting his death for years. He had it
planned down to the last detail. I am surprised there were no
processions and banners proclaiming the sad event and nam-
ing that upstart to the throne. If there was one thing Pavis had,
it was time." Corbin raised his hard, dark gaze to Lathric's
face. The color was slowly returning to his aide's skin. "I
presume you could do nothing."

"Nothing."

"Then we must deal with the consequences. You will issue
a general statement to come out by the usual roundabout
means—that will give it more credibility—that Pavis' message was a fake, a cruel joke by the rebel forces preying on a
dying man. You will seal the palace and keep the king's death
a question until tomorrow. Bend everything to make it look as
if Marc staged that little show in order to usurp the throne."

"I cannot vouch for its effectiveness."

Corbin tossed this aside with a look. "It is not supposed to be effective. It is supposed to be official. No one with a mind will believe it, but it will do as a policy statement. Since I hold the power it will not be disputed."

"Yes, sir." Lathric began to see his imminent death receding from view.

"Go ahead, as planned, with my appointment as regent. I will retain the title "seneschal" as a courtesy to the royal house. I shall merely care for another's property until the heir appears to claim it." Corbin grimaced, but continued. It galled him to have to submit to Pavis' victory twice in one day. "You will have to do something about the trappings of office. Pavis seems to have made arrangements for those as well."

"I shall see to it, sir."

Lathric sounded almost cheerful, and Corbin realized how relieved he was at his commander's reaction.

"I do not condemn a man, Lathric, for something which is not his fault."

"Yes, sir."

Lathric's reply was immediate, but Corbin detected a reserve of distrust in his voice. He filed Lathric's reaction in the back of his mind.

"Carry on. I shall expect to see reports within the hour."

"At once, sir."

Corbin terminated the conversation, and the six-inch screen went blank. He locked his hands on the aerfoil guidance control and sent the craft forward at an unsafe speed. Such reckless flying was not his wont, but his aerfoil was immediately recognized and the traffic parted before him. Corbin directed his craft toward headquarters. It dodged obstacles like a homing pigeon, sending a flock of geese in a wildly squawking tangle across the street, and causing more than one pedestrian to jump for safety. Corbin was so deeply engrossed in his own thoughts he did not care how he flew.

That old man, sitting in his scholarly retreat, dreaming an impossible scheme of revolt, puzzled Corbin. A mouse had turned in its tracks and bared its teeth at the lion. It was so incomprehensible, so ludicrous, he almost did not believe it had happened. The fatalist in him accepted the fact and placed it in context. Give the most innocuous creature a reason and it will fight any odds. He would be ready for Marc. No machinations of the old king's would be enough to place the boy on the throne. Corbin projected the consequences of Pavis' death.

First and foremost, he must find the last refuge of the resistance forces. There could be no more than a handful left, but Pavis must have had some contact with them, some link to his chosen heir. Every visitor, every piece of correspondence from the last few years would be studied until it disintegrated under scrutiny. In the end he would find them.

Once located, the resistance would be crushed, but not openly as he had originally planned. It would be better to create a mysterious accident in space or some natural disaster to camouflage the demise of the prince, for Pavis' acknowledgment made it difficult to disown Marc. It would be better to find him swiftly and dispatch him, shedding a few crocodile tears as he delivered a tribute to the prince who had died so young, regretting he could not turn the reins of government over to the rightful king. He would exhort the people to regard his rule with tolerance as he tried to fill the royal shoes until such time as another legitimate heir was found. He was writing the speech as his aerfoil landed on the security pad of administrative headquarters.

Admiral Fafnir heard the computer announcement in the privacy of his apartment. He expected the king's death, so the news was no shock. The manner of its telling was. Fafnir's glass froze halfway to his lips as he listened to Pavis' endorsement of the boy he tried so hard to destroy. The sight of Pavis' hand sealing the old-fashioned sheepskin document into law made him set his drink down.

He knew it was no hoax. Pavis had bested Corbin. The thought put a sarcastic smile on Fafnir's thin lips. There would be trouble before things were straightened out, but Corbin would see to it and win in the end.

One by one the old guard were falling by the way. The royal family was gone. Marc was no real part of them, and even if he were, his followers were scattered or dead. He was powerless. The enemies Corbin had fought so long were fading, leaving everything in his hands, making him a target.

The idea was a new one for Fafnir, and he turned it over

slowly, savoring its possibilities. It was amazingly thoughtful of Corbin to so consolidate things that his strength stood in the way of a revolution. Amazingly thoughtful. One man, no matter how formidable, can be trapped or deceived eventually, yet Fafnir was shy of Corbin's power. As Corbin's fleet commander he came into frequent contact with the Seneschal's complex mind. He had been fortunate never to meet his sword arm, not even as a sparring partner. In physical skill, Corbin had no equal.

His thoughts teased Fafnir with the sweetness of possibility, but simple fear held it in check. It was an idea to be savored, a pleasure to be prolonged. He closed his eyes and allowed it to flow through his mind, indulging his sensibilities in lascivious ease. The sarcastic quality left his smile, to be replaced by the replete expression of a weasel sucking the meat from a goose egg.

"Grandmother, what's the matter?" The boy's voice was shrill with alarm.

His grandmother reached out a gentle hand and caressed his hair. "No great matter, Georg. The king is dead."

"I am sorry, Grandmother."

There was formal regret in the boyish voice. He did not understand the old lady's tears. For her part, she let her grief run down her cheeks in quiet rivulets as she stroked the boy's hair.

"Georg, it is fitting to cry over the death of a king. This time it is even more fitting, for the royal house is dead."

"Yes, Grandmother."

There was even less understanding in Georg's tone, and the old lady smiled through her grief.

"Do you not know, Georg, with all your learning at the village school, that the king is the hope of the people?"

Georg's expression answered her.

"I thought not. The king is one of us. So many hundreds of years ago people have forgotten, except for old crones like me who have nothing better to do than remember, the king was chosen from a cage of slaves. He was given his crown to rule for us, and always he has been our hope and voice in the government of Dynt. Now he is no more."

"But Grandmother, there is the prince. Surely he . . ."

"The prince, as you call him, was not born of the royal house. How can he know of its cares or responsibilities? How can we expect him to care for our sorrows?"

"But Grandmother, the Lady Tenebrae . . ."

". . . raised him, I know. I know. No doubt she tried, but to raise a child is not always to give him the strengths you have developed or the choices you have made." She shook her head. "No, it means nothing."

"But if the Lady Tenebrae believed in him, he must be like her."

"I do not know. Perhaps I weep for the loss of the order I knew. This boy is so young, so unknown. He does not have my faith."

Georg's shoulders straightened, and he stretched to the full span his twelve years had given him. "I believe him, Grandmother. He fought for Dynt with the black fox. When I am old enough, I will follow him."

The old woman patted the boy's flushed cheek. "I do not doubt you, Georg. Perhaps it is just as well. A young man to lead the young. That is as it should be. And the king did give the prince his blessing."

Surprise and scorn dawned in the youth's eyes. "Then it's all right," he said, dismissing her sorrow.

"I suppose it is," answered his grandmother, and sighed.

Georg regarded her with affection, but no comprehension. What was she worried about, if the king named Marc after him? It would be all right. A woman could find tears on a donkey's ear. It was a saying he now understood.

In the flushed morning sky of Kingsfalden a lopsided phalanx flew a tired approach pattern to the overgrown landing field. As the motley knot of ships stooped to earth, they lost the silver beauty the early-morning sun had given them. Their battered, scarred sides, blackened by enemy fire, drew them heavily toward earth. Not one craft looked as if she could fly again, yet they would be instantly aloft at need.

The men and women who disembarked moved heavily, fatigue in their slow movements and silence. They left no guard with the ships, attempted no camouflage. They had not the strength. The next day, if they survived, they would face the business of living. Until then they crawled to shelter. As the sun bloomed over Kingsfalden, they retreated from its beauty. They had seen too much loss, too much suffering. For the present they felt no part of the pastel-tinted morning. Beauty would come back with rest and the remembrance of what had been saved as well as lost. Supporting each other, helping each other, the companions of the king withdrew to his refuge and shut the door.

CHAPTER 27

The hum of idle conversation rippled outside the open door of Marc's sanctum. It was originally made to facilitate serving the gentry, and at the same time keep the help from underfoot. For Marc's purpose it was ideal. Lined with bookshelves, it still housed a sizable library. Inspi managed to insert computer facilities and a miniature communications center into one corner. The polished dark wood of the old paneling caught the light of the slow-burning fire in a rosy glow. A light panel illumined a pile of papers on his desk with clear artificial energy. He ignored them.

Marc sank deeper into the one overstuffed chair in the room. Its fat, solid arms held him impassively. The years had left the mark of their passing on his face. Still young in contour, in repose an air of sadness hung over it. The faint shadow of evening stubble that darkened his cheeks accentuated the hollows under them. His dark hair was still untouched by silver, but it was somewhat longer than he had worn it as a boy, better balancing the added bulk of manhood. He was not a heavily built man, but beneath the dark material of his tunic muscles rippled when he breathed. There was the grace of a natural athlete in his unaffected posture, the power of a trained athlete in its spring-steel relaxation. His change-able hazel eyes shone silver in the firelight, picking up the silver metal of the signet ring on his hand.

He twisted the ring around his finger, enjoying the feel of smooth metal against his skin. He turned the crimson stone up, instead of to the inside of his palm, where he so often wore it to protect his identity. It shone brightly, like a drop of fresh blood. He spread his hands and stared at the device carved into its surface.

Swooping from the center of the stone came the dynteryx, its wings raised, and its feet frozen in suspended animation, a living creature caught in the stone for all time. It might have been some prehistoric insect trapped in amber. He knew how it felt. All his life had been a preparation for this lonely destiny, outlawed with his followers, sought by the hand of authority. Yet in spite of the drawbacks, there was a purpose which drew him on. He stared at the flying horse, mesmerized.

If he were to succeed . . . the possibilities intoxicated him. Not riches, not honor had power to claim him, but the good he could accomplish if he had the opportunity staggered him, especially since he felt responsible for the destruction of so many lives. They must count for something, they must be made an investment in a future where men would treat each other as brothers. He wanted this as fiercely as he had ever wanted anything, even Coryelle.

"Bleeeeep."

Marc looked up, startled. The soft electronic comment surprised him. The android Fido was awake. Its sensor eye was fixed on Marc's hand.

"Bloop," it said in a satisfied tone.

Marc was never sure of Fido's reactions, or purpose, for that matter. He simply knew it followed him since abandoning Stella. If he did not want a constant companion he had to order it away. Several times it performed the function Stella had described of flying in front of him in a protective zigzag. He came to respect the actions of his mechanical familiar, and if Fido wished to examine something Marc was quick to let him have his way.

Fido swooped closer, his eye beaming out a blast of red

light toward Marc's ring. "Bloop, oop, oop, oop," it muttered softly, and the beam vanished.

Marc stared at the circular metal object floating above his hand. Fido hovered, apparently waiting for some move on his part. His interest was piqued. He watched the flattened sphere slowly turn until an impression of the dynteryx was directly in front of him. The decoration had the look of a wax seal, and as Marc studied it he suddenly realized it was the reverse of the sunken image on his ring. He held the ring up to the impression to be sure.

Beasts of myth, one depressed, one raised, they were twins. The implications of the match were legion. The ring he wore was Tenebrae's, but he knew it had a long history in the royal family. Gisarme had told him it belonged to the queens of Dynt, that it was the only signet left to the royal house. Originally two coronation rings were designed for the king and queen. Down the years the king's signet was lost, to be replaced by a standard seal for use on public documents. Looking at the impression on Fido's smooth hide, he knew it had been made by the ring on his hand. On impulse, he doubled his fingers into a fist and set the ring into the impression.

Fido emitted the same whirring sound which prefaced its original activation at Stella's hands. There was a click, and the sound of another mechanism activated within the body of the android. Marc pulled his hand back as the seal slid down the face of the robot leaving an oblong opening. The whirring noise continued, and a platform was pushed forward like a wide, flat tongue. Reposing on it was a worn leatherbound book and a leather bag. The controlled atmosphere of the android's interior sealed them from the ravages of the years, but it was plain to Marc's eyes they were ancient. Such leather pouches had not been used for four hundred years. Leather lacing had been discarded in favor of more efficient sewing methods.

He touched the bag gently, afraid it would crumble under his fingers, but it was as supple as the day it had been entrusted to Fido's care. He thought of Fido's faithful watch, smiling at the whimsical name given in jest, which turned out to be so apt. He untied the bag's drawstring and emptied the contents into his hand. Rolling heavily onto his palm was a ring, similar to the one he wore, but with a heavier, squarer setting. The king's ring. The dynteryx reared across its surface with the same arrogant grace that characterized the image on the stone he wore. He had no doubt they were made by the same hand. He placed the ring on the table, and reached for the book.

As he lifted the volume from its resting place, he heard Fido's interior mechanism activate and the tongue of metal withdrew into the robot's interior. The opening closed, leaving the android a sealed, flattened sphere, innocent and enigmatic. Marc smoothed the surface of the book and gently undid the leather strap that held it. He opened the cover carefully, trying not to crack the stiff pages. The flyleaf was blank, its yellowed edges a clue to its age. He turned it over even more carefully, to be confronted with an inscription.

The handwriting was spidery, elegant, and so archaic he had difficulty deciphering it. The spelling was somewhat creative, characteristic of the early history of the kingdom. It had a charm that always made him smile, and wonder why language was a hidebound vehicle instead of a more personal form of expression. The construction of the letters gave him pause as well, but after some concentration he began to sort out the familiar, and the inscription coalesced. "This be the story of the first king of Dynt, Auric Dynteryx, and ends with his death," he read. Beneath this statement was a signature in the same dainty hand. The name Sangaree Dynteryx touched his imagination with a prophetic hand. This was the personal account, by the first queen of Dynt, of her husband's rule and demise. It was a prize for scholars, one Pavis would have loved, yet he felt more in the volume than historical reminiscences. It was an electric force drawing him, this story of Auric's rise to power.

"If I let you, you'd starve to death."

The words were prosaic, but the softness of Coryelle's voice was not. Marc looked up, startled out of his thoughts. With her waist-length golden hair loose behind her, she was a vision backed in gold, a perfect icon out of the past.

"Don't look at me like that."

Marc's quick smile flashed. "How am I supposed to look at you?" he questioned, setting the book aside.

"As if I were real."

"But you are real. That is the wonder of it."

Coryelle set down her tray and stood in front of him, her hands on her hips. It was a defiant posture she had used as a child, and it made him smile all the more.

"And not like that either!"

Marc's eyes were innocent.

"I am no child to be indulged or . . . idol to be admired."

"What, then?"

"You are an idiot."

"No doubt. That is an opinion you have expressed before."

Coryelle uttered an unintelligible exclamation and threw up her hands. She turned back to the open door and closed it firmly against the crowd. When she returned there was a light in her eyes he did not dare believe.

"We are going to have this out."

Marc was incapable of a flippant reply. He could not pretend to misunderstand. "Coryelle . . ." His voice was broken, pleading against the continuation of the conversation. "Coryelle, I will put an end to this before it starts, before you say something you do not mean." He raised his eyes to hers, and in their warmth and pain she read the truth. She knew she had won. "I cannot remember a time when I have not loved you. I am a thick, hardheaded clod, and it was not until I almost lost you I realized the child I loved unconsciously had become the woman my heart turned upon." Coryelle moved slowly nearer, her eyes surging black seas of emotion. Marc struggled for words. "I spoke the truth when I said I was your slave—in everything—but I will not let you carry the burden of the life I have chosen. Death and destruction will follow me everywhere."

"And so will I."

"No matter what title chance has handed me, I am a slave, born of unknown parentage, and you are the child of a noble house."

"Then it should be more than fitting. You said once each man is a slave to what he cares about. That is even more true of a woman. I care about you. I do not want to face life without you, yet if that should come to pass, my heart would not die if I had your children beside me."

Marc touched her hand. The effort he made to remain where he was, not to coerce her with emotion, left him trembling. He wanted a clear head for this decision, wanted her complete understanding of it.

"Marc, don't you see? All the years you loved me, I loved you back. You were the foundation of my world. Because of you, I learned to build my own foundation. Now all I ask is to give you joy."

"You have always given me that."

"Then let me come home." Coryelle's voice was forlorn.

Marc reached out and she was in his arms. He wrapped them around her and rested his cheek against the flossy silk of her hair. It smelled of sunshine. She gave a satisfied little exhalation of breath that touched him. He sighed, a deep release of years of emotional restraint. He was free. Free to love her and free to accept her love. Her complete trust and the yielding curves of her body sent a flush of warmth through him. He tightened his grip, clinging to her like the child he had never been allowed to be.

Coryelle, cuddled against his broad chest, felt the tears rise in her throat. Her love for him, for his loneliness and pain, for the man who faced heralds of death with defiance, flooded her, but this innocent reaching out sent a bolt securely through her heart. The wonder dawned on her that as much as she needed Marc, he needed her, needed the comfort of a touch, a word, a look. His hunger was deep, from the heart of his soul and blood. Everything in her leaped to answer it, and she knew she would never be the same. She had knowledge of him now. It was a fragile bond she would strengthen with each day of their lives, and to feel him reaching out to her would be the joy of her days.

"Now you can't go off and have adventures without me," she said into the soft wool of his tunic.

Marc chuckled and eased his hold, his arms a cradle.

"I admit it," he said. "Even when I am alone, you are with me."

Coryelle snuggled closer. Her fingers stole up his back. She could feel the smooth muscles ripple at her touch.

"Then why," she asked, "am I not being kissed?"

Marc's chuckle sounded again. "All in good time," he answered. "All in good time."

He drew one hand across her body in a sensual caress that roused her to him, and time slipped away as silently as grains of sand in the sealed interior of an hourglass. The room held their love in similar isolation, beyond the confines of the mundane world. It was a secret life they shared, as secret as the depths of the forest on Adyton.

Racque eyed the closed door to Marc's study with a worldly air. The book he was attempting to read lay open on his lap, the pages undisturbed.

"You look exactly like an overprotective mother hen!" Gisarme's voice held laughter.

Racque reacted with a piercing flash of annoyance. "She is my sister," he snapped.

"True."

"She is tying herself to a man doomed to destruction."

"Also probably true. As are we all."

Racque made a quick, brusque gesture.

"It is her choice, Racque." Gisarme's voice was gentle. "She has loved him all her life."

"I know."

Gisarme's eyes were amused. "I never thought to see you behave like an overzealous parent."

"It took me a long time to discover the things that matter. I am loath to lose them."

"I wish I could tell you you will not."

Racque looked full at Gisarme and weighed his words, not wanting to utter them, yet desiring the warrior's opinion. "What do you think of our chances for survival? I don't ask what we can accomplish. That is finished."

"If we were to withdraw, find some place to hide and give up the attempt to defeat Corbin, we might live out our natural lives. That will not happen."

"He won't give up?"

"Not until he has tried every last avenue, including personal sacrifice. In the end he may try to save us, but I suspect we will not let him. For my part, I am not sure I want to outlive this conflict."

"It is an impossible impasse. There is nothing left to be done. We are defeated in our victory."

"Don't be so quick to discount victory. We did succeed, you know, against impossible odds."

Racque nodded. "But we have nothing left to fight with."

"Somewhere in the depths of each of us lies one last kernel of strength. When all seems lost, that tiny grain can make the difference. I cannot believe a man who spent ten years of his life trying to find a sister he never knew would give in so easily."

"Perhaps I am tired."

"Then you should do as they are," answered Gisarme with a nod toward the closed door. "Take your happiness as you find it, revel in it, let it give you rest. Face the day with the sunrise, not before."

Racque digested the older man's words. They rang true. He could see them etched in the sanity of Gisarme's face. Racque's cryptic smile was wry.

"You know," he said, "that I can't help being dramatic."

A low chuckle was his answer. Gisarme reached out a broad, capable hand and grasped the young man's arm. "You have lived too much for atonement," he said. "It is time to live for yourself."

Racque's eyes widened. It was an idea too new for immediate comprehension, but the warmth behind Gisarme's voice was real. For the first time in his life, Racque understood what it was to have a friend.

Coryelle drowsed in Marc's arms, content in their protective circle. Marc caressed the heavy mane of golden hair, loving the feel of it sliding through his fingers. He was relaxed, almost happy for the first time in months, yet a voice of doubt picked at the back of his mind. The slow rhythm of his breathing was a natural anesthetic, pushing the doubt away, but it was not entirely successful.

Marc's eyes strayed to Sangaree's journal. It was a magnet drawing his thoughts. The worn volume with its pages made fat by numerous inserts was pregnant with the story of another age. Auric had been the first king of Dynt, a name so shrouded in mystery to be almost a legend. He might well be the last, and equally obscured by history. They were linked, he and Auric, down through years of rule.

The battle in front of him was hopeless. He was outgunned, and he knew it. There was simply no way to succeed against Corbin's superior military machine. Foxxe had come the closest, but the best he could manage was a stalemate, even with his years of experience and an intimate knowledge of his opponent. Marc, for his part, had run, scattering the lives of his followers like so much spoiled grain. In their deaths he found an agony of responsibility, for without the standard, the soldiers would not have fought.

Yet he could not turn aside. He was drawn forward. He had to admit continued opposition to Corbin's authority meant destruction, yet he did not feel suicidal. His mind grasped the fact and held it. If he did not desire his own death, then he was no suicide, and he did not. He knew himself too well.

He thought of the other side, and of Corbin. Corbin was the key to Dynt's military machine. In the short span of his years in power he built that machine into an autonomous entity capable of maintaining itself. He had ruthlessly used it to force Dynt into a more efficient economy. It added greatly to his wealth.

He saw Corbin's face in his mind's eye, the chiseled features, their beauty untouched by expression, and the dead, hollow eyes. Looking into those eyes was like staring death in the face. Their emptiness was hypnotic, an abyss into which a man could pour hatred or love with equal abandon and see it sink and dissipate into nothing. He found it hard to imagine the man Tenebrae and Gisarme knew, the passionate and gifted youth. What would have been the history of Dynt, he wondered, if that youth had prospered as the old king had wished?

He sighed and wrapped Coryelle closer. It was useless to speculate on what might have been. His sanity lay in the reality of Coryelle's love, and he held on to it with the fierce strength of a man whose options are dwindling before his eyes.

In the mid-afternoon sunshine the forest of Adyton glowed with the green brilliance of full summer. Patches of sunlight filtered through the heavy foliage to dot branches and forest floor with spots of brilliant yellow. A dynteryx dozed in a sunspot, one heel cocked and his head lowered to the ground. His hide shone in the sun, yellow as the light itself, rippling with the iridescence of health. His heavy crest was lowered and the tangle of his cottony mane fell around his head, protecting his sensitive eyes and ears from swarms of biting insects.

Power was evident in every contour even in repose. His muscles were thick and hard from years of flying, and his complete relaxation did not lack alertness. Like a warrior of old, he rested on his lance at a break in battle. Given cause, he would be in motion before the eye could blink, but there was no cause. There was only sun and the hum of insects and the twittering calls of birds. The dynteryx rippled his hide at a gnitfly, and the movement sent a sympathetic ruffle through his folded silver wing feathers. Then the little wings drooped and relaxed, spreading protectively over his body. The dynteryx sighed and slept.